"A WINNINGLY EASYGOING AND HEARTFELT DEBUT."
—Esquire

"A Cuba libre mixed with baseball, revolution, and moonlight, wonderfully evocative of a time that was and a pitcher that might have been."

—FRANK DEFORD
Author of *Everybody's All-American*

"The baseball scenes are . . . easily the strongest passages of *Castro's Curveball*, along with Mr. Wendel's vivid depictions of prerevolutionary Havana's decadence and corruption."

—*The Wall Street Journal*

"In *Castro's Curveball*, Tim Wendel gives us a sparkling novel about baseball, a country on the brink of revolution, and the man who links them together—Fidel Castro. With remarkable ease and clarity, Wendel draws us into that world and into the lives of the fascinating and diverse characters who populate it. It's a fast-paced, entertaining, and suspenseful read. But for me, one of the most important things about this fine book is that it reminds us all of the 'what ifs' that might have altered the course of our own lives."

—CAROLYN DOTY
Author of *Whisper: A Novel*

TIM WENDEL

BALLANTINE BOOKS

NEW YORK

A Ballantine Book
Published by The Ballantine Publishing Group

Published in the United States by The Ballantine
Publishing Group, a division of
Random House, Inc., New York, and simultaneously in Canada by
Random House of Canada Limited, Toronto.

www.randomhouse.com/BB/

Library of Congress Catalog Card Number: 99-91815

ISBN 0-345-43474-9

Manufactured in the United States of America

Cover design by Heather Kern
Cover inset photos of Fidel Castro courtesy of AP/Wide World Photos
Cover photo (top) courtesy of Hulton Getty/Liaison Agency
Cover photo of baseball fielder's mitt by Edward Vebell

First Trade Paperback Edition: February 2000

10 9 8 7 6 5 4 3 2 1

IN MEMORY OF JOHN AND ERIC,
FOR MY CHILDREN, SARAH AND CHRISTOPHER,
AND, AGAIN, FOR MY WIFE, JACQUELINE

And to live in a world without grays, where all decisions were final: Balls and strikes, safe and out, the game won or lost beyond question or appeal.   —Eric Rolfe Greenberg

His fastball has long since died. He still has a few curveballs which he throws at us routinely.
                                           —State Department spokesman Nicholas Burns

AUTHOR'S NOTE

Maybe the best place to start, at least with a novel, is with a tale that simply won't go away, no matter how much scrutiny has been brought to bear on it.

Was Fidel Castro a legitimate baseball prospect? It depends on whom you talk to or what you choose to believe. Still, there's little doubt that Castro was an impressive athlete growing up—track star, basketball player, Ping-Pong champion, and promising pitcher. At the age of eighteen, he was considered in some quarters as one of Cuba's outstanding schoolboy athletes.

Whether or not Castro signed a professional baseball contract has never been resolved. Castro, through a spokesman, says no. Searches by the National Baseball Library in Cooperstown, New York, have turned up nothing. Still, rumors persist in Cuba that Castro did sign, or want to sign, soon after entering the University of Havana in the late 1940s.

The only other clue to Castro's pitching ability came in an account by Don Hoak, which appeared in *Sport* magazine in 1964. Hoak, who spent eleven years in the major leagues, played winter ball in Cuba in 1950–51, soon after Castro received his law degree. In those days, professional games were routinely delayed when college students came out of the stands and demonstrated on the playing field.

During one such incident, a tall, skinny student wearing a formal white dress shirt, black pants, and black suede shoes took the mound with Hoak at the plate. Hoak later claimed it was Castro.

"Left-handers as a breed are eccentric, but Castro, a right-hander, looked kookier than any southpaw I have known," Hoak wrote.

Hoak fouled off two Castro pitches before he told the umpire to clear the field. The police moved in, removing Castro and his followers from the area around the pitching mound. Except for ceremonial pitches and exhibitions later on, after he took over Cuba, it was the last time Castro threw his curveball for keeps.

Still, after all these years, the story lingers. Just when you're ready to dismiss it, something or somebody steps out of the past.

Only a few years ago, my friend Milton Jamail was talking to a few baseball fans in Havana. One old man claimed to have played baseball with Castro as a boy on the eastern end of the island. The usual questions about hometown and schooling were asked in trying to catch the old-timer in a lie. But all the queries were fielded flawlessly, leaving only the last question: What did Castro throw?

"So-so fastball, sneaky slider at the knees" was the reply. "But his best pitch was the curveball. He had a great curve."

ACKNOWLEDGMENTS

Thanks to Elizabeth Rees, Alan Cheuse, Joel Lovell, Howard Mansfield, Jim Papian, Chris Colston, and Nicholas Delbanco, not only for their insightful readings and suggestions, but for their friendship and encouragement as well.

Special thanks to Carolyn Doty, who often believes more in my stories than I do. Gary Brozek, my editor and friend, showed great courage and patience in taking on this project. Raphael Sagalyn, Ethan Kline, and Robert Bookman fought for this work in the marketplace.

Going to Cuba, especially in the "special period in time of peace," is no easy task, and I would have been lost without travel partners Milton Jamail and Rick Lawes, as well as the guidance of Tom Miller. Editors Paul White and Lee Ivory helped back my trips to Cuba, for which I'll always be in their debt.

Thanks also to the Squaw Valley Writers Workshop, Charles Eisendrath and the Michigan Journalism Fellows, and David Everett and the Johns Hopkins Writing Program for their guidance and support.

Tim Wendel
Vienna, Virginia

CASTRO'S CURVEBALL

We are up above the clouds—safe for now. Even through the plane's window, the Caribbean sun feels as hot and as dream-inducing as I remember it.

Beside me, my daughter Cassy sleeps the sleep of the innocent and the stubborn. With my fingertips, I slowly bring her head, with its fine blond hair, to rest on my shoulder. Softly, so as not to wake her, I stroke her neck, just as I did when she was a child. I listen to the roar of the jet engines, feel this southern sun again on my face for the first time in many years, and wonder what we have gotten ourselves into.

Cassy has her mother's round face and my sharp nose. Some would say that she would have been better off with a little less of each, but I don't think that. When she was seven or so, I can remember walking the fields out in back of our house and talking to God about her, wishing her plain. Please, let her be a plain girl, a plain Jane. I was convinced only that would keep her safe in this world. For I know that the pretty and the beautiful, those talented and gifted, the ones made closest to His image, always end up getting hurt. Of that you can be sure.

As with most conversations I've ever had with God, the results weren't exactly as I'd hoped for. In terms of her looks, my daughter didn't turn out to be classically beautiful. But there's something about her smile, the way her gray-blue eyes sparkle, that people, especially boys, always seem to enjoy. Even I am not immune to being carried aloft by her enthusiasm. After all, she is the one who has led me back to Cuba after all these years.

My Cassy flies all the time. She is the lone flight attendant on a commuter airline making hops from Buffalo to Cincinnati or Washington or Boston. She makes at least four round trips a day, five days a week. That's why she got such a kick out of how they do things on this Cubana Air flight. No drinks or snacks. Instead candies—peppermint, butterscotch, mango—are offered up in straw baskets to keep our ears from popping. There are no other services on this ninety-minute flight from Cancún to Havana.

Cassy's breathing is soft and relaxed. I turn from her to look out the window. Far below, in between the clouds, I catch my first glimpse of Cuba in more than forty years. It's how I remember it—a ribbon of white sand beach and then mile after mile of dark green interior. After all the times I meant to come back here, especially that night in '53, it seems strange to come back now, with a grown daughter in tow. If it weren't for Cassy, I would have stayed in Middleport, New York, living on my high school teacher's pension, learning to be a widower after thirty-seven years of marriage. I am coming to the end of many things, and, quite simply, I want to be left alone.

My wife, Laurie, died nine weeks ago this Tuesday. I especially miss her on cold mornings and late at night when every sound, real or imagined, echoes through the empty farmhouse on Slayton Settlement Road that we filled with devotion and purpose for all those years.

It's funny. Once upon a time I thought that I would enjoy being alone again. Staying married, learning to overlook the small trespasses that mount over the years, can exhaust any

A man can be married to a veritable saint, as I believe I was, and yet he can still find himself walking the fields in back of his house, wondering where he will find the strength to hold himself, hold the marriage together. That's what being married does to you. It demands penance in the form of compromise and responsibility. When you're living it, it can all seem to be too much at times. But now I find myself trying to make sense of a different kind of pain.

Here again, I think that God has fed me a breaking ball to keep me off balance. He has taught me that missing someone you loved deeply makes you long for the days of making adjustments, enduring the rounds of petty disagreements that can dim any marriage. Though she is gone, my wife remains, as she always did, very much with me. As I sit here, suspended above an island that once held great promise for me, I don't feel worthy of such devotion.

I feel this and simply want to fade away; I want to try and wrestle those feelings to some kind of stalemate. That's what I had planned to do until Cassy found that damn scrapbook.

Leave it to my whirling dervish of a daughter to take it upon herself to clean my house, attic to basement, days after her mother's death. I had told her nothing of Cuba, the years I spent playing baseball there. It was her mother, even though she had every reason to want to forget those years I spent in Cuba, who put those scrapbooks together, kept them tucked away where I couldn't get at them. It was only when she lay in a foggy shroud of painkillers near the end that she mentioned Cuba again, told me how proud she would have been if she could have seen me that last year. All I could do was squeeze her hand in thanks.

After the discovery of the scrapbook, one thing led to another.

Cassy especially liked a photo she found from those times of a farm boy struggling to lead a pack of plow horses. She had it framed, and after I reluctantly told her who took it, she wrote repeatedly to Cuba, eager to locate more of this photographer's work. To my amazement, her efforts were rewarded.

First came the letters, with stamps of orange-tipped butter-flies and old generals. In a neat script, the photographer's daughter, Evangelina Fonseca, told a fantastic tale, one in which her mother, Malena Fonseca, and I were companions in that time before the revolution. She told my daughter that we should visit. How there were plenty of Americans down here. How she met them every day on the streets.

To further convince us, she sent cheaply made books of her mother's works. Published in Spain and Mexico, they were filled with black-and-white photographs of Cuba before the revolution. Then came the volume simply titled *Fidel*. In flipping through the shots of the Cuban president, my Cassy came to a picture of me and my best friend at the time, Chuck Cochrane, and, standing between us, a boyish Fidel Castro. Yes, that Fidel Castro.

He was so skinny back then. No bushy beard. Just a wisp of a mustache that I remember he had only started to grow. At times he was so self-conscious and unsure of himself that he constantly covered his upper lip with his hands, looking more like a blushing teenager than a budding revolutionary. Other times he was as brash as a schoolyard bully.

In the photograph, all of us were smiling like fools in the bright midday sun. The caption said the picture was taken in 1947.

Our plane banks and we begin our descent into Havana. Americans aren't legally permitted to enter Cuba. Back in Can-cún, we bribed who we hoped were the right people. We were told repeatedly what to say, how to act, when we reach customs in Cuba. Sitting by the side of the Mexicana Hilton's pool, a gentle breeze sweeping in from the Gulf, it seemed so easy. But now, as I look again at my precious daughter, I worry that this trip will bring us only heartbreak and sorrow. When you're as old as I am, you can sense trouble coming from a long ways off. It is another curse of growing old. Often you can see the future, but nobody ever heeds your warnings.

Around my neck, tucked inside my shirt, hangs a pouch with one thousand dollars in it. Another thousand dollars, also in small bills, is in my money belt, with the final thousand underneath Cassy's left armpit, riding in a shoulder holster contraption.

Because Americans cannot draw on U.S. banks in Cuba, we won't be able to use credit cards or traveler's checks there. We plan on paying cash for everything.

My daughter awakens and smiles at me.

"You said you would tell me more about Cuba on this flight," Cassy says, yawning.

"But you fell asleep."

"I'm awake now."

She leans forward, looking past me out the window. "So that's Havana?" Cassy turns back to me, her eyes now intense, drawing me in. I think about the two of them in the kitchen, sitting knee to knee in chairs facing each other, their heads tilted forward, sharing some revelation or another. I should have pulled up a seat and joined them, but I chose the company of my regrets instead.

I can't hold her gaze, so I turn toward the window and the skyscrapers and the patchwork of neighborhoods hugging the sea.

"Yes. That's it."

"Is it like you remember it?"

"Who can tell from here, hon? Memories fade, places change."

"Tell me about what it was like back then," she says, refusing to let me mire myself in gloom.

"We're almost on the ground."

"C'mon, Dad. We've got plenty of time."

"Where to start?" I say, trying again to beg off. "It was so long ago."

"Start at the beginning," Cassy tells me, refusing to let it drop.

"All right," say I, Billy Bryan, who was once the starting catcher for the Habana Lions, personal pitching coach to Fidel Castro, and lover of the beautiful Malena Fonseca. "Somewhere near the beginning, then."

CHAPTER ONE

My first mistake in Havana was trying to score from second base on Sammy Dion's weak single to right field. I ran right through Willie Gómez's stop sign at third, past his raised arms, his shouts for me to halt. I'll admit it—I was only thinking of the celebration at home plate. The hugs and the affectionate thumps on the head I would receive from my teammates. How the crowd would have cheered, their noise swelling into one delirious roar of joy, as I crossed with the winning run.

In my own mind, I had already won the game, was ready to take my place as the hero.

Instead, I was out by four steps.

Louie Lacomb, my opposite number with Marianao, was waiting with the ball in his mitt, his free hand protecting it, so I couldn't have knocked the pill loose even with my best Ty Cobb slide. But that stupid grin on Lacomb's face as he stood there waiting for me made me come in with spikes high just on general principle. There was only one out when I was gunned down at the plate. And when Cochrane, never passing up a chance to turn the knife, singled down the left-field line, I knew I was going to hear it if we didn't score. When we couldn't bring Dion around, the chants started, as I knew they would: "Bo-lo, Bo-lo, Bo-lo."

With the game already four hours old and spinning into the fourteenth inning, what remained of the sellout crowd at the Gran Estadio de la Habana needed somebody to blame. And seeing how I had been out at the plate, the last great screwup, I was the scapegoat. I was now the Bolo of the moment. Traditionally, when the real Bolo left for the night, anybody who failed to score took his place.

You see, the real Bolo was our team mascot. He prowled the stands wearing only frayed shorts and sandals, banging a small drum in time with the rumba band and chasing after the fire-eater with small cups of water. With his snarled, Medusa-like hair and wild-eyed look, Bolo wasn't the kind of Cuban we socialized with. But you had to give him credit. Nobody could whip a crowd into a frenzy better than our Bolo.

He had already done his classic tricks for the night, including my favorite, when he stood atop our dugout and wedged two baseballs into his mouth, looking like a deranged gopher, and then led the fans in booing and jeering the opposition. During the seventh-inning stretch, Bolo had come out of the stands, waving our team banner in one hand, and chugged around the bases. Rounding third, he'd handed the red and white striped streamer to Gómez, our dim-witted third-base coach, and then rumbled toward home plate. There the amazing Bolo had belly-flopped across the lid to loud groans and laughter. Bolo was long gone by this hour—down in Vedado, the new western section of Havana, where gleaming skyscrapers stood a few blocks from a silk-warm sea.

That was where the rest of us wanted to be, too. Except we would be in the casinos, rolling dice or playing blackjack, or watching the nightly shows at the Capri or the Lodi, with the fabulous house bands that could pump and massage a melody until dawn, places where Bolo would be out front, begging for change from American tourists. "Bo-lo, Bo-lo, Bo-lo," the remaining fans shouted, many of them standing. As I strapped on my shin guards I could hear them pounding on the roof of the dugout, waiting for me to come out. I wasn't in any hurry.

Broken fingers, balls ricocheting off your cup, pitchers who can't think straight, your legs so cramped you can't score from second base anymore—these are only a few of the occupational hazards of being a catcher. The crowd I could take. In a minute or so, after a couple of pitches, they would cool off. What got my goat was having my own teammates, especially Chuck Cochrane, our first baseman, give me the business, too.

"Hey, Bolo, I mean Bryan, get out here," Cochrane shouted over his shoulder at me. He was snagging throws from the infielders. It was a warm-up drill he performed effortlessly, with a bemused look on his face. For a big man, six foot three, easily 250 pounds, he moved like a cat when he had a leather baseball glove on his right hand. Like all of us, he still loved this game. We bitched about it, especially when a contest like this one kept barreling into the night like a car with a drunk behind the wheel. But come the next day, steer us between the lines and we would be happy, even with a hangover.

Out on the field, an out was always an out. That may not sound like much, but compared with the rest of the world, the lousy shape the war had left it in—well, that's saying something. I've come to know that the whole world is full of lies. So it all comes down to what lie you choose to follow. Long ago, I chose baseball.

That's how this thirty-one-year-old baseball lifer found

himself in Cuba playing winter ball after nearly a dozen years of trying and failing to win a full-time job at the major-league level.

Maybe it's a good thing, at least when you're young, to be desperate for something. So desperate that you will give up anything, go anywhere to chase it. Even though you tell yourself not to get too wrapped up in it all, somehow you still do. Just because you've put so much effort into this doesn't mean it will work out. That's what your head tells you. That's what it's *supposed* to tell you. But, of course, your heart has other plans. No matter which one I used, I believed that the world should behave logically. That if I paid my dues, I would be rewarded— someday.

So there I was playing baseball on that humid night in Havana, weighed down by a sweat-drenched wool uniform and fading dreams. But I still believed that this world of mine held a place for me; what I did not realize was that another world was about ready to reel me in.

"Billy, get out here. I mean it," Cochrane said, serious this time. "Get a move on, they're coming."

I glanced at the outfield bleachers. Sure enough, the kids' banners were up. A round of firecrackers went off, announcing their charge. This game seemed doomed to take all night.

"C'mon, c'mon," Cochrane said, his mitt popping with another warm-up throw. "If we get this inning started, maybe they'll crawl back in their cages."

"I'm coming," I said, clicking the last strap in place. I tapped at the shin guards with an open palm, making sure both of them were snug against my legs.

The crowd hooted once I cleared the dugout's shadow. I kept my eyes on my feet.

Tyga, the clubhouse kid, a mulatto Cuban, was catching

Happy Nelson, a Negro with a nice fastball and nothing else. He'd come in to pitch the new inning. There was nobody else in the bullpen except Skipper Charles, who was scheduled to start the next day's game. That's how desperate we were.

I motioned to Tyga that I was ready, and he got up from behind the plate.

"*Mil gracias,*" I said as he handed me my glove. But like everybody I've ever met in baseball, he couldn't resist a smart-ass remark.

He showed me those pearly whites of his. "How about a few less thanks and a little more speed?"

I ignored him and his grin, pounding the mitt's pocket with my bare right hand, trying to rid myself of any sense of him. If I could have scored from second on a bloop hit like Dion's, would I have been there in the off-season, trying to survive as a ballplayer? But try explaining that to an unruly bunch who wants your head. Back in the dugout, Gómez was getting an earful from Ángel González, our manager. About how I wasn't fast. What catcher is? That's why this position was created in the first place. It's for smart guys who have a good arm, who talk a good game, who like to be in the center of it all. It's a great job—God's view of baseball, with everything set out there in front of you. An ideal way to make a living, if it weren't for all the idiots surrounding you.

I had just caught Nelson's last warm-up toss when Cochrane yelled, "Too late. Here they come."

The umpire, old Raúl Atan, was ready to settle in behind me to call balls and strikes. When he saw the kids sweeping out of the stands, he straightened up and strutted toward the backstop for a smoke.

"*Haz algo,*" I told him in Spanish. "Do something."

Atan shrugged. He wasn't any taller than five foot two. A

little general, he hated being told what to do. Delays didn't bother Atan. He was always eager to share another dirty joke with the rich folks left in the box seats. Baseball had no clock, and he loved it.

He sauntered back toward the open area between our dugout and the backstop. He gestured at a fat, red-faced guy in a polo shirt who was puffing happily on a cigar. Next to him was a nice babe in a yellow summer dress. The American smiled, waving Atan over like they were bosom buddies—the way most tourists treat the natives down here. Old Atan leaned against the rail, jawing away, in perfect position to check out the lady's endowments.

The demonstrators were out of the stands, heading toward the infield.

"There goes Virtue Street," Cochrane moaned.

"It's Virtudes Street," I replied.

"Virtue, Virtudes, who cares?" Cochrane laughed. "Billy, you know too much *español* for your own good. All I know is 'turn out the lights.' That's English for 'the party's over.' "

Trying to get a dig back at him, I replied, "The ladies of the night will wait up for you."

"They'll be too tired," he complained, tugging at his groin. "Too spent for my *mucho* action."

I stood up, the mask resting on top of my head. The protesters were students from the University of Havana. A ragtag bunch, they unfurled banners that denounced Grau, the country's president, as well as United Fruit. Unlike most of my teammates, I at least took a passing interest in the local color. I knew that Grau and United Fruit held down either end of a system that was a boon to foreign investors and a burden to many Cubans.

On this night, there were about two hundred demonstrators—

big shots trying to steal a scene right here on our shimmering green field, with the golden city lying in the distance. They looked far more interested in having a good time than in bringing down any government.

Cochrane and my teammates headed for the dugout, content to let this storm blow over.

"If Bryan had held up at third . . . ," I heard Nelson saying.

He was right. If only I could have gotten lucky playing this game, we would have been getting ready for a night on the town—hobnobbing with the wealthy and the famous, being treated like kings and heroes. In short, we would have been lapping up another glorious night in a town we owned, a reward we deserved after riding so many buses in the bush leagues.

"Billy, Billy, let's go sit down," our left fielder, Oscar Artemino, teased me, running in from the outfield. "I think your legs need the rest."

"Not you too," I grumbled.

Oscar's coffee-brown face broke into a wide grin.

"What's a few insults between friends?" he asked.

"That's right. What the hell? Kick me while I'm down."

I always loved Oscar's lilting accent, the way his Spanish could float and tease, taking the sting out of anything he said. My first year down here, Cochrane and I had roomed with Oscar, one of three Cubans who were in our everyday lineup. Our apartments weren't ready yet, and staying with Oscar was management's idea. Chuck had lasted only a few nights before blowing his cash on a suite at the Nacional. But I had stayed at Oscar's for almost a month.

His family was sweet. I paid only a few dollars for the room, so I slipped him pocket change whenever he taught me a phrase or two that I liked. The result was that while I had known some Spanish coming down here, after being with Oscar, being on this team for more seasons than I cared to remember, I was damn near fluent.

Oscar also was a great host. He didn't meddle in my business and kept most of his opinions to himself. Only occasionally he talked about politics. Usually I had to wait until he was a bit drunk, sitting out on his front porch, after his kids had gone to sleep. Only then would Oscar tell me how Grau was president only because Fulgencio Batista had retired to Daytona Beach. Everybody expected Batista to return someday. Oscar also told me about United Fruit. How the Boston-based company had operations throughout the Caribbean and had more political clout on the island than any other American industry or bank. He had several cousins who worked for them, men who got paid little more than slave wages. That's what kept him in the game, knowing what he'd escaped and not wanting to jeopardize his family.

"So, Billy, we sitting down?" Oscar asked. "You know this game could take all night."

"You go ahead," I told him. "You need your wheels more than me. Besides, I'm not taking off this gear after I just got it on."

Oscar gave me a curious look.

"Go on," I told him. "I'm sticking around. Something's in the wind tonight."

Rory Guild, a big rookie with good power and forearms like hams, also lingered near the plate. He was the first hitter due up that inning for Marianao. Guild hadn't been in Cuba long enough to know that such interruptions could go on for an hour or more. He didn't know he should head for the dugout and relax.

Catching my eye, he asked, "They do this every night?"

I shook my head. "Only at full moons, when the price of sugar falls, or the government jails another of their brethren."

Guild nodded dumbly. "Oh," he said.

Guild was like most ballplayers—oblivious to what was going on around him. To guys like him, it didn't matter if they were playing in Havana or Hartford as long as their uniforms fit, the weather held, and there was a place to grab dinner after the game.

I stuck around, hoping things might burn themselves out quick enough. It didn't appear likely.

Many of the demonstrators beat small drums or shining cymbals or cowbells. They stretched in a snake line from first base around to third, swaying back and forth, proud of their own self-importance, singing something like, "Die, die, die. Grau must die."

Then they easily moved on to another catchy number with the same relentless beat, a noise that gave anybody over the age of thirty a headache. This chant was about Batista, Cuba's president until 1944. What a devil he was, their protest song went. He had raped their land, and if he returned to Havana, blood would flow until justice was done. Real cheery stuff.

What was so strange about these interruptions was that from a distance the demonstrators seemed like nice enough kids. They dressed pretty well. Their parents were obviously well-off. The protesters' faces had that youthful shine, a refreshing eagerness that was open to anything that could possibly happen. Most nights they crowded the bleachers down the right- and left-field lines, helping to fill this glorious bowl of a ballpark. Beyond their sections, in the distance, you could see the hotels and casinos. At night much of Havana came alive, pulsating in red, white, and pink neon. Those lights, that energy, never shut down. The show went on until dawn every night of the week in Cuba.

The demonstrators may have wanted to change all that—bring down the government, do God knows what with the casinos and the clubs. But whether they wanted to admit it or not, they fit right into the madness that was this place. They were as much a part of this Cuba as the floor show at the Capri Hotel or the surf along the Malecón. Down deep, I had the feeling they knew this. They cheered the good plays and were as ready as the rest to ride somebody about being Bolo. Like many things in this country, their conduct didn't make sense on some basic level.

While most of them sang away, a smaller group of students surrounded the pitching mound and clapped rhythmically while an *hombre* with a muscular upper torso and matchstick legs started pawing the pitching rubber. He wore thick, black-framed glasses and dark slipperlike shoes, with a white dress shirt and ruffles and frills coming untucked from his black pants. He looked like a combination of a maître d' and a matador. The guy went into an elaborate windup, windmilling his arm around and around before pretending to let one fly toward the plate. The motion was ridiculous. Still, after each effort he marched in place, and his nest of admirers cooed and whistled. It was enough to make you sick.

After he had done this a couple times, I'd had enough. I rolled the ball out to the mound and motioned for him to throw it in to me. "*No comas mierda, lanza de verdad,*" I shouted out to him. "Don't pretend, pitch the ball for real."

I could hear Oscar laughing back in the dugout.

The kid stared at the ball lying at his feet. I figured he was chicken. But with the crowd beginning to buzz, he reached down and picked up the ball and studied it like he had stumbled across the Hope diamond. I got down into my crouch, and he looked from the ball to me and back to the ball. His face became serious and angry, and the way he glared in at me I got a bit concerned, wondering what he might do next.

He waved his fan club back a couple steps and then went into his delivery for real. Now, this windup resembled something right out of a Bugs Bunny cartoon—plenty of grimacing, with his arm flying around. Yet when he let the ball go, he had something on it. When the ball hit leather, there was a reassuring pop. His admirers cheered, and the crowd got a little interested.

The demonstrator threw a couple more before Guild surprisingly stepped into the batter's box.

"Let me take care of this knucklehead," he muttered. "The way you're going, they'll crown him king by morning."

The crowd was on its feet. At least they'd forgotten about me being Bolo.

The demonstrators moved to either side of the foul line, and Atan, welcoming a big show, slowly walked up behind me to call balls and strikes once again. In my dugout, talk about the newest act at the Shanghai Theater died down and the other players began to watch, too.

From my crouch, I signaled one finger, wanting a fastball, but I was ready for anything. The kid went into his whole act, letting his arm go around a half dozen times before he lifted his left leg, rotated his hips, and followed through toward home plate.

This pitch was his fastest yet, and Guild was lucky to pop it foul, off into the right-field stands.

"Fuck that," Guild said underneath his breath.

It was as if my man heard him, because his next pitch came in high and hard, aimed at Guild's head. It was a fine piece of chin music, and Guild barely spun out of the way, dropping to one knee, the crowd gasping with delight.

"Brass-balled motherfucker," Guild said, digging back into the batter's box. "That's it, Bryan. I'm taking your *amigo* over the fence."

I signaled for the fastball again and set up inside. But the pitch caught too much of the plate and Guild almost made him pay, pulling the ball hard, barely foul, deep over the left-field fence. The protesters scattered like somebody had fired a gun at them.

"Strike two," Raúl shouted as the crowd roared.

"When did you wake up?" I asked.

"This is better than anything else I've seen tonight, except maybe that lovely lady in the box seats," he replied. "This pitcher your discovery? I enjoy."

I signaled two fingers, curveball, and the guy nodded. I chuckled. Guild glared back at me. This was getting good. The guy seemed to know the game.

When he let the ball go, I could tell by the rotation that it was going to be a beauty. The curveball came in like it was heading for Guild's head and shoulders, but it had plenty of bite. I could sense Guild's knees begin to buckle. He was a goner on this one. About twenty feet from the plate, the ball's spin caused it to begin to fall downward and in toward the plate.

I'm convinced there are moments when time does slow down, as if the gods themselves can't believe what they are seeing and make the world pause a beat or two so that they can all gather around and get a better look. As soon as that ball started to break, I was silently rooting it home. The rotation was so tight that I saw a red dot appear on its hide—the result of the seams spinning so fast that their jagged lines become a pin-prick of execution.

All Guild could do was watch that pitch break beautifully, down and over the inside corner and into my glove. The pitch must have broken a good three feet, and I never had to move to catch it.

When the ball fell into my glove, like a feather dropped from above, the first thing that came into my head was a question: How could this Cuban kid deliver such a great pitch when we had yahoos with years of instruction in the minor leagues who would never come close to throwing a baseball this well?

"Strike three," the umpire shouted, and the crowd went crazy.

"Get him out of here," Guild said, starting for the mound with his bat in hand.

Atan waved the security cops out from behind the backstop. They reluctantly began to clear the field. Usually this took a while. But whether it was Guild with a bat in his hand or the satisfaction that one of their own had gotten the best of us, that night the protesters quickly moved back to the sidelines.

The only one who wanted more time in the limelight was this kid pitcher. When the cops reached him on the mound, he stood his ground. As the cops pushed him along, he continued to stare in at me, like he was still waiting for my next signal.

The smug smile that had been on his face disappeared. He straightened and tried to gather a group of men around him. They all stood with their arms linked. Then a flashbulb popped. I saw a raven-haired woman sling a camera bag over her shoulder and yell at a policeman who was about to prod her with a nightstick. Her eyes lit up like one of her flashbulbs. The cop backed off. The protester put his arm around her and started to lead her away.

I tore off my mask and went halfway out to him.

"What's your name?" I yelled.

He stood high on tiptoe for another look at me, like he was memorizing my face.

"Castro," he shouted back. "Fidel Castro."

As it turned out, I would never forget his name, or the woman's face. No matter how hard I tried.

CHAPTER TWO

The morning after Castro struck out Guild, I was in bed when a loud ring pierced my alcohol-induced deep sleep. Once I figured out that the ringing was from the phone and not inside my head, I lifted the receiver off the cradle.

"Busy?" asked Papa Joe Hanrahan, the chief Caribbean scout for the Washington Senators, the major-league team that employed me.

"Nope," I said, squinting at the alarm clock. It was a little after nine, an hour of the morning that I rarely saw.

"Billy, do you have any idea who that pitcher was last night? The one who came onto the field?"

"Just some kid," I said, rolling out of bed. I began to pace with the receiver tight to my ear. I didn't want to miss a word. I cleared my throat, trying to sound awake. "He was one of those fool protesters. We didn't leave the ballpark until past two because of them."

"I heard he struck out Guild," Papa Joe said with a hint of eagerness.

"Guild didn't know what hit him," I said. The phone cord grew taut, so I turned in the opposite direction, still pacing. Through the sliver parting the curtains, I saw blue sky, with only a few stray clouds out over the turquoise ocean. "Guild has no experience playing ball down here."

I heard voices in the background on Papa Joe's end, and I realized that he was holding court in his suite at the Hotel Nacional. Once a month he brought together his scouts from across the Caribbean and they compared notes about prospective baseball talent. Papa Joe was famous for never leaving a stone unturned when it came to signing light-skinned Latins for the big leagues. Before the war, hardly any had gone to the States to play ball. But by 1947, thanks in large part to Papa Joe, there were fifty in the majors and their presence was growing.

"So, you don't think much of this pitcher?" he said.

The voices in the background became louder, and my voice rose as I tried to hold Papa Joe's attention.

"N-No, I didn't say that. The kid had an OK fastball. But you know what impressed me most? His curve. That's how he rang up Guild. With a gorgeous curve. I wish all of our guys had an Uncle Charlie like that."

"How old would you say he was, Billy?"

"I'd guess twenty, twenty-one."

"Colored? Mulatto?" Papa Joe continued.

"No, he's light-skinned. Old Spanish family, I'd bet. He looks like Cochrane with a better tan."

Papa Joe chuckled. "That's interesting. Good curve, right makeup. You know, the Dodgers may be ready to bring coloreds into the big leagues with this Robinson kid, but I doubt if the world in general is ready for that just yet."

The voices in the background again grew louder, and Papa Joe barked at them before returning to me.

"Billy, I'm intrigued by your prospect," he said.

I couldn't decide if I liked the sound of that—*my* prospect.

"Did you get his name?"

"Castro. Fidel Castro."

"I've never heard of him," Papa Joe said. "Any idea where he lives?"

"No."

"Do me a favor, Billy," Papa Joe said. "I have to go back up to the States for a week. We have our annual organizational meetings. Keep an eye out for this Castro character while I'm gone. I'll reserve a couple seats for him behind the plate. I'd appreciate anything more you find out."

"Is my name going to come up at these meetings?" I asked.

"Everybody under contract will be discussed," Papa Joe said. "It's that time of year."

The players had nicknamed Papa Joe "the Storm Cloud." He routinely dressed in white suits and a Panama hat. During a game, he appeared without warning somewhere in the crowd, writing down a tendency or a bad habit that would cost a guy dearly at contract time. Years earlier the Senators had moved him down here from Washington, and he reveled in the change of scenery. He frequented the clubs, the Capri, the Lodi, and the Tropicana, as much as we did.

There was more commotion on his end. For a moment I thought I recognized one of the voices in the background, but I couldn't quite place it.

"Billy, I'll see you in a week," Papa Joe said.

I stopped pacing. I wanted to talk more, about me and where I was going within this organization. Rarely in a ballplayer's life do you know where you stand—if your stock is on the rise, or if you should be looking for another job. I hardly ever spoke with Papa Joe, so I had to ask about my status with the Senators.

"What will you say when my name comes up?"

"Me?" he replied, sounding surprised and then annoyed. "I

can't say for certain. Maybe I'll say what a good job you're doing scouting for us. You know, a good scout is worth more to a team than another backup catcher any day."

■ ■ ■

Señor Canillo, my landlord, kept two fishing poles in the small closet by the back door. He had told me to borrow them anytime I wanted.

I selected the long bamboo model and walked a few blocks over to the breakwater that marked the boundary between Miramar, where I lived, and the city of Havana.

Cochrane and a couple others were scheduled to tee off about noon at the Río country club, and I had told them I'd complete their foursome. But after my discussion with Papa Joe, I wasn't in any hurry to play golf. For you see, it was happening to me again. No matter how much I begged and wooed this game of baseball, once again it wasn't going to give me a decent shot at cracking the starting lineup.

The gulls circled over me until they saw that I wasn't landing anything. Below me, the channel soon emptied into the ocean, and I saw the square white rigs of sailboats hugging the coast and, farther out, the dark spots of cabin cruisers trolling for marlins.

My dream had always been to be the first-string catcher for the Washington Senators. Such aspirations were over if Papa Joe now considered me more valuable as a scout than as a player.

Six years earlier, before the war, I'd been certain I'd made the Senators. I had had a great spring. Yet on the last day of camp, before the team headed north, management traded for Cecil Sanders. They told the newspapers they needed another veteran. I was twenty-four, Sanders thirty-two.

At the time everybody told me I would get another chance. But I should have sounded off to the reporters and anybody else who would listen. That had been my opportunity to stick with the big club, but all I had done was smile and let them take my chance away from me. Looking back on it, it was like leaving the door open and an itemized list on the table with the location of all my valuables to make it easier for the burglars to rob me. All because I was too scared to make a big fuss. Too scared to be considered anything but a team player.

When the war came, I thought I'd get another chance at playing regularly in the majors. I flunked my army physical, so it seemed I was destined to play ball. But leave it to the Senators to be so deep at catcher that I rarely made it up, except when somebody was hurt or it was the end of the season. Heck, other teams were so desperate for players that the Reds brought in a fifteen-year-old, Joey Nuxhall, to pitch. There was Pete Gray, a one-armed outfielder, playing for the St. Louis Browns. We had holes to fill, too. Old Bert Shepard, who'd lost part of his leg from being wounded in the European theater, pitched some relief for us. But when it came to catching, the Senators were set. Sanders didn't go anywhere, and in 1944 Rick Ferrel, a Hall of Famer, was traded back to Washington.

Sometimes the coaches would mumble something about moving me to third base, even the outfield, to take advantage of my arm. But I was a catcher, pure and simple. Being less than that might have kept me in the majors, but in my view it didn't seem worth it. So I stayed in the minors or rode the pine on my few call-ups to the majors.

I'm convinced there's nothing more painful than to know you're ready to do something great, ready to take charge, and then never get the chance to play. It changes you. It could possibly make you edgy or more determined; worse, if you're not careful, you could become more bitter. All my life, it seems, I've been waiting for people to notice me. To give me a chance when it counts.

At the time I thought that maybe it was fitting that my career might end there, in Cuba. The best money I ever received for playing ball came on that crazy island.

To play winter ball was to live the life of a king. The Habana Lions ball club paid me $1,000 a month, plus $400 for expenses. I had a two-story apartment with a beautiful view of the ocean. Then there were such fringe benefits as being able to walk into any nightclub in Havana without paying a cover, and having a fishing pole anytime I wanted one. After eight years of professional ball, I'd played for more teams than I have fingers, been on enough overnight bus rides to give me a permanent backache, and spent enough money on hotel whores to fund my own pension plan.

"Hey, stud," I heard a voice say. It was Cochrane. He stood on the gray rocks, looking down at me. He wore a golden polo shirt and yellow and black checkered knickers. "The deep blue can wait. The golf course wants *gringo* blood."

"Not today," I said, shaking my head.

"The hell you say," Cochrane said. "So what are you catching that's so god-awful important? Stingrays? Sharks? Maybe new wheels so you can score from second base?"

"Nothing that important," I said.

Cochrane scrambled down the stone breakwater and took the pole from my hand. He reeled in the line and held up the hook for a closer inspection.

"I may not be much of a fisherman," he said, "but I do know a losing proposition when I see it. I'd imagine big fish are a lot like women. You have to bait the hook to land one."

"I'm just thinking," I said.

"Billy, if you ask me," Cochrane said, handing back the pole, "you're already doing too much thinking. Anybody can see that. Think too much and you never hit the ball. That's one of God's rules to live by: Thou shalt not think. It should be one of the Ten Commandments."

I sat down on a large rock. Cochrane dusted off a spot and joined me.

"I got a call from Papa Joe this morning," I said.

Cochrane nodded as I cast, putting the baitless hook as far out as I could.

"He asked me about that protester who struck out Guild last night."

"Stupid kids. They're the reason why I've got these bags under my eyes. Hell, I didn't get down to the casinos until almost two in the morning because of them."

"They're sticking up for the peasants, the nation's poor," I teased.

"Billy, don't even start. Besides, with them bastards cutting into my casino time, I'm going to wind up poor. A man needs time to make up his losses."

"I don't know about that, but I do know that Grau isn't doing much for them. And everybody is probably right. Batista's just biding his time until he comes back to run the whole show again."

"And I'll be long gone by then. So unless this Grau fella is on the hill tonight, I got better things to think about," Cochrane said. "So what's Papa Joe so interested in a fool protester for?"

"Because he struck out Guild."

Cochrane gazed out toward the ocean, shielding his eyes with one of his large hands. "I guess that's why Papa Joe is where he is in the world and we're down here fishing with no bait on the hook," he said. "You've got to give the man credit. He is relentless."

The sun beat down on us, and for a moment it felt like everything stood still. The gulls had disappeared on the last of the morning breeze, and the only sounds were the waves in the distance and the slow clicks of me reeling in the fishing line.

"So, I bet Papa Joe told you to keep your eyes open for this crazy protester, right?"

I nodded.

"I don't see how that's serious enough to kiss off a round of golf at the Río," Cochrane said.

"That's not all we talked about," I said, pulling the hook out of the water. "He told me he was going up to Washington next week. He said it's time to grade everybody in the organization."

"That it is," Cochrane said, looking at me. "So you're worried, right? That's why you've got the hangdog face? That's why you're casting for minnows instead of playing golf?"

"Chuck, I'd feel a lot better if I'd scored that fuckin' run last night. Something like that happens and it can get you to—"

"Thinking," Cochrane snapped. He stood up and glanced back at the seat of his pants, making sure they were clean. "I've already told you that thinking, at least too much of it, never did a stud any damn good." He picked up a stone and flicked it out toward the middle of the channel. "Just because you gave up that honey back home—"

"Hey."

"What was her name?"

"Leave it alone, Cochrane."

"Now, don't bite my head off. I'm just trying to bring a few rays of sunshine into your cloudy day. It was Laurie, wasn't it?"

I grunted in agreement.

"Sweet name. But just because you left her for ball doesn't mean ball's going to pay you back. It doesn't work that way."

I still sat staring out to sea.

"If you think that way long enough, you start to believe it yourself. Don't you see?" Cochrane said. "Think too much about the past, and buddy, you might as well be putting things in your way to trip over. Forget her. Turn the page. That's the best medicine any doctor ever prescribed."

I could feel the desperation welling up inside me. In my mind, I pictured the bus terminal back home where Laurie had dropped me off a few months before on the first part of my journey back down to Cuba to play more ball. Another stop in pursuit of an elusive dream.

We hadn't said a word to each other on the drive over. That's how mad she was. She didn't move when I went inside to buy my ticket. She was still sitting there when they called my bus. I walked back over to her father's old Kaiser sedan. She rolled down the window and held out her hand, palm up. I grasped it and leaned in long enough to kiss her on the forehead before she turned away.

"I'll be back," I told her.

"But I won't be," she said. "I told you I could compete with another woman, but baseball's got a hold on you and it won't ever let go. I'm tired, Billy. I've let too many opportunities pass me by, and my father's made you a good offer. If you can't take it, that means you don't want me."

She rolled the window back up and sat there staring. I took some consolation in the fact that she stayed there until I got on the bus and rolled south out of sight.

God, I was beginning to believe that I was cursed. Every

gamble I made in those days, from leaving Laurie to trying to score from second base the previous night, seemed certain to blow up in my face.

Cochrane crouched down and picked up another rock. With a sidearm snap he sent it skipping across the calm water.

"I bet you were just mooning about Cecil Sanders, too." He laughed. "Heck, I can read you like a book. You were thinking about that big chance with the Senators that got away. Admit it, now. Am I right or am I right?"

I laughed too, in spite of myself. "Good guess."

"Guess, hell. Face it, Bryan, we've known each other too long to have any secrets between us."

"You're right about that."

"And you know, sitting in the shadows ain't going to cut it when you're feeling low. C'mon, you need to at least play a round with me and the boys. You can pretend that old Cecil's face, all wide-eyed, with that goofy grin of his, is on every ball you hit. Maybe you'll break a hundred for once."

"All right," I said, reeling in the rest of the line. "The fish don't seem to be biting, anyway."

"That's my boy," Cochrane said. He eyed the bamboo pole one more time. "I never could figure this fishing game out," he said. "Why be alone when there's always somebody else to share your misery?"

"Hey, Chuck—about you being able to read me like a book? Just when exactly was it that you learned to read?"

CHAPTER THREE

"What is it about women?" Cochrane asked me that night in the clubhouse. "I mean, in the dark, when you're all liquored up, hornier than hell, every one of them looks fine. But come the morning . . ."

"Two-bagger?" I offered.

He nodded.

Cochrane had popularized the term "two-bagger." He even had the Cuban clubhouse kids using it. To Cochrane, a two-bagger meant a girl so noontime ugly that you needed two bags: one over your head in case the one over hers fell off. Cochrane had a tendency to gravitate toward two-bag honeys, and too often I followed my friend's example.

"Chuck, you've tried to drink too many women pretty."

"Ain't it the truth," he said. "But I'll tell ya, Billy Bryan, someday I'm going to find her. When I wake up with her in the morning, I'm going to be even more crazy about her than in the dark. Some guys dream about hitting three hundred in the big leagues. Hell, I've done that. That's nothing compared with finding a real gorgeous woman. One that's pretty and right for you all the hours of the day."

It was almost eleven. We had lost—again. Not that defeat

was holding many of us back from the rest of the evening. Almost the entire team was crowded in front of the cracked mirror that hung lengthwise over the two sinks near the showers. In quick order, we were slicking back our hair with Wild Root or water and smoothing over the shaving cuts with a bit of bay rum. The more desperate ones among us were splashing on Wild Musk cologne for good measure.

"Phew, what a stink," said Skipper Charles, that night's starting pitcher. He hadn't even showered yet and was still walking around with his pitching arm wrapped in an Ace bandage and melting ice. He had gone the distance, giving up three runs. We hadn't helped him out much, plating only one.

"I don't know what impresses me more about this team," Skipper added. "How sweet it smells or how fast it can shower and dress after a game."

"That's enough, rookie," said Cochrane, studying his reflection one more time before stepping back from the mirror. "You're halfway there when it comes to priorities in Cuba. You pitched a timely ball game, thank you very much. But you need to improve your shit-shower-and-shave act. By the time you get downtown, there will be a severe dent in the action. That is, if Bryan and I have anything to say about it."

Most of the guys were wearing guayabera shirts, the white pleated numbers many Cubans favored. But long ago Cochrane and I had decided that such attire was too native for a night on the town. We went top drawer—polo shirts and blue blazers with khakis.

"You two could be twins," Skipper said.

"The veteran touch," Cochrane said, slipping his long black comb into his back pocket. "You'd be good to emulate it, son. Casual yet stylish. Comfortable yet slightly suggestive."

Then Cochrane turned to me. "You ready yet, hoss?"

I nodded. "Let's go."

I noticed Oscar sitting by his locker, smoking a cigar with a dreamy look on his face. It was about as much celebrating as he was going to do that night. Cubans, especially dark-skinned ones, didn't frequent the clubs and casinos. It wasn't that there were any rules against them going in. It's just they weren't made to feel particularly welcome once they got there. Anywhere you went at that hour—the Capri, the Jockey Club, the Bodeguita, Sloppy Joe's, the Nacional—you would find mostly corn-bred Americans with money to burn.

"We'll return telling tall tales and big lies," I told Oscar.

Oscar blinked like he was waking up from a sweet dream.

"I know you will," he said with a smile. "You and Big Chuck never let me down."

Cochrane and I shared a cab downtown, racing along the long boulevards toward the lights of the hotels and casinos. The doorman at the Capri, dressed in the hotel-issue emerald green uniform, smiled and tipped his cap when Cochrane and I pulled up in front. Inside, the crowds at the baccarat and roulette tables were three rows deep. The women wore evening gowns, and some of the men were in tuxedos. Every fifteen feet or so, another crystal chandelier hung down from the high dark ceiling. When the Capri was packed, like it was that night, the chandeliers turned slightly with the vibrations and noise, reflecting haphazard sparkles of light across the gambling tables.

Up near the stage, I saw Señor Canillo sitting at his regular table. He was surveying the wide expanse of greed and laughter with a bemused look on his face. Canillo was a small guy, with a neatly trimmed, pencil-thin mustache, and he had that rare ability to look a little crazy and very serious at the same time. Canillo smiled when he saw us, sending over one of his henchmen to usher us to his table.

That night Canillo's party included five businessmen from New York, who rose eagerly to shake our hands. Cochrane was already checking out the two women in low-cut gowns who were with them. The darlings were smoking long cigarettes from holders and batting their eyes—trying to look desirable and unavailable at the same time. That all seemed so ridiculous in Havana, where women were available, calling to you, on almost any street corner.

After introductions all around, Cochrane waded right in among the tuxedos. With his huge hands, he moved one of the girls directly onto his lap. The businessmen immediately took a liking to his initiative. People usually did.

One of the tuxedos endeared himself right away to Cochrane by talking about some homer my buddy had hit a couple seasons before at the Polo Grounds in New York. Cochrane sat there, grinning from ear to ear, looking like he might kiss the guy.

"So, Billy, how did your fishing go today?" Señor Canillo asked me after I pulled up a chair next to him.

"How'd you know about that?"

Canillo shrugged. "I heard."

"I didn't catch anything," I said. The rest were listening to Cochrane describe how he had driven in our only run that night. How he had guessed exactly what the pitcher was going to throw. In the swell of mambo music and chitchat, Señor Canillo and I were alone in our conversation.

Now, I didn't know that night what Canillo did for a living. But I remember he was never at a loss for the good things in life—women, drink, tables near the dance floor. He followed his own schedule, too. I admired how he could stay detached and cool about things, even when he had something riding on the outcome. Every night his table had American businessmen, sometimes a Hollywood actor, hovering around it. Two of his bodyguards stood back in the shadows, not sitting at the table like other high rollers' muscle men.

A tuxedo began to talk about the latest on Wall Street, but Canillo cut him off, wanting to discuss baseball with Cochrane and me.

"So, my sluggers." He beamed. I had taught him a couple baseball terms, and he never failed to trot them out.

"Yes, sir," Cochrane said, always respectful toward somebody who could pick up the tab.

"So, my sluggers," Canillo said again. "Why have we lost three in a row? This appears to be too good a team for such things to happen."

"Every team, no matter how good, goes through slumps," Cochrane said, rolling back his shoulders like he was ready to campaign for town sheriff.

Canillo appeared genuinely puzzled. "These losses are unavoidable?"

"Afraid so." Cochrane shrugged. "You can't stop the rain, you can't stop the sun, and you can't stop slumps. Every team gets them. It should end tomorrow, but who knows? The hard times roll when Lady Luck turns her back."

"That's so interesting," said the blonde sitting on Cochrane's lap.

"Why, thank you, honey," he said. "That means something coming from you."

"Sounds like baseball's like sugar prices," said one of the tuxedos. "Can't figure when they'll go up, can't figure when they'll go down."

"Baseball is like sugar?" Canillo sighed. "I was so hoping it'd be more predictable than that."

The conversation was interrupted by a drumroll from the stage.

"It's Lola," Cochrane said.

"Yes." Canillo smiled. "Our Lola." Turning to a couple of the businessmen, he explained, "It's time for our favorite."

Lola Lagal had come to Havana as Shirley Patterson of Elkhart, Indiana, a no-name singer who had been fired from her last gig in the Catskills. She'd sworn me to secrecy about that my first season down here. With a change in hair color from everyday brunette to bottle blond, a crucial fashion switch to glittering, low-cut gowns with an intriguing slit up one side, and her old repertoire of Broadway show tunes now backed by a lively Cuban band, suddenly she was packing them in.

Even though none of us said it aloud, the house band at the Capri was what sold Lola's act. Beautiful soaring trumpets, an all-male chorus that could charm the dead from the grave, and a beat—a bit savage, a bit sweet—that was distinctively Cuban. During the week the house band cooked until the wee hours, and I often went down there alone and let it lap over me like waves on a beach.

One reason we never gave the house band too much credit was that Cochrane appreciated Lola in the worst way. I didn't have the heart to tell him that I had beaten him to the punch almost two years before that.

Shirley and I had met on the night ferry from Miami, both of us too poor to fly down to Havana. That was before she changed her name, changed her act, changed her taste in men. Now it was like I knew too much.

"This girl's like fine wine," Cochrane said to nobody in particular. "She just keeps getting better and better."

Canillo seemed genuinely surprised by the insight. He and Cochrane shared a smile, like they had discovered a similar taste in fine cigars.

Lola launched into "Chicago, Chicago, that toddling town"— changing the words to "Habana, Habana." It was a little twist she did every night. Still, it never failed to win over the crowd. You had to hoot for anybody with that much breast and showing that much leg.

Her rendition of the sweet native ballad "Perfidia" was another crowd favorite. The room grew quiet as she told the song's story: how a poor boy from the mountain country couldn't win the love of a beautiful woman from the city. From there, Lola's act pounded along into the night with the grace of a runaway locomotive. It held lots of brass and sax solos, Lola keeping rhythm with a rhinestone tambourine. The hour-long set ended with her speaking heart to heart to the audience, a single spotlight overhead, and Lola telling the rich drunks how much she loved them. Before coming to Cuba, "this island paradise," as she called it, Lola Lagal had been "nothing, simply nothing, until this beautiful, beautiful city believed in me."

Then came the bit about her threatening to coldcock a nameless nightclub manager (everybody knew it was Artie over at the Lodi) if he didn't give her one last chance. The way she curled up her fist and looked up into the lone white spotlight, like she was staring down the Lord himself, was worth the price of admission. Not that ballplayers ever paid to get into these places, anyway.

Lola's performance came "straight from the soul" two times a night, five nights a week.

After she finished, she sat down at Canillo's table. Lola sipped a Tom Collins, gave me a shy smile, and laughed at anything Cochrane or Canillo said. She held her cigarette out to be lighted and the tuxedos tripped over themselves to reach it, almost setting fire to the linen tablecloth. Cochrane had shuffled the blonde off to another lap so he could give Lola his undivided attention.

"So, when are you going to run away with me?" Cochrane began.

"Charles, if only you meant it," she replied. Lola was the only one who could get away with calling Cochrane by his given name and live to see the morning sun.

"I do, I do," Cochrane said.

"I bet," she joked, and the tuxedos chuckled along with her.

"What brings you gentlemen to Havana?" she asked, turning her attention to them.

"Business," replied one of the tuxedos dryly, eager to move on.

Now, that could mean sugar or gambling or the Mafia. "Business" summed up why a lot of people came to Havana.

"What kind of business?" Lola asked, and for a minute she sounded like old naive Shirley Patterson, who had plunked down her last dollar for a ride on that night ferry to Cuba and a final shot at nightclub glory.

She had made a mistake and she knew it. There was an awkward pause, with none of the tuxedos answering.

"Lola, darling, just business," said Canillo, smoothing things over. "Business is business."

Lola tried to smile.

"When are you going to add those songs from *Oklahoma!* to your act? You have kept us waiting long enough, don't you think?"

I loved to watch Canillo operate. He had a hand in everything. Nothing seemed to surprise him. When things hit a snag, needed a little nudge, he easily moved it all along.

When Cochrane and Lola went out on the dance floor, Canillo sat back and smiled like he had seen it coming and had approved the whole ball of wax long before. We watched them as the tuxedos, a bit disappointed she was gone, began to glance at each other, trying to decide if they dared to cut in.

"I heard Papa Joe called you today," Canillo said.

"How did you know that?"

"Billy, how many times do I have to tell you? I know everything of importance in Havana. Now, how is the major leagues' best bird dog? That's the right term, isn't it?"

"That's right," I said. "He's still got the best eye for talent in the game."

"So it was a social call," Canillo said as he ran his index finger around the lip of his gin and tonic. "When are we going to see Mr. Papa Joe again?"

"He's back up in the States for a week or so."

"That is too bad."

"He was asking me about a kid pitcher, that demonstrator who came out on the field last night. The one who struck out Guild."

"A fluke, as you would say," Canillo offered.

"No, not really," I said, looking at him. "The kid had good stuff. A great curveball. You've got to give Papa Joe credit—he's always there when he hears about talent."

Out on the dance floor, one of the tuxedos was dancing with a blonde, looking to steer close to the beautiful Lola. But Cochrane glared at him and the tuxedo didn't stray any closer.

"Papa Joe wants me to find this kid," I said. "You have any ideas about where I should look?"

"Billy, that wouldn't be the wisest thing to do," Canillo advised. He placed his hands on the table, tracing his index fingers around the surface like he was drawing a strange map. "Those demonstrators are not like us. They're wild, almost animals. I doubt if any of them could have a civil conversation like you and me, or be as brothers to one another, the way you and Mr. Cochrane are. I think our Papa Joe forgets such matters sometimes."

"All he knows is the kid can throw a helluva curveball. I told him that."

Canillo flinched, a barely perceptible flicker running across his face, like he had bitten his tongue. "But Billy, often things aren't that simple."

I shook my head. "Those were just kids last night. What can be so dangerous about kids?"

Canillo looked toward the dance floor. "You don't understand, Billy."

"If I can help out Papa Joe, I will," I said. "The way I see it, my career may ride on this."

"It's dangerous," Canillo said.

"University kids are dangerous?"

"That's right," he said, pointing at me. "Why can't you Americans ever understand? It's like one big joke to you people. You don't know what is going on out there, do you? How these kids, as you call them, will stop at nothing. They will make friends with anyone who will help them bring down our government. Communists, Socialists, gun merchants—they wouldn't think twice if it helps them and their precious cause."

I sat there, waiting him out. It wasn't often that I got to see Canillo lose his cool, so I decided to enjoy the show.

He looked out at the dance floor and shook his head. I could tell he didn't like to lose his composure. "I apologize," he said to me, still watching Chuck and Lola dance. "It's just that our country is more complicated than you can ever understand."

"But I've got to at least make the effort for Papa Joe," I said. "He's a guy I need to be on the good side of. Especially right now."

Canillo nodded, his eyes back on me.

"You're a sharp young man, Billy," he said. "I enjoy your company. But you need to remember that this is Habana. This is Cuba. Things aren't always as they seem."

CHAPTER FOUR

Socialismo o Muerte reads the sign, a warning in blunt red and black block letters, marking the entrance to customs in Havana.

"Socialism or death?" Cassy asks me, and I nod, looking around us once again.

We stand at the end of a long line of tourists.

"Cass, hon, we can always go back," I say, knowing how she will hate the concern that has crept into my voice.

"No, we can't," she says in a harsh whisper. "You know that."

Up ahead, the line is moving briskly. Four inspection stations are open, and clean-shaven customs officers in green fatigues routinely inspect every third or fourth bag and then motion the next tourist through with well-rehearsed nods.

"We're going to have to go through separately," I tell her.

"That's OK," Cassy replies. "My Spanish is good enough."

We remain quiet until we reach the yellow line that extends across the worn tile floor. When the next station opens up, I walk slowly toward it.

The customs officer is in his late twenties. He remains stone-faced and silent as I slide the two Lands' End bags atop the table without being asked. I hand him my passport and watch him nervously lick his lips when he sees that it is American. He tries to chuckle but coughs instead, flipping impatiently back to the opening page.

"Why do you come here?" he asks. "It's not allowed for you."

"I used to play baseball here, for the Habana Lions. Curiosity got the best of me. I had to see the place again, you know, while I still could."

He nods, thinking this over.

"They say our president, Castro, used to play baseball."

"I've heard that, too."

"I don't know if I believe it," the customs officer says. "That could just be old people talking." He begins to laugh again and then stops, embarrassed. After all, he is questioning an old man. A man who will be seventy-five next month. "Pardon me," he says. "But some believe in such stories."

"Fidel Castro playing ball," I joke, trying to put him at ease again. "That would have been something."

He looks at me, puzzled.

"Your Spanish is very good," he says.

"Like I said, I used to live down here, back when I played ball."

"Maybe, but you must have learned to speak well before that," he says. "Those who learn when they are older, they don't talk as well as you. Your accent is very good."

"*Mil gracias,*" I tell him.

He waits for me to go on, but I raise my eyebrows and smile faintly. After all, how do I explain all that happened so long ago? How do I tell him that every time I decide there is no connection between this land and upstate New York, where I grew up, something presents itself, reminding me once again that I am part of both worlds? I remember how the water in the channel where I used to fish in Miramar was always muddy, with few ripples. It was the same brown color of my family's fields in the fall, when the first of the cold rains came and everybody hurried to get the crops in before winter arrived.

"*Señor?*" the customs officer calls out, regaining my attention. He holds up a gold-colored imprint like he is wielding a weapon.

"You want your passport stamped?" he asks, smiling.

"No, an insert, please," I reply. "In Cancún they said you could do that."

"Yes, I suppose I can."

He waits while I reach into my pocket and come up with a twenty-dollar bill. The transaction works precisely as the people in Cancún said it would.

The customs officer doesn't even look around before taking the money from me.

"All right, then," he says with a bored expression. "No stamp." Instead, he punches a piece of paper that carries an official-looking letterhead and slides it inside the front cover of my passport.

"Enjoy your stay," he says, returning my papers to me and then looking to see if there is anybody else in line. There isn't, and by the time I have gathered up my bags he has disappeared.

Outside, on the street, I find Cassy sitting atop my old Louis Vuitton suitcase. Actually it is my wife's old suitcase. I bought it for her, for us, the day before our honeymoon to Niagara Falls and Toronto. Is there no escaping her ghost?

"What took you so long?" Cassy says.

"A little history, a little bribery."

"Dad, I don't know why we thought this would be so tough. My guy just wanted to give me the once-over. He was more interested in my boobs than my bags. It was no problem getting into this country."

"Did he stamp your passport?"

"No, a piece of paper. Just like they said in Cancún. I was careful."

I look around us. Our fellow passengers are boarding buses bound for the beach resorts.

"She said she would be here, right?" I say. "Any sign of a welcoming committee?"

"No. Nobody."

"Well, we'll make our own way in the world, then," I tell my daughter. "I think I can still find my way around this town."

I look down toward the end of the terminal and wave. In a few moments a 1959 Chevrolet sedan, a Cuban taxi, rolls up to us. We get in and head toward Havana.

Soon the heat falls over us like a thick blanket and we grow quiet, lost again in our questions and fears about what we're doing. Out the open windows, we see the long, wide boulevard that reaches out to gather us into the capital. It is dusk, and the old Chevy roars past flocks of bicycles, donkeys pulling carts, Ladas belching white smoke, and, here and there, like rare diamonds in the rubble, a new, shining Honda or Audi. If it weren't for those cars, I could pretend that it was '47 again, and if I squint my eyes just right, it's Laurie by my side and not Cassy.

Everyone is in a hurry to get home before the sun sets and the world rolls over upon itself. For at night, it is said, Havana can sink into the earth. At night, the waiting might come to an end, the prayers for something better might be answered.

At the city limits, the poorer barrios begin. Our ride barely slows as we pass rows of shacks with corrugated steel roofs and tar-paper walls. But soon enough we are caught up in the narrow streets, following the trail around traffic circle after traffic circle. On either side of us are the familiar hotels and colonial-style apartment buildings, with their stone columns, shuttered windows, and iron-grille balconies.

But I know that the real Havana lies in the shadows, winking like a whore from another alleyway. This place rides the night air like a piece of music that grabs your attention, only to dissolve when you stop and try to determine where the tune is coming from. Except for the cathedral, El Morro Castle, and the capitol dome, Old Havana rolls out as a city of low-slung buildings. They carry on like old men who go to the park every day. No matter how weathered by the decades of salt air and lack of government money for paint or any upkeep, these old buildings remain, a stubborn reminder. Like the wedding ring I still wear—slightly misshapen, but in the right light a perfect circle.

A block down from the capitol building, with its ivory dome, looking so much like the one that stands in Washington, our cab stops in front of the Hotel Inglaterra. A red-uniformed bellhop hurries to gather our bags from the trunk. As we walk past the sidewalk café, other tourists stop for a moment to look us over.

My daughter and I check in and, with the elevator out, walk up the narrow white marble staircase five flights to our room. It is a corner suite, with a small balcony that looks out onto the park and Old Havana. Below us, the twisting streets fan out like an old catcher's fingers, crooked and broken, toward the Malecón breakwater. A yellow biplane is the only thing in the darkening sky, and we watch as it heads north over the Straits of Florida. Soon it will break off and return. It must return, or it will be shot down.

Cassy stands with both hands on the balcony rail, peering down at the streets below.

"Dad, will you look at that?" she says.

Clots of bicycles fill the wide lanes. We've been told that most of the traffic lights in Havana have been turned off. There is no point to having them. There are not enough cars, not enough gasoline to bother anymore. The bicycles, imported from China in exchange for tons of unrefined sugar, go anywhere they want.

I ask her for the old photo album. The family heirloom that helped put this insane trip in motion.

I slowly turn the pages, fingering the brittle yellow newspaper clippings—all that remains of my baseball career. In the back, poorly mounted with glue and tape, are pictures from my life down here. A photo of me and Skipper Charles grinning by the players' entrance to the stadium. One of Papa Joe looking friendly yet businesslike. Another of that lonely cantina outside of Santa Clara. And, finally, Chuck Cochrane, standing proudly alongside his powder blue Hudson convertible in the driveway of my old flat in Miramar. She took all of these photos and then forced me to go home with them and nothing else.

Some people can keep their past neatly bottled up and at a distance. I admire them for that. After so many years, my past has risen like Lazarus and threatens to overwhelm me.

I hand the album back to Cassy and she slips it, almost lovingly, back inside a brown accordion file. Alongside it sit the books of Malena Fonseca's photographs, all bound with paper covers and held together by staples.

"So, you didn't listen to Señor Canillo, did you?" she says.

"No, I didn't."

"So what happened next?"

"Cassy, my Cassy, it's getting late. I'm an old man who needs his beauty rest. Besides, it took us forever to land and get to the terminal. That should be enough stories for one day."

"Dad, I'm warning you. I can wait you out."

"What, are you a little girl again?" I say harshly. "You still need fairy tales to fall asleep?"

"And I'm not going to let you get me mad, either," she replies. "Look around you, Dad. We've got all night. There doesn't seem to be much going on here. I'm too wound up to sleep, and I imagine you are, too."

"Yeah, I suppose I am," I say, looking beyond her to the darkening city of my past.

CHAPTER *FIVE*

The street leading up to the University of Havana was steep, and I was left gasping for breath. Ballplayers aren't in the kind of shape track and football players are in. We don't pretend to be. In our game, the emphasis is on big moments—the clutch home run, the perfect pitch—and not simply running for running's sake.

When I reached the top of the hill, where the campus began, I sat down on a stone bench. I set aside my blue blazer and unbuttoned my polo shirt, trying to cool off.

Below me, somewhere in downtown Havana, Cochrane and my teammates were carrying on into the night. Viewed from on high, the Cuban capital was an amusement park of blaring neon lights, car horns, and a thumping, jazz-infected downbeat. The Good Book says that all good things, especially sinful ones, must come to an end. In another land that notion could have made the people more prudent. But here in Cuba, it was an invitation to live large and live loud.

Every night the tuxedos, their dates in evening gowns, the beggars, and the whores crowded the strip that stretched from the casinos down to the Hotel Nacional and the Malecón and the sea. Like toy tops set loose on a marble floor, they bounced off each other, going faster and faster, eagerly urging each other onward. Only here could a visitor dance and drink, gamble and cavort, laugh and love, with total disregard of the consequences. It was a dreamworld, too good to last. Everybody knew that. So every night the whole operation cranked into gear, desperate to be more frenzied, more fun, than the night before.

I didn't have any particular plan. Castro was from the university, and I hoped I could find him up here. The campus, with its towering royal palm trees protecting the grounds like giant umbrellas, was larger than I had expected. For a moment I found myself wondering what it would have been like to go to college. I had had the chance. My family had urged me to do so. Instead I'd signed a minor-league contract just days after graduating from high school.

I got up and began walking again. Up ahead there was a huge white building with a series of wide steps leading up to it. Kids, holding their books tight to their chest or hips, hurried by and up those stairs and past thick oak doors. Peering inside, I saw that every corridor was lined with bookshelves up to the ceiling, illuminated by metal fixtures holding bright bulbs.

I didn't go in. I didn't belong there. Instead I sat down on the steps and asked kids if they had heard of Fidel Castro. Eventually I was directed to the Café Carmen, a small dive just off campus. Castro was a regular there, I was told.

The Carmen grew uglier and uglier the farther you went into it. The air smelled of cheap beer, piss, and cigarettes. It was dark and smoky. With my blazer hanging over one shoulder, I stayed near the bar, feeling lost and plenty scared. Conversation around me died down, so I sat on the nearest stool and ordered a beer, trying to fade into the background.

Away from the bar was a larger room of tables and chairs. Every seat seemed to be taken. At the far end of the room was a small stage and a lone microphone. I looked around, anxious not to make eye contact. I had to be the only American within a quarter mile of this hole. I was beginning to wonder if coming here was worth the risk.

I never saw her coming. Suddenly she was in my face with that small camera of hers, which I would soon learn she carried everywhere.

The flash went off, and my only reaction was to put up my hands to protect myself, like a foul tip was coming back at me.

"Jumpy?" she said.

"Now, wait a minute—"

"The American should remember where he is," she said. "That he is far away from the fancy clubs and tourist hotels. That he is near the university, where anything can happen."

She had dark, closely cropped hair whose tips reflected the reddish light of the café.

"This isn't a good place for a tourist," she warned me in English.

God, she was all bristle and movement, talking with her hands. So different from the chiffon-and-diamond babes down at the casino.

"I'm not a tourist," I replied in Spanish. "I live here half of the year."

"So I'm only supposed to dislike you half as much?" She smiled flirtatiously, but her smile quickly snapped off. "You speak the language," she said, "but you obviously don't know this place, or else you wouldn't be here."

"What do you care?"

"That's right," she said nonchalantly, shrugging and looking around the room as if she was losing interest in me. "What should I care?"

I found myself bewitched by her heart-shaped face and the proud way she carried herself. I couldn't just let her slip away.

"I-I'm looking for somebody," I stammered. "Maybe you can help me."

Her dark brown eyes, almonds in the smoke, mocked me.

"Here? You?" she said. "An American?"

"I'm looking for a guy named Castro. You heard of him?"

She smiled and looked away. How I wanted her to continue to flirt with me, and me with her, and let the whole crazy thing carry us somewhere we had never imagined.

"I see his reputation grows," she said, looking me over. "Now Americans come to hear him talk."

She wore a dark linen jacket, tight black pants, leather boots, and little makeup. I decided she was unlike any woman I had ever met before, and all I wanted was to keep her talking to me, just me.

"So Castro will be here tonight? That's what I was told."

"He'll be here," she replied. "But Castro follows his own clock. With him, you wait and see."

"So we should have a drink, then?" I offered. "While we wait."

"Only if you're buying," she said, signaling for the bartender. We both ordered a draft beer.

At a nearby table somebody talked about Batista. How he was only an hour's flight away in Miami, ready to sweep in and take over at any time. My Spanish was better suited to swearing in a dugout and telling the clubhouse kid to fetch me a clean towel. Still, I understood much of it.

"You are either very brave or very foolish," she said.

That night I thought she had only contempt for me and where I was from. It wasn't until much later that I realized she was studying me, as she did everything in the world. She was observing me, trying to decide if I was worthy.

Her beer disappeared in a few gulps. Trying to lighten the mood, I stared wide-eyed at her empty glass. That made her giggle. While the rest of her was so edgy and street-smart, her laughter reminded me of the birds in the early morning back home. The red-winged blackbirds. The blue jays and the finches. Not exactly songbirds, but they have a song, and when they choose to sing it their music can reach you even after you have drawn up the covers and buried yourself deep in the pillows. All it takes is a hint of that sweetness to settle into your brain, for there it will always lie, planted so deep that you can hear the call years later and in the quietest of times.

I see now that I fell in love that night, even though it would be a long time before I realized how head over heels I had tumbled. Her taunting voice, even her aggressive manner, were the things that first drew me. The eyes had held me. But, in the end, it was her laughter that I could never forget.

"What's your name?" I said, calling for another round.

"Malena Fonseca."

"A name so good that it rhymes."

"It has a rhythm to it. It rolls off the tongue of anybody who was born on this island."

"Obviously, I wasn't born on this island."

"No," Malena said, leaning closer to me, "you're an American. Everybody here knows they bring nothing but trouble."

She wasn't a knockout by any means—maybe five foot four, with smallish breasts. But when her eyes locked onto you, it was as if you were the only one in the world who mattered. Her face, milk white with a small mole on the left cheek, was like a crescent moon moving through the clouds at night. While she sometimes tried to enrage you, there was something about her that begged to be pampered and held.

"So you're one of those who think that if the Americans left, everything would be great here," I said.

"Most in this room believe that," she said. "But I'm not one of them."

"No?"

"No, you don't simply throw the Americans out. That's a waste. The night before they go, you have them leave all their money and their hearts at the casinos and the brothels. Then you throw them out—broke and brokenhearted. That way they will never cause us trouble again."

"You would make a great general," I said.

She laughed and finally seemed to relax. "That's right," Malena said. "I would make a great general. But I'll never have the opportunity. As they say, I don't have the balls for the job."

There was a smattering of applause as a guy dressed in a dark blue suit, wearing the only tie in the place, began to snake his way through the tables toward the stage. He stopped to shake hands, make a joke, or slap somebody on the back, and as he neared the stage the applause spread.

"Castro?" I asked.

Malena nodded. "Now the show begins."

Castro stood at the center of the stage and waited until the room grew silent. Then he slowly removed his black-rimmed glasses and folded them away in an inside pocket. He wasn't a handsome man. His brown hair was thick and unruly. Still, he offered a presence. He seemed unafraid of anything, whether it was pitching in front of a ballpark full of people or speaking to a room of smart-ass college kids. Maybe that's why I wanted to

believe in him, or at least believe in what he could do on the diamond. He seemed courageous enough and foolish enough to try anything.

Castro began slowly, his voice low, the words almost stumbling out of him. But instead of losing interest, the people leaned toward him, paying closer attention to what he was saying. Sidling up near the microphone, he bent his knees to it, almost like someone praying to God.

He stroked his bare chin, then ran an index finger down the side of his face. All of these moves, done one after the other, made him look like a shy schoolboy. Soon, though, I realized we were in the hands of a real con man—part snake-oil salesman, all genius. I could picture him at home, practicing his moves in front of his bedroom mirror. For as Castro skillfully reeled us all in, his voice built in volume and anger. There was no doubt that he knew what he was doing.

Castro talked about the government and how it allowed its own people to starve.

"Our representatives are evil," he said. "There is no other word to describe their treachery. The only way to deal with such traitors is to kill them quickly and with no mercy."

Several in the crowd jumped to their feet, cheering, and everybody in the room, except for me, the bartender, and Malena, applauded.

"We have more power than we know," Castro said, his voice still building. "If we stay together and join with our brothers and sisters in the streets, join with our families in the countryside, join with those around the world who are ready to help us, then it doesn't matter who stands in our way. We will destroy Grau. If Batista returns, we will destroy him as well. If the U.S. army invades tomorrow, we will stop them on our beaches. The blue waters will turn red with their blood."

I couldn't believe what I was hearing. I couldn't believe that the kid spouting this nonsense was the same pitcher who had struck out Guild. I nodded at Malena and then walked to the end of the bar, farther into that smoky room, to get a closer look. Castro saw me, and our eyes locked for a moment. I like to think he smiled before turning away to finish his speech of angry revolution.

The room was with him. Most of his audience was ready to storm the presidential palace that night, if he asked. Castro was stone-faced as he waited for the noise to die down. When he spoke again, his voice was as soothing and sweet as a lover's.

"But nothing righteous is ever easy," he cautioned. "We will march someday, but not tonight."

He held both arms out as some in the room cried, "No!"

"Our time is coming," he said. "There is much work to be done. Everyone has a job. It is one thing to cheer. It is another thing to organize, to prepare, to be ready to kill. There is tremendous enthusiasm in this room. But the next step is harder. This passion has to take root. We must care for it, help it grow; only then can we reap its glorious harvest. The country will be ours. But only if we accept all that must be done. Only if we are strong.

"*Hasta la victoria siempre,*" Castro shouted, which meant "ever onward to victory."

"*Patria o muerte!*" Homeland or death!

"*Venceremos!*" We will win!

With that he walked offstage, his shoulders stooped, again the shy schoolboy. The people were on their feet, wanting more.

I felt a finger running up the inside of my forearm. I turned to find her beside me.

"He angers you?" Malena asked. "You don't clap."

"Neither do you."

"I've seen Fidel speak many times before. But you, an American, should be afraid. If he has his way, your great U.S. of A. wouldn't be allowed in this country anymore."

I smiled, now wishing she would go away. I felt angry and disappointed. Why couldn't this kid be some hick from the farm instead of somebody who was involved in all of this? It would have been so much easier to convince him to give baseball a shot.

Still, deep down, I understood Castro's readiness to make his own private war and bring his *amigos* along with him. The day after Pearl Harbor I had led my buddies down to the local recruiting office, regaling them with tales about the emperor of Japan and Hitler. We were doing our patriotic duty. But who would have guessed I would be rejected, deemed physically unacceptable, and they would be sent overseas, many of them never to return.

"Come, let's go see your friend," Malena said, leading me by the arm.

In a back room, Castro was surrounded by a knot of his admirers. I figured we would be waiting awhile, but Malena elbowed her way to the front, with me in tow. She had her camera back out and was taking more pictures. As soon as he heard the shutter, Castro smiled in her direction.

"My Malena," he murmured. "How good of you to come."

He was a bigger man than I had first thought, more solidly built. And in spite of myself, I was soon scheming about the best training routine for him.

"An American," Malena said, nodding at me. "Now they come to hear you. Can you believe it, Fidel?"

"Our movement grows," Castro said, opening his arms wide like he wanted to hug me. But then he dropped them to his sides.

"You talk as well as you pitch," I said, extending my hand.

"The two are in many ways the same," he said, clasping my hand after a slight hesitation. "You were my catcher last night?"

"That's right. You're one of the best arms on the island."

I could almost see him puffing out his chest—proud as a kid after a sandlot game.

"You're good," I said. "We should throw more on a regular basis. It might prove beneficial to both of us."

Malena stopped shooting pictures. "What's all this, Fidel?" she demanded.

"Baseball," Castro declared, like he was getting ready to make another speech. "It's our national game as well. Did you know that when this country was first fighting for its independence, the student rebels played baseball?" He looked around him, only to find questioning faces. "It's true. The Spanish wanted everybody at the bullfights. The true rebels went off to the countryside to play baseball."

"You could make a pretty good living playing baseball," I said. "In the States."

Castro smiled. "You're being too kind."

"No, I'm serious."

"Baseball," said Malena. "Fidel, what are you saying?"

"You saw me last night," Castro told her. "At the ballpark. I struck out one of their best."

"A real good hitter," I chimed in.

"An effective demonstration, too," Castro said. "Didn't you capture it all with your camera, Malena?"

"I don't believe this," she replied. "It was just a silly show."

"You've got a great curveball," I said. "Work with me. You could turn pro. You're that good."

"Unfortunately, I have no time for this now," Castro said, then, in a lower voice, "Please, your flattery is becoming embarrassing."

I held out a piece of paper on which I'd scribbled my name, telephone number, and address.

"For when you find the time," I said.

"Billy Bryan," he read.

"That's right. The most promising catcher in the game."

"Really?" Castro said. "I've never heard the name."

"Think about it," I told him. "We'll talk again soon."

On the way out, I extended an invitation to Malena as well. "If you'll allow me, I'll show you that baseball can be as exciting as politics."

"Baseball?" she replied, puzzled by what she had just witnessed. "I don't know what to make of you. An American friend of Castro's."

"And ready to be a friend of yours, too."

On the way out, I heard Castro laughing among his followers. "Do you believe that?" he said. "The Americans want me to play baseball for them."

CHAPTER SIX

Right on schedule, Cochrane pulled up to my doorstep, driving that beautiful Hudson Super-Six convertible of his. I was loading my golf clubs into the backseat when I saw Castro walking up my white gravel drive. His eyes were bloodshot. His hair was a mess. But he was smiling away, flipping a tattered ball into a glove that had to be older than Babe Ruth.

"Billy Bryan, I'm here for lesson number one," he announced.

"Who's the native son?" Cochrane said.

"How can you remember every skirt you chase and forget the next Cuban Cy Young?" I asked. "This is the young right-hander who struck out Rory Guild."

Cochrane slid his sunglasses down his twice-broken nose and glared at me. "What are you talking about?" he asked.

"Our kid revolutionary," I said, putting my arm around Castro's square shoulders. "You remember the protester who came out of the stands to pitch."

"So?" replied Cochrane. "Unless he's here to caddie, he's busting up our golf game."

"Señor Bryan says he'll be my pitching coach," Castro said. "I'm ready to learn what it takes to be a professional ballplayer."

"Billy boy, can I have a word with you?" Cochrane said, waving me over. He tapped a nervous beat with his fingers on the steering wheel, looking past me to Castro, who stood there, still smiling. I crouched down next to the door, ready to hear him out.

"You know what they say about these Latins," Cochrane whispered. "How they haven't got the heart for the game. Why waste your time with this local?"

"Papa Joe thinks he's got potential."

"How does Papa Joe know that?" Cochrane demanded. "He wasn't there that night."

"I told him," I said. "Remember?"

"You told him," Cochrane said. "How could I forget? Bryan, you've always got a scheme going. You're worse than me."

"I'll take that as a compliment," I said.

For some crazy reason, I was happy that Castro had taken me up on my offer. I stood up, and Castro lobbed the ball to me.

Cochrane sighed, glancing at the open trunk. "So that shoots golf this morning, huh?"

"Afraid so," I said. "At my invitation, Señor Fidel Castro has been good enough to show up. He wants a baseball lesson, and I'm going to give him one."

"Unbelievable," Cochrane said. "Next thing you know we'll be helping nuns across the street, saving orphan kids—"

"Drop us off at the park?" I asked.

"Have you lost your mind? Take your island brother there and you're asking for trouble. They aren't going to allow a kid who isn't under contract—a Cuban, for Christ's sake—in there because he's your new *amigo*. Tell you what, we'll pull by and grab some gear. A better ball than that chewed-up coconut, for starters. We'll find some field and you can work with him. I'm sure this Castro character knows someplace discreet. He seems like the type."

We settled on a lonely stretch of beach twenty minutes out of town. It was sheltered by palm trees and had a small rise that would do for a mound. As I was getting things set up, a couple of kids came out of the tall grass to watch us. They were barefoot, with alert dark eyes, taking everything in. Cochrane gestured for them to fan out across the open area where the sand turned to jungle. The kids would be Castro's outfielders, Cochrane decided.

Once we built up the mound, I put on my chest protector and shin guards. I had Castro throw nice and easy, honing his windup so it didn't look like something out of the cartoons. He had good movement on the ball, and I could tell Cochrane was impressed. Cochrane stood off to one side, a couple bats on his shoulder, simply watching. Whenever Cochrane didn't have his mouth running, something big had gotten his attention.

Castro threw for fifteen minutes or so, calling out his pitches before throwing them. Cochrane hit some fungoes to the kids, having a good belly laugh as they scurried around after the ball like so many hungry pups.

Every now and then I'd go out to our makeshift mound and try to refine Castro's windup. He was tipping his pitches: Before throwing the curve, he would rear back a little too much.

"Keep everything the same," I told him. "Anything that's slightly off, they'll nail you on it."

I could see Castro wasn't much for taking advice. When I talked, he looked down at his feet, going into a deep sulk. But I did my best to keep him up.

"Just little stuff," I said, turning back toward the chrome hubcap we had found for home plate. "You look beautiful out there, babe. Unhittable."

Finally Cochrane couldn't take it anymore. Ever since I'd

reminded him that Castro had struck out Guild, I knew Cochrane would want a couple hacks off my prospect. I waved back our ragtag outfielders and looked out at Castro.

"You ready to pitch a little BP?" I asked.

Castro tapped his chest with his fist. "Am I not unhittable?"

Cochrane snickered. "What a joker," he said, digging into the sand with both feet. "I hate to do this to you, buddy. But it's time to take your prospect downtown."

For a moment Castro fell back into his dipsy-do windup. I motioned with my glove for him to settle down and he caught himself, firing a nice low hummer across the outside of our circular plate.

"That's ball one," Cochrane declared.

"Maybe in this ballpark," I said, flipping the ball back to Castro. "But anywhere else on God's green earth, you're in the hole, oh and one."

I signaled for another fastball and settled down into my crouch. But Castro shook me off. He wanted the curve. I liked that. The kid had some moxie. He had an idea of what he wanted to throw and wasn't afraid to tell you about it. If I'd been able to get some of our pitchers on the Lions, especially Happy Nelson and Skipper Charles, to think at all, my world would have been a lot better place.

Cochrane backed out, a little perturbed.

"C'mon, get it together, huh?" he ordered. "Remember, I'm out here on my own time."

"Your efforts won't be forgotten at bonus time," I said.

With Cochrane ready again, I signaled for the curve. The pitch came in a little ragged, too far inside, and Cochrane ducked out of the way, falling on his ass in the sand. He was swearing to himself when he got up and wiped off his backside with both hands. Out in the field, the kids laughed.

"Since when do Latins throw inside?" he grumbled to himself. "Fuck me. I find the one in the world who does."

Then he motioned with the bat out at Castro while talking to me.

"One more like that and I'm leaving," he warned. "You and this pineapple-head try to get along without me."

"OK, OK," I said. "Simmer down. He's just a little wild."

I caught a faint smile on Castro's face before he turned his back to us.

The next curve was a beauty, breaking in right across the hubcap for a strike. Cochrane was caught bailing out, certain it was another brushback pitch.

"Well, I'll be—" he said, seeing where the ball had landed, nestled in my glove. "That's a killer pitch. I haven't seen a curve like that in a long time."

"Something to behold, isn't it?" I said.

I signaled for another curve, and Castro kept shaking me off. He wanted to throw his change-up, of all things. I let him have his way and, as I expected, Cochrane teed off and crushed it far over the kids' heads and into the tall grass.

"Revenge," crowed Cochrane.

I went out to Castro, who was shaking his head, all in a lather.

"I appreciate your initiative," I said. "A pitcher's got to believe he can throw anything in his repertoire at any time. But I'll tell you what—let me call the pitches for a while, OK?"

"Let's throw that pitch until we get it right," Castro urged.

I glanced back at Cochrane, who was grinning from ear to ear. He would scald every change-up. Our kid outfielders would be on an African safari in the tall grass forever.

"Not now. Not with that pitch," I said. "Like I said, let me do the thinking for a while. We'll need that pitch someday. I don't want you to lose confidence in it."

"So we work on it now."

"No, we don't."

Castro didn't say a word.

"You with me?" I said, in his face now. "That pitch first needs work between you and me. A couple of private lessons before we trot it out for the world to see. If you keep up this pouting act, I'm pulling the plug right now. We'll go home."

That woke him up. "OK, OK," he said. "I'll pitch whatever you want. I'm with you, Billy Bryan."

I returned to the plate. Cochrane was still grinning.

"Jeez, one dinger and you two are fighting like a pimp and his whore," he said. "You take things too seriously, you know that, buddy?"

For almost a half hour I called the pitches and Castro had Cochrane under his thumb. About all the famed cleanup hitter for the Habana Lions could do was line a couple balls foul. He couldn't time Castro's curve, especially when we set it up with a few inside fastballs. Cochrane knew that the curve was coming and he still couldn't do a thing about it.

Every curve Castro threw was as good as the one before. The kid was a fast learner. And with each curve he missed, Cochrane got more and more bent out of shape.

"Last batter," I shouted.

"Here we go, honey," Cochrane said, talking to himself. He dug in with both feet, so deep that the sand was almost up to his ankles. His face was flushed and he wiped the sweat away from his eyes with the back of his hand. "Hang in there. Let's knock the hell out of his fuckin' curve."

Castro and I began to set up Cochrane one last time. After

moving the fastball around, getting a couple foul-ball strikes, I was ready for the curve to punch him out. Castro nodded and went into his motion. But this time his curve came in flat, with no sharp drop. Cochrane was on it in an instant, turning beautifully at the hips, head down over the plate, and the ball flew out of there with the crack of the bat, soaring so high over the kids' heads they simply stood and watched with their mouths open.

Laughing away, Cochrane began to run the imaginary bases in the sand. He clasped his arms over his head like a prize-fighter, and the kids first giggled and then clapped and cheered, falling into line behind him and following his huge footprints in the sand.

I didn't get what had happened until I looked out at Castro, who was good-naturedly watching Cochrane's antics. He caught my eye and gave me a big wink. That's when I learned that Castro was wiser than his years. This kid, maybe twenty-one years old, knew better than to let Cochrane go home with a bruised ego. After all, Cochrane might be useful as a friend somewhere down the road.

CHAPTER SEVEN

The next evening I watched the two box seats behind home plate that Papa Joe had reserved for Castro. They remained empty, two holes in a patchwork of bobbing heads, into the middle innings.

Before the bottom of every frame, as I made my way out to home plate, I glanced over there.

"What's with you?" Cochrane asked when we later went out to our positions.

Together we looked up toward the seats, and there they were—Castro and Malena—settling in. It was like they had appeared out of thin air.

"I get it." Cochrane grinned. "Your big-time pitcher's delivering a little leg on the side. Billy boy, you never cease to amaze me. What's her name?"

"Malena Fonseca," I said softly.

"She is something," Cochrane said, jogging past me to first base. He flapped his glove like he was touching something red-hot.

I nodded at my two fans before flipping down my mask and getting into my crouch. Castro was talking to Malena, and he waved back, with a big smile. Malena glanced at me and then turned her attention back to Castro.

Somewhere after the seventh inning, Castro departed, leaving Malena to shepherd me. Castro and I had made a deal: He'd strut his stuff for Papa Joe, work with me in preparation for the big tryout, if I attended a few of his speeches. Tonight was political lesson number one.

I was feeling pretty good after the game. We had won, ending our losing streak, and I'd gone three for four with two RBI. Any other night I would have headed straight to the casinos with Cochrane and the rest of the guys. But that night I begged off, saying I was worn out. Having seen my friends in the stands, however, Cochrane knew better.

"He's got better fish to fry, better tracks to lay," Cochrane was telling Fermín and Hollins while I shaved. "My man's getting a little action on the side. Cuban action."

Then Cochrane called to me, "Señor Canillo isn't going to be happy. You know how much he likes having the stud of the night sitting at his table."

"He'll understand," I replied.

I was the last player to leave the clubhouse, moving slowly in the warm afterglow that comes with being the hero of the day. The clubhouse kids scurried around the place, cleaning up the crumpled rolls of white adhesive tape and piles of towels that had been scattered on the floor. By the time we returned for the next day's game, the clubhouse would be beautiful again, everything in the players' stalls neatly arranged, a fresh uniform waiting on every hanger. Whatever I'd done that night, no matter how impressive, would be nothing more than a statistic, a trend that I needed to keep improving upon if I was going to stay in the game.

Malena was waiting impatiently when I came out of the tunnel between the clubhouse and the street.

"You take as long to dress as an old woman," she said. "We're very late."

"Hey, the night's young. After all, this is Habana," I said. "How about a little detour, maybe a drink at the Jockey Club?"

"A deal is a deal, Billy Bryan," she said, picking up her canvas camera bag and draping it over one shoulder. "I don't know what Fidel is thinking, but I'm to take you to him. Let's go."

"Here, we can grab a cab down the street," I offered, hoping it would impress her as much as it did Castro.

"No cabs," she said, entwining her free arm around my elbow. She looked up at me with angry eyes. "You Americans don't know anything. Cabs won't go near that part of the university. It's too dangerous. We have to start walking. We're already late."

She began to stride off, and I had no choice but to fall into step beside her.

Malena was in good shape, a fast walker, and as we started up the hill to campus I was soon breathing hard.

"I thought you were an athlete," she said scornfully.

"Not an athlete," I gasped. "A baseball player."

I wanted to talk more, maybe warm things up between us, but my lungs were burning from half running merely to stay next to her.

We had just come to the stone wall that ran along the outside of the campus when she suddenly stopped and pulled me by the hand into the bushes.

"What the hell?" I said.

"Shhh," she ordered. "I don't know if they saw us."

"Who?"

"The MRI."

"What?"

"Hush." Reaching into her camera bag, she pulled out a small pistol.

"Whoa, darling," I said. "I'm not too crazy about this."

"Shut up," she warned. Nodding down the street, she whispered, "There they are."

A black DeSoto slowly approached us. We got down on our bellies; Malena had the pistol cocked, holding it with both hands, ready to fire.

The car cruised closer, its windows down and two faces peering out, searching the darkness. They were kids. Each held a machine gun, the barrels half out the window.

Both of us held our breath as the DeSoto slowed to an idle in front of our hiding place. It sat there for what seemed forever. We could hear them talking. There were three of them—the driver and the two gunmen. One started to get out, but the driver told him he was wasting his time. They argued, with one of the gunmen saying he was sure he had seen us disappear somewhere around here. The driver laughed, not believing him. Then the driver said that if they got out of the car, he was going to leave. He wanted a beer, he told the others.

Pissed off, one of the gunmen squeezed off a round inches above our heads. Twigs and shredded leaves rained down on us. I pressed my face into the soggy grass, thinking I was going to die.

Far off in my head, I heard the DeSoto speeding away. The idiot laughter lingered on the night air.

Malena helped me to my feet.

"Hurry," she said. "In case they come back."

We ran through a maze of back alleys beyond the beautiful

campus plaza. We didn't stop until we reached a wooden door and she knocked twice in a hurry. I looked up and down the street, certain that the DeSoto would return at any moment. The front of our clothes were dark with mud. Shredded leaves were still caught in Malena's hair.

A small slate opened in the door and a pair of eyes peered out at us. Malena said, "Fidel," a password, and the door opened and we were hustled into the darkness. Brushing ourselves off, we entered a crowded, smoky room. Only when we saw Castro coming toward us did Malena put the pistol back into her bag.

Castro had a table reserved for us. We were still in shock as he ushered us to our seats and poured us tall glasses of beer. My heart was in my throat. The world around me was shadows and blasts of white light. My mind kept reminding me that I was lucky to be alive. This was a long way from upstate New York and the string of ballparks and minor-league teams that had somehow led me to Cuba. My life was busting out of its small box, careening out of control faster than I could pick up the pieces. Somewhere in this city, not too far away, my buddies were doing the usual—tooling around town with a couple ladies on their arms, buying them drinks, and seeing how far their money and looks could take them. Here I was running through the back streets near the campus with a girl who packed a gun, while others tried to hunt us down.

Somebody had shot at me. Somebody had tried to kill me.

A voice inside me told me to run. Go back to my old life, play ball, and never open the door again when Castro came calling, his ratty glove in hand. With a little luck, I could find Cochrane and the others before the night was over.

But I stayed. Even though I was still shaking, still angry and d, I couldn't tear myself away. I couldn't help feeling that there was something for me here. Maybe in this world I could be a hero. Maybe here I would at least get the chance.

Years later I told myself I'd been too tired to leave, too much in shock. And what if I ran into the DeSoto on my own? But those were only excuses. A part of me wanted to stick around and watch Castro and, more important, be with Malena. After so many years of knowing what I was doing and not seeing things work out, that night I said the hell with it. I'd gotten on this roller coaster, and I wasn't going to step off. Not now.

"It makes no sense, does it, Billy?" Castro said later, returning to our table. "The MRI are our cousins in revolution."

"Cousins," I replied dumbly.

"A rival political group," he added. "We disagree on philosophy. That's all. Yet they would love to see everybody in this room, except you, dead. The feeling's mutual. Silly, isn't it? We fight among ourselves, while the country sinks deeper into the quicksand." He leaned closer to me. "You offer me an alternative, a way out of all this madness. For that I will always be thankful."

"You won't play ball," Malena said. "You like to talk too much."

"Maybe, maybe not," Castro said. "Billy, I remember the first time I was shot at. Just a couple months ago, after I declared myself politically active. Our struggle has no reason, I think. Not only does the government want to see us dead, so do the MRI, the Orthodoxes, the Communists, all the political parties. Crazy, isn't it?"

He was still sky high from his speech. His eyes were bright, his hands flailing around.

"Then there's Malena. A true warrior woman. Nothing usually shocks her, yet tonight she looks as drained as you are.

You're both pale from seeing your own ghosts walk before you."

"Fidel, shut up," Malena said, sounding tired and disappointed. "You'll get us all killed one day, won't you?"

He ignored her and turned his attention back to me.

"Billy, you know what I dream of sometimes?"

I shrugged. "I don't have a clue."

"I dream that things weren't so crazy," Castro said. "That we didn't have so many choices. I think that's where primitive cultures were healthier. They didn't kill themselves over what could have been, because they had no choice. You did as your father did before you. That's how things were. Now we strive for a better future, and in the process we simply drive ourselves insane. I dream of attending one of your fine universities, a school like Columbia. In a city that's much safer than this. A city like your New York."

"New York," I said, shaking my head. "We're a long way from New York." Then I looked at him and back to her. "They shot at us. They could have killed us."

"And tomorrow you'll awaken happy, my friend," Castro said. "Mark my words. I know. Tomorrow you'll be happy to be alive."

About two in the morning, when we were about the only ones left in the club, Castro and Malena walked me to the edge of campus, where I flagged down a cab. Before I left them, Malena handed me her revolver. Its polished surface glistened under the streetlights.

I tried to refuse it, but she wouldn't hear of it.

"I have others," she said.

Castro laughed. "This is perfect. Billy, now you have two friends in this dangerous place. That's something your teammates will never know or understand."

From his pants pocket, he pulled out a gun that was newer, more deadly.

"Billy, we'll be fine. I'll make sure our Malena gets home safely. Good night, my friend."

I got into the cab, and when I turned back to look for them they were already gone. The cabbie was happy to have an American under his dome light. Somebody who could pay him in dollars.

CHAPTER EIGHT

Papa Joe was back in town, and that night he was at our game against Cienfuegos. Dressed in his white suit and steamer hat, he looked a bit silly, a white whale of a man surrounded by our Latin brothers. But there remained a sharpness about him that you always had to respect.

His eyes, greenish with flecks of gold, were a warning. They saw what others could only guess at: the hitch in a batter's swing, the off-balance rock in a pitcher's delivery. The small clues that suggest why one ballplayer is worthy of the majors, while another will never get past double-A ball.

Papa Joe was in his regular seat behind home plate, taking notes on his clipboard. When he finished with an assessment of a player, he would carefully remove that sheet from under the spring clamp, fold it twice, and slide it into the inside pocket of his jacket. When he was especially busy, the pockets on both sides, swelling with his opinions and directives, pushed his jacket out so much that he looked like another harmless old man who had grown small breasts as his body went to seed.

We won handily that night, with Castro and Malena looking on. They were back in those seats down the right-field line. Not far from the bleachers, where a handful of student demonstrators were carrying on. But nobody came on the field. Nobody had interrupted one of our games since Castro and I had started working out together.

Cochrane's philosophy about the ebb and flow of the game had panned out once again. Where a week earlier we hadn't been able to buy a break, in this game, against a normally good Cienfuegos ball club, we rallied for four runs in the eighth and another two in the ninth. Passed balls, a couple errors, throwing to the wrong base: We took advantage of every one of our opposition's mistakes.

Near the end of the game, Papa Joe moved down the line and sat in an empty seat in back of Castro. That's where I found them when Jumping Johnny Albert fanned the last batter to nail down the victory.

"Hello, Billy," Papa Joe said as I approached. Much of the sellout crowd had already filed out. "Fidel's been telling me about the extra work you two have been putting in. Neat arrangement—you learn about Cuban politics and Fidel works on the finer points of his game."

"I think I got the short end," I said. "Castro's speeches go much longer than any of our practices."

"My tongue's stronger than my arm," Castro joked. He was excited by all the attention. "Billy's a fine teacher. With him, I'll go far."

I smiled at Malena. "You picking up the game?"

"It seems like a lot of waiting around for things that happen too fast," she said.

The rest of us laughed.

"She knows more than she realizes," said Papa Joe.

She turned to Castro. "Can we go now?"

"In a minute," Papa Joe said. "Fidel, I was wondering if you could throw a little right now. Billy's still got his gear on. I'd love to see what you have."

Castro was undecided. "I don't have my glove. Besides, Malena is right, we are late—"

"It won't take but a sec," Papa Joe said. "Billy's told me so much about you that I'm kind of chomping at the bit. He really believes that you have major-league stuff."

"I'll pitch tomorrow," Castro announced. "Ten o'clock in the morning. That OK?"

"Fair enough," Papa Joe said. "I'll clear my calendar. We'll meet here?"

Castro nodded. "Fine. Tomorrow, then."

"Here at ten. I'll be waiting with bells on," replied Papa Joe.

Castro smiled and then motioned to Malena. Papa Joe and I watched them go up through the deserted aisles.

When they were out of sight, Papa Joe said, "Billy, I can't figure your prospect out."

"How's that?"

"That's never happened to me before. I've had kids shinny down banana trees or leave a mule and plow halfway up a row in a field to show me what they've got. That's the first time I've made an appointment like that to see a kid throw a baseball."

"He's worth it," I told Papa Joe. "You'll see."

■　■　■

The next morning I was back at the ballpark by nine-thirty. Papa Joe was already there. He had his brown leather briefcase in hand. It was open like a gaping mouth, packed with files. Papa Joe had his clipboard out, and a stopwatch hung by a cord around his neck. From a distance he looked like a doctor or a veterinarian, ready for an examination.

Papa Joe wielded his tools of the trade with precision and a taste for blood. What he wrote down on that clipboard could stay with a person as long as a tattoo. His opinion carried weight right on up to the top of the Senators' organization. His scouting reports were never questioned. After all, Papa Joe was the best in the business.

I came out of the clubhouse and sat down on the home team bench, putting on my shin guards. Papa Joe came over and stood beside me, one foot up on the bench. He cupped his hands against the overhanging edge of the dugout, revealing huge half-moons of sweat under each arm.

"I'm impressed with how you've brought this together," Papa Joe said. "Boy, am I excited."

"You haven't seen him yet," I cautioned. I didn't want him too enthusiastic.

Papa Joe walked a few feet from the dugout and surveyed the field.

"I realized last night you must have been real patient with this Castro kid," he told me. "That's good. It shows good judgment on your part."

I sat there listening, trying not to get too full of myself.

"I won't forget this, Billy," he said. "You can count on that." He looked back out at the field and then up into the stands. "Now where's our boy?" he wondered aloud.

"Castro runs on his own clock," I said.

"Some do," said Papa Joe. "Until you break them in. Teach them the bottom line."

He began to pace in front of the dugout. He opened his right hand and I flipped him a ball, which he rubbed hard with both hands.

I almost told him about the other day at the beach. How Castro had pitched to Cochrane. How he had followed his own game plan, but when it came time to kick something back into the pot, scratch somebody else's back, Castro had played along. If Papa Joe wanted to believe that I had some control over my talkative Cuban, I thought that was well and good. Yet the way Castro had gone along with the show, kept everybody happy, showed me he loved this silly game as much as Papa Joe and I did. He simply had a different way of showing it.

Still, I didn't tell Papa Joe that story. I realized only then that it had become my favorite time in all the wild ones going back over three winters down here. It somehow outranked my two-homer game against Almendares, the night I caught Jumping Johnny's second straight shutout and he kissed me right out there on the mound like I had thrown every pitch for him, the time Cochrane and I homered in consecutive at-bats. That day on the beach, with kids running in the tall grass chasing down the balls, looking like little puppies in front of a barn somewhere in the sun, had been just about perfect. Two guys as different as Castro and Cochrane had gotten along for a spell, and I was there, able to see it all laid out in front of me like it was some great puzzle falling into place for my personal enjoyment.

The memory was mine, and on this day I didn't feel like sharing it.

"I need to warm up," I said.

"Sure," Papa Joe said, grabbing a glove. We moved out along the first-base line.

He threw a looping floater and I lobbed it back, feeling the tightness in my shoulder that was always there for the first couple minutes after I picked up a ball. Soon Papa Joe was putting a little extra on it, and I returned the ball in kind. I had forgotten that he had been a big-time prospect until he tore up a knee in class A ball and began scouting to stay in the game.

Papa Joe broke out laughing. "Sometimes I forget how much

fun this is," he said. "Just throwing a ball. Simple minds, simple joys."

He was humming to himself when Castro arrived, carrying his old glove and wearing a faded green jersey with gold stripes down the shoulders.

"It's from home," Castro said, pulling down the jersey with both hands as Papa Joe gave him the once-over. "Back then I wanted to play on the best team in town, but they didn't want me. So I put together my own team. This was the uniform. We were undefeated."

"Is that right?" Papa Joe said.

We walked out to the pitching mound and Papa Joe set a small bucket of balls down to one side. There was really nothing else to say.

I nodded at Castro and he smiled. In a few minutes it would be determined if he had a future in baseball. He didn't appear to be the least bit nervous. There was a spring in his step. He kept smiling and smiling, and I began to think he was too worked up for his own good. Papa Joe lobbed a ball and Castro kept flipping it in the air as he turned his back to us, gazing out at something beyond the center-field fence.

Papa Joe walked with me back to the plate. The faded green seats were our only audience. The box seats and grandstand waited silently. It seemed strange to have so much riding on something out here, on the field, and not to have anybody ready to cheer things along.

I hoped that Castro would fill this place with expectations about his baseball future. And that his good fortune would sweep me along in its wake, leading me to something far different and far better than what the last couple years had delivered. That was my prayer on this day.

Papa Joe had a small catcher's mask. It was a speck of a thing

riding a fleshy face with a double chin. Coming back from the mound, hurrying a bit now that Castro was ready, had gotten him flushed. He clutched his clipboard in his right hand, the stopwatch hanging from his neck. He was ready for what he did best: dissect a man's strengths and weaknesses and then project if such talents would be of any use to him and his organization, the Washington Senators.

"Let's see some fastballs," he shouted to Castro. His voice was crisp and direct.

Castro began to throw—slow and measured at first, and then cutting it loose with regularity. His fastball was good, not great, and I could tell from Papa Joe's low grunts that he was far from won over.

"OK, now the change," he said. The pitches began tumbling across the plate like they had a limp, lopsided-looking efforts that were less impressive than the fastball.

"OK," Papa Joe said, head down over his notes. "We'd better see that curve."

I got out of my crouch and started toward the mound, wanting to tell Castro this was it, not to hold back.

"Stay here," Papa Joe ordered. "Let's see how he handles this on his own."

Castro's first curve was in the dirt. I tried to block it with my body, but it kicked away because of the topspin and bounced past me to the screen.

"Try again," said Papa Joe. He was putting his pen back in his shirt pocket. That was a bad sign.

Castro's next curve had no bite, none, and it was all I could do to stretch out and snag it.

"We need it now," I said, throwing the ball back at him with authority. Castro caught it nonchalantly and then took a stroll by himself off the back of the mound.

We had one, maybe two more pitches left before Papa Joe would shut down the whole show.

Castro peered back in at me. He went into his windup, and as soon as he turned his torso and his arm came through, I knew this was going to be a beautiful pitch. The ball spun through space, its path a perfect downward hook. A pitch that would have handcuffed Babe Ruth, Ty Cobb, Jimmie Foxx—any of the great ones.

"Again," said Papa Joe, as if he couldn't believe what he'd just seen.

The next curve was as gorgeous as the first, breaking nicely down and across the plate. A batter could know it was coming and still have a tough time hitting it.

"Yes," Papa Joe said, scribbling volumes now on his clipboard. He was sold, but he wanted to see more, maybe just for his own enjoyment. And Castro indulged him.

Curve after curve he delivered, each as perfect as the one before.

"Jeez-us," Papa Joe said at one point, and then both of us started laughing. That's when I went out to the mound and told Castro to stop.

Later, the three of us sat in the dugout, Castro with a towel over his head. We each had a beer, while Papa Joe went into his sales pitch.

"A couple seasons, maybe one and a half, and you'll be ready for the majors," he told Castro.

Castro nodded like he'd known it all along.

"I'd play in Washington?" Castro's voice was low, curious. I couldn't tell what he thought of the idea.

"That's right. The District of Columbia, the nation's capital. Fidel, my boy, you'll love Washington. The hubbub, the politics—you'll feel right at home."

"Yes, I believe I would." Castro smiled, but I noticed that his eyes were far away. He was gazing out past the center-field fence at the tall buildings of the new quarter of Havana. What was he thinking? This was the opportunity I'd been waiting for my whole life, and here it was being handed to this crazy kid. I felt a mix of envy, anger, and, yes, joy wash through me. After all, he was still my prospect.

"Now, I can offer you a thousand dollars U.S. to sign, another five thousand bonus when you reach the majors," Papa Joe said, his voice gaining momentum. "We'll start you at fifty a week, double that easy once you reach the Senators."

"The money's fine, Señor Joe," Castro said. "The only condition I have is that Billy be my private catcher, a special coach."

"Personal coach?" Papa Joe looked at me. "Did you put him up to this?"

"It's my idea," Castro replied. "Without Billy, I wouldn't have come this far. He must be part of this."

"Well, Fidel, that's grand of you," I said, not sure what he was up to. "But don't knock yourself out on my account. Papa Joe will look out for you. It's in his best interests, remember."

"This condition is non-negotiable," Castro said, putting his half-empty bottle down on the dugout bench. His eyes had hardened. He folded his arms, and I got the feeling that he had used this stance many times before.

"I see," Papa Joe said. "All right, give me some time to work on it. I had a deal already drawn up. Had it right here," he said, flipping through his clipboard. "Give me until tomorrow. Can we meet tomorrow afternoon at my office? We'll do the paperwork then."

"That's fine," Castro said.

"All right, then," Papa Joe said, getting up to shake Castro's hand and then, reluctantly, mine. "We'll nail this down tomorrow."

Papa Joe put his clipboard and stopwatch back in his worn briefcase and disappeared into the clubhouse.

After he was gone, Castro and I sat there for a while, finishing our beers.

"You didn't have to do that," I told him. "You know, he's pretty upset."

Castro didn't say a word. He just sat there, staring out at the empty ball field.

"No, Billy, I had to ask for that," he finally said. "Loyalty is important. Sometimes it's the only thing we have."

CHAPTER NINE

The view from Papa Joe's office, on the tenth floor of the Hotel Nacional, never failed to impress me. First I would focus on the cars and people hugging the Malecón, that wide boulevard and adjoining breakwater that wrapped themselves along the city's border with the sea like an arm draped over a pretty woman's shoulder. Then my gaze moved farther out, across the glimmering blue water, to the whitecaps in the distance.

It could be perfectly calm in Miramar, where I lived, only a mile or so away, but the water was always far rougher here. The waves, especially beginning in the late afternoon, smashed against the breakwater with such force that a blanket of mist and spray could extend six blocks or more into Old Havana itself. Almost every time I came here I saw at least one city truck along the edge, bringing more limestone from the countryside, trying to replace what had been swept away the night before.

From Papa Joe's window, the land looked like a giant hook, ready to snag any storm that blew across the gulf separating Cuba from the United States.

"It's a good contract," Papa Joe told me. He was behind his desk, flipping through a large stack of scouting reports. His phone rang, and from the directions he gave I gathered he was going on another trip, sounded like to Pinar del Río on the western end of the island, to scout more talent. Papa Joe carried a pad of contracts, with the traditional boilerplate, in his briefcase. Castro would be one of a dozen or more ballplayers he would sign this month.

"I don't care if there's no flights this afternoon," Papa Joe said into the receiver. "I need to be there by Wednesday morning. All right, then, if need be I'll go by car. Hell, I could use the fresh air."

He set the receiver of teak and gold flake back in its cradle.

"There's times when I get fed up with this world," he complained. "It's always *mañana*, we'll do it *mañana*. That's how they deal with everything. I betcha your boy Castro's no different. He'll be here. But he'll keep us cooling our heels for a while. Most of the time I let it roll off my back. But sometimes . . ."

As we waited for Castro, Papa Joe offered me a cigar and dug through his bottom desk drawer, fishing out a pint of whiskey.

Indeed, the hour of Castro's appointment slipped by, and I grew impatient. Things were so close to being tied up in a nice bow. Yet Papa Joe wasn't bothered by the morning vanishing without a trace, so I tried to follow his lead. Getting a bit fuzzy-headed on the booze, I got to thinking about how, beginning that night at the ballpark, I was going to start looking out for myself, concentrating on my game. Maybe scouting wasn't the direction I needed to go in just then. I could still peg the ball to second base with something on it. A few corrections in my batting stance and I would start hammering the ball again. I would forget about trying to pull everything and start going to right field more often. I would use the entire ballpark, like the smart guys did. Like Cochrane did.

Just before noon there was a soft knock on Papa Joe's door.

"There's our boy," he said, rising unsteadily from his chair.

At the door, though, he took a half step backward when he opened it to find Malena Fonseca. She raised her camera like a weapon and took a photograph of Papa Joe, with me standing in the background. Both of us had dumb-ass expressions on our faces.

"What the hell?" Papa Joe exclaimed.

Malena laughed. "An effort to preserve the moment."

"Where's Castro?" Papa Joe demanded. "And what are you doing here?" He was angry and stepped toward her like he was going to snatch the camera out of her hands and break it in half.

"I'm delivering this," Malena said, holding out a small white envelope.

Papa Joe ripped it open and read aloud:

" 'Papa Joe and Billy: Sometimes the heavens open and drop a gift. At such times, you must beg your friends for forgiveness.

" 'This morning I left on a great adventure. I've gone to Holguín, in the interior, to train with my university comrades-in-arms to overthrow the corrupt government of the Dominican Republic. We plan to oust the truant Trujillo.

" 'For now *beisbol* must be delayed but not forgotten. I'm sorry I cannot sign the contract at the present moment.

" 'Malena will relay any message you have for me.

" 'Sincerely, Fidel Castro.' "

Papa Joe wadded the letter into a ball and threw it toward his metal-mesh wastepaper basket.

"He's crazy," he said. "The best curveball I've seen in years, and the boy wants to play soldier."

"Not soldier," corrected Malena. "Revolutionary." She had a smirk on her face, obviously happy that her beloved Fidel was out of our grasp.

"Any message?" she said.

"Wait here a minute," Papa Joe said. "And if you take any more pictures, I'll personally throw that camera out the window. Got it, young lady?"

Malena shrugged and sat down on the brown leather couch against the far wall. Above her were framed photographs of Papa Joe, in his distinctive white suit, posing with various Latin prospects he had spirited away to the United States.

Papa Joe led the way out to the balcony and the view I admired so much. He closed the wooden shutter door behind us. From below came the noise of car horns and an occasional voice.

"Did you know about this?" said Papa Joe.

"No," I said. "We both know he's into politics. But I figured it was all talk with him. I didn't think he'd try to be this big a hero."

"Nobody should get this worked up about politics," Papa Joe said. "This worries me. Some of the things they do in Washington may turn my stomach, but I don't throw away my livelihood because of it. You can't be that foolish. Somebody's got to tell Castro that."

Papa Joe walked over to the railing, and I followed. Below us, a siren blared; he looked up and down the Malecón but couldn't find where it was coming from.

"We can still sign him," Papa Joe said. "I'm sure of it. We have to show the proper enthusiasm, though." Then he paused, looking out at the blue ocean. "He said we're supposed to give a message to his girlfriend," he finally continued, thinking out loud.

I remained quiet. I didn't think Malena was exactly Castro's girlfriend. At least not in the regular sense.

"A letter won't do it," Papa Joe added, turning toward me. "Our next move has to have some clout. We need a face, a face in his. Somebody to show him the light."

"What are you saying?" I said, stepping back.

"Calm down. It'll only be a courtesy visit. If anybody is going to talk him out of this, it's you."

"I'm a ballplayer," I said. "I've never been outside of Havana except to play ball or go to the beach. Where the hell's Holguín?"

"Who cares?" exclaimed Papa Joe. "If that's where our boy is, well, then we have to follow. Billy, you're the only one who can reason with him right now. You're his American *amigo*, right? Anybody who can throw like that—my God, his heart has got to be in baseball, not a revolution."

From his coat pocket, he took out Castro's contract.

"Your name's on here as his personal coach," he said. "You might as well earn that distinction. Listen, I'll sign my end of this right now. Even initial in another two hundred dollars for his signing bonus. That'll show Castro we're serious. Tell him to run around the jungle for a week or so, get this revolution business out of his system, and then sign. Tell our boy we'll still ship him off to the States, no questions asked."

"But what about my career?" I said angrily. "If I'm not mistaken, the Lions are playing tonight. Hell, I'm hitting four-eleven over the last week. I need to up my game before spring camp."

Papa Joe nodded and looked down at his patent-leather wingtips.

"I've been meaning to talk with you about that," he said. "When I was up in Washington, your name was mentioned." He paused, nodding again. "The fact of the matter is that your contract won't be renewed by the Senators. We're feeling the effects of the war finally being over. It took a couple years, but they're here, in shape, all the stars."

Finally it had happened. My dream was slipping away.

"But I'm batting almost three hundred for the season down here," I blurted out.

"You're batting two-eighty—in winter ball," Papa Joe said. "Frankly, you could hit a thousand between now and the end of the season and it wouldn't matter one iota. At least not with the Senators."

"Then I'll find another team."

"The prospect of you making a deal with any major-league club would be extremely remote, Billy. Trust me."

"I've been hitting the ball. I'm doing good," I argued. "Doesn't anybody notice that? After all the years I've given to this organization, this is how it ends?"

Papa Joe frowned. "Billy," he said, "it's time for you to consider other options."

Other options? I couldn't believe what I was being told. When I had gone fishing, only a few days before, I'd been preparing myself for this day. But now that it was here, I refused to accept it. Sure, it added up. All the big boys were back from overseas. Not only were they war heroes, but now they would fill up the big leagues, taking my job as well.

Papa Joe had opened the door. Malena was still sitting on the couch, awaiting our reply.

"God damn it," I shouted, slamming my palm against the

door frame. "I'm better than this," I said, glaring at Papa Joe, "and you know it."

"Simmer down," Papa Joe warned. Then he leaned closer to me, talking in a low voice. "Show a little class, will ya? The writing's on the wall, my boy. Keep working with me on this Castro kid and I'll see what I can do."

"Screw you, Hanrahan."

"Get ahold of yourself, Billy. You might as well go; you've got nothing to lose."

"Screw it, screw it, screw it. Screw it all."

Papa Joe took me by the arm and steered me back toward the balcony.

"Use your head," he whispered. "You bring Castro in and you'd be off to a great start at staying in baseball. You'll still have your job here for the rest of the season. I'll smooth things over with the club. I'll tell them you're a bit nicked up. That you'll only be out of the lineup for a couple days."

"I want to finish the season in the starting lineup," I said. "I'm not riding the bench ever again."

"I'll see what I can do," Papa Joe replied.

When we reentered the room, Malena was on her feet, anxious to go.

"So, what do I tell Fidel?" she asked.

"We'd like to give him a message in person," Papa Joe began.

"You'll take me to him?" I asked.

"Take you? You're crazy," she said. "To reach Castro right now is very hard. Holguín is many hours away, on the eastern end of the island. He's in hiding."

"I've discovered I suddenly have the time."

Malena didn't know what to make of this.

"Write me something," she said, her voice becoming strained. "I will get it to him. I promise you both."

"Too many people between his ears and our message," said Papa Joe. "It's not that we don't trust you, darling, but the gist of it could get lost in the translation."

"And I'm supposed to trust you two? Two Americans?"

Papa Joe shrugged. "It appears we have to trust each other for Castro to hear our offer. That is your function here, isn't it? To deliver our message. Not to take so many pictures. So what choice do you have if we wish to send our own emissary?"

"We could be gone for a couple days. Doesn't he have his baseball to play?"

"That will be taken care of," Papa Joe said. "Well, what do you think, darling?"

She nodded at me. "Your hand," she said.

Blood was flowing from a four-inch-long cut on my palm, down my fingertips, and onto the Persian rug.

"Oh, my God," said Papa Joe.

He hurried over to his desk and returned with a dirty washcloth and the nearly empty pint of whiskey. At first I thought the liquor was for me, to clean my wound. But Papa Joe simply handed me the cloth. While eyeing his rug, he gulped down the rest of the whiskey.

"Do you know how much that rug cost?" he moaned. "I just got it last year."

After wiping off my hand, I crouched down to see what I could do about the rug.

"Don't," said Malena. "He can find somebody else to do that. Here, let me see."

I held out my palm.

With both hands, she pulled the wound open briefly.

"Hey, that smarts," I said.

"Shhh," she replied. "It's not deep. But you'll have to keep an eye on it. In this heat, any cut can get infected almost overnight."

She looked at me, and for the first time I noticed a hint of concern for me.

"You have no idea what you're getting into," she said.

I nodded. "Sometimes it's better that way."

CHAPTER TEN

I grew up in a cold, cold country, and that is why I sometimes act the way I do. I don't use that as an excuse. Just an attempt at some sort of explanation.

The morning after my return to Cuba, Cassy is up early, talking away, as excited as a magpie. Only cold water snakes through the ancient pipes to our shower. I begin to complain about it, but then I see there's no use. Cassy is so excited, can't believe that we are actually here, in Cuba, that she doesn't want to hear it.

By seven-thirty that morning we are sitting in the Hotel Inglaterra's dining room. Bananas, peeled grapefruit, sliced mangoes, and oranges have been set out on a long table. On an adjoining table baskets overflow with small loaves of white bread. An hour later, we are still sitting there waiting for her. The white-uniformed waiters begin to tear down the setting. Only one other table, where an elderly couple talk in Portuguese, remains occupied.

"So we just wait?" Cassy says, stirring more white sugar into her coffee.

"Sometimes that's all you can do in Cuba," I tell her.

We watch the old ones get up to leave. They slowly walk by our table, hand in hand.

"How sweet," Cassy whispers. "They remind me of you and Mom."

"You miss her a lot, don't you?"

"Just like you do."

"I miss your mother's tenderness, her sense of humor," I say, surprising myself. "She knew how to smooth over all my rough edges. Looking back on it, I was so hard on you kids. Thank God for your mother."

Cassy's eyes begin to brim with tears. "You're so silly. You two were perfect together. You're a lot better father than you give yourself credit for." She wipes her eyes briefly with a tissue from her purse.

"You know what's funny?" I say.

"What, Dad?"

"If your mother was still alive, we wouldn't be here. She wouldn't have let us do this. I mean, sneaking back into Cuba?"

"Don't be so sure. Mom believed in finding a way to let things heal. If she thought this trip could do that, maybe she would have even come along."

"Now you're dreaming," I tell my youngest.

The morning sun streams through the hotel restaurant's round stained-glass windows. Hues of canary yellow, emerald green, and bloodred spill across the dining room's marble floor and tables topped with white linen. Outside, Havana is awake, the noise of tourists, bicycles, and vehicles building on the streets. The peddlers are setting up their wares beneath the red stone columns that begin near the hotel and continue almost two blocks, past the old post office, to the capitol dome.

I am thinking about the city, remembering how this particular street flows into another, when I see her. The waiters whisper among themselves as she stands by the hostess table. She is taller than any man in the room, with a round face, large brown eyes, and lips as ripe as the fruit the men are carefully wrapping up in clear plastic. It appears she has been traveling for some time to reach this place. Small bags mar the smooth skin underneath her eyes, and her long black hair is matted and pushed back from her face, as if she fought a steady breeze in coming here to meet us.

Her long, flowing dress is frayed at the hem and her sandals are weathered, with one of the clasps broken. Anyone here can see she is just another Cuban. And in this "special period in time of peace," the nation's people have become second-class citizens. To keep Cuba financially afloat, the land's precious beaches and premier hotels, stores, and restaurants are off-limits to them. Only tourists, with their coveted foreign currencies, are allowed inside.

One of the waiters steps forward to tell her the dining room is closed. Breakfast is over for the day. But she brushes past him and strides confidently toward our table with the waiter trailing her.

"My God, she looks just like her mother," I say, marveling at the resemblance.

"You said Malena Fonseca wasn't that tall," Cassy says. "She only came up to your shoulder."

"Yeah? So?"

"Dad, this girl isn't exactly petite."

Indeed, she has a slight paunch and thick legs that the long skirt cannot fully conceal. Her rear end is ample, a characteristic that a woman in New York or Los Angeles would strive to reduce and conceal. But this, after all, is Cuba. A place where women fear becoming too thin. A land where they routinely take in the waists of their dresses and jeans so their buttocks jut out like the fins on an old Chevy.

Even with several waiters now in her wake, she still heads toward us. While she may hide nature a good bit with the flowing skirt, her walk is rolling and brassy. Anywhere else in the world she could be mistaken for a hooker.

Around her neck are layers of bead necklaces. Two golden hoop earrings set off her almost angelic face. But what takes my breath away is her dark eyes. There is a pride, an anger, there that I haven't seen in decades.

I stand as she draws closer. Behind her, the waiter points at the clock on the restaurant wall.

"Closing now," he says.

"Not yet," I reply, reaching into my pocket and handing him a five-dollar bill.

"Dad," wonders Cassy, "did he need to be bought off?"

"*Gracias*," the waiter says, stepping back, satisfied for now.

The woman sits down and pries off her sandals with one hand. Her feet are blistered and dirty.

"Thank you, Billy Bryan," she says. "It is good to finally meet you."

Turning to my daughter, she adds, "And you must be Cassy. The courageous Cassandra. The one who writes such beautiful letters that the censors have no choice but to let them through. The one who brought her father back to the country that never forgot him."

I laugh. "Never forgot. Now you're being too kind."

She stares at me, her eyes taking me in. "No, you would be surprised."

"And you are Evangelina?" I ask.

"Of course, I am Evangelina Heydee Fonseca. But, please,

call me Eván, as my friends do. The past seems to have left me with so many promises and so many names."

"You must be starved," Cassy says.

"Yes, some food would be nice. Traveling has never been easy in this country, but it has become almost unbearable since the Russians left. The bus ride from Santa Clara is maybe five hours. But when there is no petrol, there are not many buses."

"So, how long did it take you to get here?" I ask.

"Two days."

"Two days?" I say.

"Then rest a minute," says Cassy, springing to her feet. She soon returns with a heaping plate of fruit. Together we watch our visitor attempt to eat slowly, politely, but her shaking hands betray her.

"Take your time," I tell her.

She licks the juice off her fingers as she finishes what's on her plate.

Cassy looks over to the buffet table, ready to gather more, but the food has disappeared. The waiters have taken the rest of it back into the kitchen.

Chewing the last morsel, Eván stands, gathering her sandals up with one hand.

"We should go," she says, "before this becomes more difficult."

"All right," I say, leaving a few bucks on the table.

"That will be another fortune to them," she says, nodding at the waiters, who are watching us from the kitchen door. "I'm tempted to stay to watch them fight over it. Unfortunately, it won't buy us any more time here. Come, let's go. We can always talk as we walk."

We hurry through the hotel lobby. Outside the door, alongside the sidewalk café, two bellhops are joined by a green-uniformed security guard and they begin barking questions at us. "Who is this one?" they ask, pointing at Evangelina. "Why is she with you? Two Americans?"

I stop to answer, but this girl entwines her arm with mine, much in the same way her mother used to, and she gathers up Cassy, too, half pushing us, half pulling us, bearing us out into the street and away from the men who want to know so much.

"Who are you?" the guard shouts.

"One big happy family," Eván cries over her shoulder, and with that we are half running, still three abreast, arm in arm, the two women giggling, down beneath the columns, past the old post office, and into the labyrinth of streets below the capitol. God damn, how my back aches and my knees creak. Still, it feels good to run again in the Cuban heat.

Above us the sky is a bright blue, with the first clouds of the day racing past. The wind is so strong that the statues of politicians and angels perched on the ledges of the capitol high above us appear to be flying, coming with us, heralding our escape and arrival.

"Do you think those guards will come after us?" Cassy asks.

"No," says Eván, slowing to a walk. My daughter still stands on one side of her, and I am on the other. Only after we've slowed does this mysterious woman let her arms disengage from ours.

Cassy looks back, ready to run again if we are being followed.

"We're safe," Eván says. "Safe for now."

Up ahead there is a one-story cigar store, wedged between a shoe repair shop and an apartment building, and I wave the girls inside.

A bell atop the door rings when the three of us enter. A small table covered with broad-leaf tobacco is in the corner. Two old men sit on either side of it, rolling cigars and cutting away at the leaves with small knives. They raise their heads briefly and then return to their work when a middle-aged woman dressed in a finely tailored, Western-style dress appears from behind a bead curtain and takes up her position behind the glass counters. She smiles at me and Cassy and then studies our companion.

"Can I help you?"

"Do you have any Mineros?" I ask.

"Mineros? You know a lot about cigars, *señor,* if you want Mineros."

"Maybe a Superfine Negros."

"You know those only come from the eastern end of the island. Where our Fidel was from."

"I know."

"Let me look in the back. Such cigars are very rare."

"I'm only looking for a few. Three at the most. We're celebrating a special occasion. They would be perfect."

"Let me see."

The saleslady disappears behind the curtain of rose-colored beads.

"You look a lot like your mother," I tell Eván.

"I have her face, her hair," she says. "But physically, I think I'm more like my father."

"Your father?"

"Yes, my father."

"Castro, right? He's your father?"

"That's what I was told by my family for many years. But my mother never told me Fidel was my father. Their relationship, as you surely know, was more of brother and sister, not lovers."

I nod as Cassy watches me. "Lord knows the two of them could fight like brother and sister."

"My mother was beautiful when she was young, wasn't she?" Eván says.

I smile. "Yes, she was. She was the type of woman men dream of falling in love with."

"But whom did she love?" she asks me.

"She loved this country," I reply. "It took me years to figure that out. I've always thought that it was too bad she wasn't in charge of the revolution. It would have been more just and right somehow."

Eván is nearly as tall as I am. From the shoulders down, she has my build—hard and thick, ready to take on whatever comes her way.

"I know I hate it when sorrows aren't shared equally," she tells us. "When I was a little girl, they used to tease me that I wanted everything to be right with the world. I wanted justice in the next breath."

Cassy says, "I don't see anything wrong with that."

"But dreams and reality are so different," Eván says. "Sometimes I think I've spent too much of my life deciding between the two."

"In your letters, you said you're a teacher," Cassy says. "But where? What do you teach?"

She smiles broadly. "I've taught for almost twenty years in Santa Clara, where my mother's family is from. I teach younger children. Grade school—is that how you say it?"

Cassy nods. "That's right. Grade school."

"And maybe that's why I spend so much time thinking about dreams and reality," Eván says, the big smile beginning to fade from her beautiful, sad face. "How do I tell the children about the world around them? Even the United States, a country so close? Such places few of them will ever see. It all exists out there, as though it is behind some curtain. It's like we can hear the noise of the world, but do we participate? No. You learn that very early in life here."

"What I find so strange about returning," I say, "is that to me nothing seems to have changed. The city, the people— nothing."

"But of course everything has." Eván laughs. "Habana is falling apart. The revolution? Well, who knows what has happened to that."

The two cigar makers glance up from their work like rodents poking their heads out of holes to catch the morning air.

"You have no idea, you two," she says, looking from me to Cassy and then back to me. "Señor Bryan, how long has it been since you were here?"

"More than forty years."

"A lifetime for some."

"Yes, for some."

"I was born in 1948," she says. "Forty-five years ago."

"That can't be true," Cassy says. "You look barely thirty. No more than thirty-two."

"Cassy, you're too kind," she replies. "Our Fidel would love to hear you talk this way. He's always telling us that hard work, volunteering to bring in the cane from the fields, keeps a person young. Now you're giving him more ammunition for his arguments."

"Does anybody see much of Castro?" I ask her. "Do you?"

"When I was younger, every now and then," she says. "When he did appear, he would always make a point of coming over to see me, asking how I was doing in school. But today? Nobody sees our Fidel, except for the times he makes speeches on television or in the plaza. He has become what he always wanted to be: another dream in the clouds that is supposed to reassure us somehow."

The saleswoman returns with a handful of slender dark cigars.

"Only a few left," she says.

"That's fine," I tell her. "Three will be fine, plus a box of Selections."

"Very good, *señor,*" the saleslady says, moving to the cash register.

"Dad, you don't smoke," says Cassy.

"No, hon, I do. Or I used to. In fact, I love to smoke. Or I used to." I shake my head and try again. "How to explain it . . . Well, as a friend of mine used to say, 'There's no better place to do the things that Mama warned you about than in Cuba.' "

The saleslady offers her lighter and I accept, flicking it alive with one stroke and leaning close to the heat as I light my Mineros. Then I hold the flame out to Eván, who inhales like an expert, and then to Cassy, who rolls her eyes and then tries to follow our example.

Through the smoke that briefly lingers between us, I smile at these two lovely women. There is Cassy, who won me over long ago with her courage and determination. Even as a child, when she found herself in a difficult situation, she could smile and make the best of things, as she is doing again now.

Cassy takes a puff from her cigar and begins to cough. Eván, who has appeared like a genie from the past, slaps her hard on the back, causing Cassy to nearly fall over. Holding on to each other, they begin to laugh. They act like sisters. They could be sisters. But I tell myself I am the only one who can decide such things. Let this Eván regale us with stories from the past about her mother and me, maybe Castro, even Cochrane and Lola and Canillo. Let her delve deep into her version of history. But the past belongs to me. Perhaps that is the only advantage of growing old: I decide what once was and how it will be remembered.

We go back outside, the bell atop the door ringing again. We are halfway down the block when a baseball rolls across the sidewalk in front of us, continuing into the street until it lodges against the curb on the far side. A boy dressed in green fatigue shorts that are several sizes too big for him, a blue T-shirt, and worn leather sandals appears in front of us. Behind him four other boys are laughing, telling him to run, to "get the ball, stupid." They grow silent when they see us.

The boy stands there—scared and watchful. He is eight or nine, I guess.

Feeling sorry for him, sorry that we've disturbed their game, sorry that his clothes aren't better, I try to smooth things over. In hurried strides that surprise me, I quickly cross the street and retrieve the ball. The hide is synthetic. It feels too slick and cheap to me. I had heard that a year or so ago, when the embargo was at its worst, the Cubans had trouble making suitable hardballs for their professional teams.

The ball bears the Batos stamp. *Industria Deportiva Pelota Official*—Official Ball of the Cuban Industrial League. The boys must have gotten it at a game. A foul ball, or maybe a home run, that they tracked down in the stands.

They undoubtedly are proud of this ball. It is as good as one can probably find in Cuba. But as for me, a former catcher, I wouldn't trust the future of anybody who has to throw this ball day after day. With its slick skin, it would make throwing a breaking ball nearly impossible. Try too hard and you could destroy a promising arm.

The boy smiles as I toss the ball to him. He catches it and then flips it back to me, asking if I want to pitch. I follow him to a thin wooden slate that serves as their pitching rubber. Behind me, Cassy and Eván smile. Sixty feet, more or less, in front of me stands a dark-skinned boy holding a short black bat. He holds the bat perfectly still, his eyes on me. He is wearing dirty sneakers and a large white T-shirt that hangs down past his hips, halfway to his knees.

Behind him squats an older boy. He flexes his catcher's mitt, the leather lips flapping at me like a clown face. He smiles, urging me to pitch it in there.

I cannot remember the last time I threw a baseball. The boy's mitt flaps again, as if it is the one doing the talking, keeping up the chatter, and not the boy himself.

"Right here, buddy," the voice says.

I eye the batter again. His eyes haven't left me, and we begin the guessing game. He looks ready. Too ready, I decide.

I make a small circle with my thumb and index finger and hold the ball loosely with my remaining fingers. I go into a bit of a windup, trying to make it seem that I am going to throw as hard as I can.

The ball spins out of my hand—a bit loopy and hesitant in flight.

The boy is too eager and swings and misses before the ball comes close to the plate. The rest of them jeer and laugh as the official ball flops into the catcher's mitt.

The catcher nods and fires the ball back out to me.

"Way to outthink him," he yells.

For the second pitch, I grip the ball hard along the seams and try to throw it past the kid. My hope is that I've set him up, but I know I haven't. No, I want to see if I can throw it hard anymore. Feel the familiar tug in my shoulder. Feel the ball take off and then, suddenly, go even faster. See if I have anything left.

Of course, the boy scalds my fastball. He swipes at it with a slight uppercut, propelling it into the air, and we all watch it soar skyward, hitting halfway up the apartment building far across the street

"Good hit," I say, even though nobody hears me. "Helluva hit."

CHAPTER ELEVEN

Malena roared up to my place in Miramar that afternoon astride a motorcycle with a sidecar hitched to its carcass.

"We're taking this?" I said, standing alongside my suitcase. She nodded.

"And that won't fit," she said, motioning to my luggage. "I believe in, how you say, traveling light?"

"I can get us any kind of car you want," I said. "Just give me an hour. We'll rent something. A Buick, a new Chevy."

"No, we're taking this," she said. "If you don't like it, just give me your message. I'll deliver it to Castro."

"Ride in this all the way to Holguín? Malena, be reasonable. That's a ten-hour drive."

"More like twelve." She smiled. "You don't like it? Stay home."

"Bitch," I muttered under my breath. I was tempted to let her go. But there was something about her—her fire, her determination—that wouldn't leave me alone.

I took my bags back inside and picked out a change of clothes and my old pair of hiking boots—nothing else. Downstairs, in the basement, I found a knapsack and stuffed it full.

Back outside, after I climbed into the sidecar, Malena handed me a pair of leather goggles.

"To save what's left of your batting eye," she joked.

"That's good, Malena," I replied. "Real good. Where did you get this bucket of bolts, anyway? Sure you can handle it?"

"Hang on, Billy," she said, popping the clutch.

We lurched out of my driveway, spraying white gravel, and headed through the Havana suburbs to the main highway leading into the interior. An hour out of Havana, my legs were cramping up. My hair was pinned back to my skull as Malena raced to make good time. The land had been transformed into a rippling emerald ocean of sugarcane stalks and fat-leafed banana trees. It felt like we were in a dinghy on a vast emerald ocean. The packed-dirt-and-cinder road rolled over the hills, and when we headed into another trough, we were overwhelmed by the intense heat.

Somewhere past Santa Clara we came around a sharp bend and arrived at a checkpoint with two sentries and a wooden swing gate blocking our way.

Malena wasn't happy. "This hasn't been manned in months," she said. "If I'd known . . ."

They signaled for her to pull over. Both of us took off our goggles, and she smoothed her dark hair back from her face. God, she was beautiful. Both of the guards wandered over and, leering from ear to ear, tried to figure out the best angle to peer down her jacket and blouse. The bigger one stood in front of us, resting one foot on the front wheel. He gave Malena a big smile.

"Yanquis?" he asked.

"I am," I told him in Spanish. "One who has always enjoyed your beautiful country."

My accent was dead-on today, and it surprised him. The big

one stopped acting so self-important and wandered around to my side.

"You look familiar," he said.

The other one started questioning Malena, and once he determined that she was Cuban, the bigger guy momentarily forgot about me, and they both went after her. In rapid-fire fashion, they wanted to know where she was going. To her mother's. Why? To introduce her new boyfriend. But he was an American; what was wrong with Cuban men?

"He has more money," Malena said.

They shared a good chuckle over that. Then they ordered both of us away from the cycle and sidecar. The smaller one kept touching his revolver, which was strapped in a holster around his waist.

"We're not armed," I told him.

But he ignored me, rubbing his chin with his free hand before joining his buddy in tearing apart the bike.

There was a small trunk in the rear of the sidecar, and they jimmied it open, pulling out a pair of small duffel bags. They opened the first one, revealing a gleaming camera, and when the little one dropped it on the ground, laughing as it clattered and bounced, Malena was on him in an instant.

The bigger guard was waiting for her. He slapped her hard, the blow catching her full on the left cheek. She fell on her side and was rising, ready to go after both of them, when I stepped in.

I began talking as fast as I could. Telling him how I was an American *gringo* who knew some people in some very high places, like Havana, like Washington, D.C.

I rattled off the entire front office for the Washington Senators, hoping he wouldn't be the wiser, banking that a quick verbal barrage of American names would make me sound like somebody who was close to how things operated in our nation's capital.

He gave me a look like, What's with this guy?

Then I rolled into baseball. Were they fans?

They both nodded. I ran through the roster for all four winter ball teams—the Habana Lions, the Almendares Scorpions, the Marianao Tigers, and the Cienfuegos Elephants. Would they like tickets? Balls? Bats?

"You play?" asked the bigger one.

"Sure thing," I told him. "I'm hitting over three hundred right now. Thanks to personal instruction from Bobby Estalella."

The big one whistled. "Tarzan?"

I'd hit pay dirt. Estalella had been Papa Joe's first signing from Cuba, and he had made the Senators in one year. He had hit mammoth home runs, mortar shots that carried forever. No ballpark could hold him, thus the nickname Tarzan. But in the field, he was an adventure. The Senators played him at third base, and balls were always bouncing off his chest and chin.

Quickly I got down in an infielder's crouch: knees bent, arms hanging loose, hands ready, eyes on the batter.

"Pow," I said, staying with Spanish—saying it in a clipped voice, like a radio play-by-play man. "It's a hard smash to third. Tarzan, oh, no."

I rocked backward like the ball had hit me square in the chest. The big guard was laughing.

"But Tarzan hangs with it . . ." I reached down for the imaginary ball, pretending I was gunning a bullet across the diamond. ". . . and throws to first. He's out."

"That's him," the bigger one said. "That's our Tarzan."

Meanwhile, the little punk shook his head, wondering if his uniformed pal was the crazy one.

I swung my imaginary bat, and all heads turned to watch

that fleeting glimpse of horsehide sail off toward the horizon. I started to run around the bases—first past the guards, then the bike—my hands waving up over my head. I had won over the big guard. He started to clap in appreciation.

"You are something," he said. "Go. Before my friend talks me into more mischief."

I hustled Malena into the sidecar (it was about time she suffered through that hell) and shoved the camera and bags back into the small trunk. Climbing aboard the bike, I revved the hand throttle. Even though I hadn't driven a motorbike in years, I somehow roared off in a flourish, while my new buddy, the big checkpoint guard, swung the gate high for us to pass underneath.

We had gone a ways down the road when Malena, her cheek still red from the blow, tugged at my sleeve and I pulled over. My heart was racing a million miles per hour. I might not have been able to score from second on a single anymore, but I had discovered I could outbluff a military man.

Malena was still holding on to my shirt. I looked down at her, all cozy in the sidecar.

"I must learn more about this baseball," she said.

I laughed. "Yes, you should."

At dusk we veered off the main highway, with Malena back behind the handlebars. She followed a dirt road into the jungle until we were well enough off the main road that no one could spot us. She shut off the engine, and I could still feel my body shaking and my ears ringing from the road.

"How much farther?"

"A couple hours," she said. "But there's no hurry. Fidel's not supposed to leave for a few more days."

She pulled out a paper sack from underneath the seat in the sidecar. There were two apples and a loaf of bread.

"If I'd known that was there, I'd have gobbled it down hours ago," I said.

"There's a stream just over that hill," she said, holding out a metal canteen. "Would you get us some water?"

Once the world stopped roaring by, it didn't appear so threatening. Our thicket was overrun with a kind of strange orange flower. Mostly it was a bush, but here and there it had grown into full-fledged trees. By the time I returned, she had rolled the bike back into a grove of white-trunked palms and squat, spreading *júcaro* trees.

"What's the orange flower?" I asked, handing her the canteen.

After taking a long swallow, she looked around us.

"Flamboyants," she replied. "When I was a little girl, they were my favorites."

I ambled over to the closest bush and plucked a flower. She watched me as I returned, bowed, and held it out to her.

"A flamboyant flower for a flamboyant lady," I said.

She took it from my fingertips and smiled in spite of herself. "Sometimes, Billy Bryan," she said, "I can't decide if you're a prince or a toad."

"Don't wait too long to make up your mind," I replied, "or I might hop away."

I lay down on the ground next to her, and it was pleasant to hear the breeze ease through the *júcaros'* pebbly leaves, sounding like the poplars that fronted the property line back home on my family's farm. In the evening I would lie awake in my bedroom and listen to that sound with my eyes closed and imagine that I was a million miles away, lost in an exotic land, a land like Cuba.

When I awoke it was dark. The two of us were hidden within the *júcaro* trees. Malena had gotten a small blanket from the bike and laid it across my legs. A few feet in front of us was a fire, still burning nicely. Its light made dancing shadows on the dark trunks of the surrounding trees, though I doubted any of that light was visible to the outside world. In this nest we were safe.

I watched Malena sleep. With her eyes closed, her face lost much of its anger. Without those fierce brown eyes staring me down, I was able to study her slightly upturned nose. On somebody less beautiful it would be a pug nose, but on her it was lovely. Her mouth was slightly open, and her lips were thin but a generous red. She had an angular look about her, like the wall at Wrigley—all crazy hops and balls lost in the ivy. Her high cheekbones were a hint of a past with more aristocracy than she would ever admit to now. Her family had to be from somewhere in Spain, and I imagined her living in a castle of gray stone, with people coming at her every beck and call. Though her face was tanned, below the solid chin and graceful neck, farther down to where the first two buttons of her blouse were open, the skin turned a more creamy white.

I settled back down next to her, shimmying in a little closer, resting my hand on her hip, and she stirred and then fell back asleep. I watched her chest rise and fall. Papa Joe could believe that he had somehow sold me a bill of goods about becoming a baseball scout, about how Fidel Castro was my first project. But deep down I knew that I would have gone on this silly motorcycle ride, left the cushy life in Havana, regardless of what Papa Joe had wanted me to do. Once Malena had agreed that I could come along for the ride, I was going. For the first time in a while I thought of Laurie and wondered what she was doing. I wondered why I could take off on this adventure but not agree to the simple things Laurie asked of me. I thought of my future, settling down, kids. In my heart I knew that as long as I chased my dreams I would be pursued by ghosts of regret. But here was another chance to forget, another opportunity to lose myself in the shadows.

Malena's connection with Castro was something I couldn't figure out. He had a hold on her in some way. There was no doubt he trusted Malena Fonseca as much as anybody in his midst. Castro had that ability to determine who was on his side and then ask them to do crazy things, dangerous things.

Still, she and Castro weren't in love. At least not in the way that I understood such things. Once Castro figured you were with him, he could somehow keep a whole city happy with attention and excitement and schemes. Malena, and any other woman so inclined, had to think he was the best thing that had ever walked into her life. But was that love? I mean real love? I hoped not.

So, that night under the trees, I decided one last time to stay in the game. In looking back, I had my chances to up and leave. But I lingered on, and it wasn't because of Papa Joe, or Castro, or my fading career. It was because of her. I decided to be with Malena as long as I could. I wanted to be a different kind of man to her than Castro could ever be, and a different kind of man than I had been before.

CHAPTER TWELVE

Outside the provincial capital of Holguín, Malena turned down a dirt road that appeared at a right angle to the Central Highway. During the long stretch from the roadblock near Santa Clara to Holguín, the route had gotten more desolate as we went east, away from Havana. The homes had no electricity out here. Dirt paths led to one-story shacks with tin roofs that had ragged blankets or burlap sheets for doors. We passed more horse carts than cars.

We roared up to another checkpoint. This one was manned by unshaved men who wore no consistent uniform. Some had boots and were dressed in dirty, pea-green fatigues. Others had sandals on their feet and were stripped to the waist, with thin ropes holding up their pants. Beyond them, more men scrambled aboard flatbed trucks, and a couple of vehicles roared out of the complex, going farther down the road, away from where we had come.

"What is this place?" I asked Malena.

"A school. They teach our people how to fix engines, machinery," she said, looking around for somebody in charge. "Fidel and the others were supposed to be training here." Her face clouded over. "I don't see him. We should have kept going last night."

"No, it was too late," I said.

We dismounted and began our search. Indeed, the place was emptying out faster than a ballpark during a rain delay in the second game of a doubleheader. The chain-link gate was opened only to allow another truck to roar past.

"What's going on? Where are you going?" she asked one of the remaining guards. He was a young kid, maybe fifteen. Hanging from his waist was a machete.

"Just walk away," he warned, gripping the blade's handle. "You saw nothing here."

"I need to find Castro, Fidel Castro," Malena continued. "Do you know him?"

"Maybe," the boy said, refusing to look at her. "Maybe not."

"You need a gun for your adventure," Malena said, nodding at his blade. "Is that why they have you holding the door instead of riding out on one of the trucks? A boy needs a gun to be a man, right?"

The kid's dark eyes glared back at her.

"Don't tease me," he warned.

"I'm not," replied Malena. "Maybe I can help you. That is, if you help me."

There were three more trucks left in the wide area in front of a mustard-brick building. Whatever had gone on here was over; the operation was moving out.

The kid followed Malena over to the motorcycle. She opened up the small trunk and began rummaging around where the sentries had been so interested. Reaching deep with one hand, the side of her face pressed against the sidecar metal, she carefully pulled out a package wrapped in rags. Putting the package

on the cycle's seat, she slowly undid it, revealing a polished revolver, a partly disassembled rifle, and a small box of bullets.

"We're running guns?" I said, trying to make it sound like a
joke. I kept smiling, but inside I felt sick. "I wonder if I can put
that on my bubble gum card. 'Hit two-sixty-eight at Rich-
mond. The next year ran guns in Cuba.' "

The kid's eyes grew wide, staring at the weapons.

"What's your name, boy?" Malena demanded.

"Arturo," he said, not taking his eyes off the guns.

"Arturo, where's Castro?"

"Gone with the others. To Antilla. Where the boats are."

"The invasion's on?"

"Yes, tonight," the boy replied. "Before the government can
stop us. Somehow they found out." He looked nervously at me.
"The Yanquis want to keep Trujillo in power."

"So the operation was moved up," said Malena.

"Yes, Castro is with the first group. They leave tonight by
boat. By dawn they plan to be in the Dominican Republic. To
fight."

"Beautiful," I said.

"How many men?" Malena wondered.

"Maybe five hundred," the boy replied.

"And what of Castro?"

"He's been named lieutenant in charge of a squad," Arturo
said. "In line to be a company commander."

Malena sighed. "That's good. At least he's safe for now." She
paused. "Did he have a weapon? Besides his pistol?"

Arturo shook his head. "No, nothing. He said once the battle
started, he would get another one from one of the MRI men.
He's confident they cannot fight, that they will run or be the
first to fall. He felt sorry for me because I had no gun. Told me

to do the same thing." Arturo pointed at the guns. "I need a gun to fight," he said. "I need a gun to go with them."

Malena picked up the revolver and held it out to the kid. "It is yours, if you help me," she said. The boy nodded, taking the gun from her.

Expertly Malena threaded the rifle's barrel into the stock. Rewrapping the assembled rifle in burlap, she handed it and the box of bullets to Arturo.

"You must promise me, on your family's Bible, that you'll deliver this rifle to Castro," she said.

"I promise."

"Tell him that the word in Habana is that he's safe from the MRI—for now. But tell him to watch his back once the invasion ends. With our student brothers, he again becomes a marked man."

"I will," Arturo said. "You have my word."

"So go and join your army," Malena told him.

Grinning, the boy ran back inside the stockade and toward the last truck on the parade ground. Somebody in a uniform stopped him, but when Arturo held out the rifle and nodded at the revolver jammed in the front of his pants he was waved aboard.

Moments later the truck roared past us and Arturo flashed us a thumbs-up from the back.

"Where to?" I asked.

"Habana," she said. "We can't do any more now."

"So when does our boy Fidel come home?" I asked.

She looked back at the last truck. It was whining along in low gear, going up the long hill out of the grounds.

"That may depend upon this other boy," she said. "If he can find his way to helping Castro."

CHAPTER THIRTEEN

The lights of Havana appeared, golden and warm, as we cleared the last of the rolling hills bearing us into the city. It was a little before midnight. The night, heavy with moisture from the ocean and riding the last of the evening breeze, hid Havana's blemishes and scars. In the dark shadows and glittering neon, the city was magically reborn into a world of mambo music and whispered conversation.

Malena was snuggled down in the sidecar, a blanket around her. While I had dreaded the long ride to Holguín only a few days before, now that we were back I didn't want our trip to end. I slowed as we swept past the bungalows on the edge of town where the natives sat on rotting wooden porches and stared with vacant eyes at the world passing by. The road eventually became a wide boulevard with tall royal palms whose tops rustled in the ocean breeze. More cars and scooters crowded the two lanes heading toward central Havana, and together we all plunged over the last small rise and down into the glowing city itself.

Branching out toward the old part of town, I brought us through a maze of narrow streets, along the harbor, to La Bodeguita del Medio, the place where Hemingway liked to hang out.

"Where are we?" Malena yawned after we came to a stop.

"La Bodeguita."

"A tourist trap," she said.

"Sorry, darling, the driver gets to choose where to stop. And I've got a hankering for a steak and a *mojito*."

"Fine, fine," she said, too tired to argue.

Inside we found a small table in the courtyard. When the *mojitos* arrived, a wonderful concoction of rum, lime juice, and sugar with a stalk of mint leaves, she peered down into her glass for a long moment. Then she raised the tumbler and downed it in one gulp.

"Unbelievable," I said.

"And so are you, Billy Bryan." She smiled. "So are you."

Malena was as hungry as I was, and we both tore into tender steaks and bowls of rice and beans.

Two more *mojitos* arrived, and I offered a toast.

"To our success."

"To our success," she said, raising her glass.

After a long sip, I said, "And to the next great Cuban baseball player—Fidel Castro."

"Billy Bryan, you live in a dreamworld," she said. Then she abruptly burped.

I started to laugh. She tried to hide her smile with her hand, but soon she dissolved into nervous, relieved laughter. Ours was the laughter of fools, those who had risked a bit of themselves and were lucky to come away unscathed. We laughed and laughed, and soon our commotion had everybody looking over at us.

"Shhh," Malena warned. "Now look who's coming."

Chuck Cochrane, his face rosy with booze, was heading our way.

"Hello, Chuck," I said, standing up.

"Now where have you been, buddy?" he said, towering over our table.

Malena was suddenly tight-lipped.

"Papa Joe said you were hurt," Cochrane said, looking from me to Malena and back again. "And here you are on the town. My, my, old hoss, we can hear you two laughing all the way out on the street."

Slightly unsteady on her feet, Malena brushed by Cochrane on her way to the ladies' room.

"You sure pick the skittish ones," Cochrane said, gazing at her backside as she disappeared around the corner.

At that remark, I wanted to pound his face in. But it was taking all my focus and determination to stand and talk. The room had gotten a little ragged around the edges. I knew I was very drunk and very stupid. I held up my hand and showed him my bandaged palm.

"I've got a bum paw. Papa Joe said to take a few days off. Get some R and R." I swayed unsteadily.

"You *are* in the bag, aren't you? Look over there. There's Lola, Canillo, a couple of his gang. We're on the prowl for chow and just got a table. You care to join us?"

Cochrane pointed across the room, and there they all were, smiling back at me.

"We're on our hind legs, ready to run," Cochrane said. "Why don't you come on over? Your lady friend will find us if she's of a mind."

Cochrane put his arm around my shoulders, and I went along with him. Canillo smiled when he saw me coming.

"I was wondering whom Chuck had found," he said.

"My buddy shows up in the damnedest places, don't you think?" Cochrane said.

"And with the most surprising company," answered Canillo.

"Billy Bryan never ceases to amaze me. He seems to have friends everywhere in Havana."

He was looking past me at Malena, who was returning.

"And good evening to you, too, my beautiful lady," Canillo said.

Malena frowned.

"You know her?" Cochrane asked Canillo.

"Certainly," he replied. "Señorita Malena Fonseca ranks as one of the outstanding photographers in Cuba. Her pictures often create a stir in the less reputable publications around Habana. Her efforts are moving portraits of the downtrodden, the forgotten Cuba. Am I correct, Señorita Fonseca?"

"You're so kind," Malena replied, an edge to her voice.

"How did your paths cross?" Canillo said. "The ballpark? Is the famous Señorita Fonseca now taking photographs of sports? This I don't believe."

"We have mutual friends," Malena said.

"Is that right?" Canillo said. "I can't imagine who they would be."

Malena turned to me. "It's getting late."

"No, it's not," Cochrane protested. His beefy face seemed to take up half the room. "Hell, hon, we're in Cuba, where the night is always young. Trust me on this. I know."

"Please, please, join us for a nightcap," urged Canillo.

Malena brushed off Canillo's attempt to take her by the elbow and steer her into an empty chair.

"Give me some money," she said to me.

Cochrane started to laugh. "Oh, my golly. She is a pistol, isn't she?"

I reached into my wallet and pulled out all the bills I had. She kissed me on the cheek after I handed them to her.

"Good night," she said. "I'll find our waiter on my way out."

"No, hey, let's stay," I said. "It's OK. They're friends."

I tried to follow her. But before I knew it, Cochrane had an arm around my shoulders again and was directing me back to Canillo's table.

"Let her go, hoss," he told me.

I sat down across from Lola. Cochrane settled into a conversation with Canillo, and just like that everything was back to normal. The two of them were talking about that night's game, which I soon gathered we had won—a come-from-behind victory over Almendares.

I ordered a black coffee and tried to let things sort themselves out.

"So you're healed?" Lola asked. "Cochrane said you were hurt."

"I'm fine," I said. "Bad hand. That's all."

"Your friend seems nice," Lola added. She was smoking a mentholated cigarette and drinking an orangeade.

I nodded dumbly. "Malena is. Nice, that is."

"The way you looked at her when she left . . . I wish you had looked at me like that once upon a time."

"Yeah. Well. What can I say?"

Lola glanced at Cochrane and Canillo, who were becoming embroiled in an argument about whether first place was a possibility for our team. The Habana Lions were playing better, but we stood ten games out with much of the season over.

"And I saw how she looked at you before she ran out of here," Lola continued. "Billy, you have something special there. Any girl can see that. And when she does, she gets a little envious."

I nursed my coffee and tried to smile.

Three musicians, two guitarists and another guy dragging a

stand-up bass, appeared at our table. Canillo handed them a couple bills and they broke into a silly number that was more Mexican than Cuban. Not that it mattered to Chuck.

"They're playing our song," he said, taking Lola by the hand and leading her out to a small space in between the tables.

"For you everything's our song," Lola said with a laugh.

"Exactly," replied Cochrane.

As they danced, Canillo slid his chair closer to mine.

"She's beautiful, isn't she?" he said.

"Sure, Lola's a dream."

"I meant your new friend. Malena Fonseca."

"Yes, she's beautiful, too."

"She's your contact with Castro?" Canillo offered.

"It's got nothing to do with Castro," I said. "Anybody ever tell you that you stick your nose into too many things sometimes?"

Canillo leaned back, arms half raised, palms up. "I'm sorry, Billy. Pardon my manners, please."

"Just drop it," I said.

But he wouldn't, of course.

"I only have your best interests in mind," Canillo said. "Please, my friend, never forget that."

I stared down at my coffee.

"Malena Fonseca is very beautiful, but she is also very dangerous," Canillo said.

I had to laugh.

"This is true," Canillo protested. "You must remember this. She will only bring trouble to a person, an American, like yourself."

I stood up, tired of his talk. "I need my beauty rest if I'm going to be in the starting lineup tomorrow."

"Tomorrow's Friday," Canillo said. "Your day off."

"And I'll need all of it to be ready on Saturday," I said, fumbling in my pants pocket for change to pay for the coffee.

"Your lady friend has all your money, remember?" Canillo said. "See how she treats you?" He held out a crisp ten-dollar bill. "Use this to get home. Everything else is taken care of."

Outside the wind was blowing in off the ocean, sweeping up the deepwater harbor that the conquistadors used centuries ago to ship the gold they found in the New World back to Spain. The evening chill gave me the shivers. I held Canillo's ten-spot in my right hand. After walking past the Havana cathedral, which stood sentry to the patchwork of restaurants and bars, I decided I wouldn't spend his money. I didn't need it. I would walk. I would head for the Malecón and follow it all the way home. It didn't matter to me, in my drunken stupor, that Miramar was almost two miles away. For a moment I imagined that I would bump into somebody famous, another fellow American, say Errol Flynn or George Raft or Ernest Hemingway. They could spot a fellow American from a block away. They would give me a ride back to my place. We would talk about making movies and great books and the grand game of baseball.

After a while I did hear an engine, idling slow, following me. But I was certain this wasn't my daydream come true. No, this sounded dangerous, and I bolted, ducking up the nearest alley. To my horror, the engine roared to life, coming after me. I tried to work my way deep into the maze of Old Havana. A right here, then a left. I ran blind, stumbling over trash cans and slipping on the cobblestones. Through it all, the engine stayed with me, its headlight drawing closer. Then I heard her voice.

"Billy, stop."

It was Malena.

"Billy, it's me."

I slowed to a jog and then halted. Bent over at the waist, I vomited the night's liquor and fear into the narrow space between two garbage cans. She shouted something above the motorcycle's roar that I didn't make out.

I held up one hand, had another good heave, and then stood up on wavering legs, wiping my mouth with my hand.

"Are you OK?" she said at my side.

With an arm around my waist, she steadied me as we made our way over to the motorcycle. I slid into the sidecar like it was my favorite bed.

"Why did you come back?" I said.

"I never left. I was waiting for you to get free of your friends. I didn't mean to scare you."

"*You* didn't scare me," I said. "The whole world scares me now."

"I'd like to show you something," she said. "Please be all right."

"I am."

We wound through the old part of town and into central Havana. The fresh air on my face felt good. Near the ballpark, she angled up through a section of small houses. We climbed a long hill until we came to a four-story white building with columns out front. Here we slowed, staying on the outside of its circular lot until she stopped around back. Malena got off the bike, camera in hand.

"I've been waiting weeks for the right night to shoot this picture," she said.

I followed her farther into the shadows. The streetlights were around front. Back here much more of the night sky, the stars and a glowing half-moon, was visible. She retrieved a tripod from the trunk and mounted the camera on it. I leaned against a small tree, watching her work.

"Isn't it too dark for pictures?" I said.

"Normally, yes," she said, turning a silver screw into the camera body to hold it steady. "With this moon, if I keep the shutter open, with no movement, we should have something."

She had lined things up so a wooden chute, coming down from the second story, was firmly in the middle of her photograph, nicely framed by the moonlit sky and dark shadow lines on either side.

"What is that?" I asked.

"It's one of the reasons I'm proud about what we did—getting those guns to Castro. He's a man who can help eliminate such things from our society."

"But what is it?"

"Hush. I'll tell you soon."

In her hand, she had a plunger device that was connected to the camera's shutter.

"Count to ten," she said. "Ready?"

I nodded.

She pushed hard on the button and the shutter clicked open.

"Begin," she said.

"Uno, dos . . ."

"Slower."

"Three Mississippi, four Mississippi . . ."

When I reached ten, she released the button. We repeated the process several times using different exposures and settings. Malena explained as we went along.

"That will work," she said, beginning to pack up the tripod and camera. "You want to see how these come out?"

"Is that the only way you'll tell me what it is?"

She nodded. "C'mon."

I was feeling much better. "I'd love to."

Malena lived back in the working-class neighborhood we had driven through on the way to the white-columned building. The ballpark was farther down toward central Havana, and a sign pointed to the city dump about a half mile out toward the airport. Hers was one of the more run-down houses. Planks stretched over long ruts in her muddy driveway, and when she rolled the cycle up on the boards, brown water oozed out with a low gurgle.

"Watch your step," she warned, climbing off the bike.

I followed her through a wrought-iron gate and up the back stairway of a two-story house.

"Who's on the first floor?"

"An old lady who sleeps soundly."

Her place upstairs had a small kitchen with a wooden table and two chairs. I sat in the living room on a ragged couch with springs that immediately took a fancy to my backside. She put the kettle on for coffee and then ducked into her darkroom for a minute to begin developing the roll of film. I found the bathroom, with its pincushions of different smells and small bars of soap. My eyes were wild and bloodshot. I washed my face, massaging my forehead with a cold cloth.

Malena was in the kitchen when I came out.

"How do you want your coffee?" she asked. "Sugar? Cream?"

"Black," I replied.

Except for the walls, the place didn't show much effort or expense. The furniture, I decided, was pretty much borrowed or used. But on the walls were a series of black-and-white photographs, behind glass and framed in gold or silver. Taking my time, I went around the room, studying each one. Many were of children, rich and poor. All were smiling, but most had the inflated balloon bellies of longtime hunger. Another photo, a larger, horizontal one, was of a sugarcane field with a row of men, their backs to the camera, bent over at the waist, attacking the crop with machetes like the one the boy in Holguín had carried. Together the men were cutting a wide swath through a dark curtain of stalks. The men were of all colors, like it is in Cuba—white, black, mulatto—brought together to do the dirty work.

Next to this one was a much smaller photograph. A boy, maybe fifteen, held in his hands at least a dozen horse reins that streamed out from all sides to farm horses. The angle was from on high, and the boy was trying his hardest to keep the beasts moving in the same direction. By the resigned look on his face, his mouth locked in a thin-lipped frown, it was apparent that he wasn't having much success. As the eye followed the reins back to all the horses and the promise of more of them in the background, the boy's situation appeared impossible.

"You like it?" Malena said, bringing out a tray with two cups of steaming coffee.

"Yes," I said, glancing around the room. "It's my favorite."

She smiled. "Mine too. Something about that boy . . . that's the way I feel too many days."

She led me by the hand over to the couch.

"How about the picture you took tonight?"

"I'll finish it tomorrow," Malena said. "It's getting late."

"So what was it, anyway? That chute? That place?"

I blew on my coffee and she sat down beside me.

"It's of something that's always bothered me," she said. "It shouldn't exist here. That was the Habana orphanage. On the second floor is the ward for abandoned babies. Many pregnant women already have too many children, so they leave the new ones there. Why not? There are so many more at home."

She picked up her coffee cup, taking a small sip.

"Many that are left there die there. The ones that die must be disposed of. It's difficult to see in the dark, but that chute has canvas flaps at either end. It ends in a metal container that is taken away every afternoon, about two. And another is slid into its place. Someday I'll take a picture of them moving that container. The men who do it, they look a bit like my horse boy up there."

She smiled at the kid in the photograph like she really knew him, knew where he lived, what he loved.

"Somehow a place like Habana, with one of the world's best universities, casinos that attract people from around the globe, the finest beaches anywhere—it can't afford to care for the unwanted ones, to keep them alive. They are thrown out like the trash."

Neither of us said anything for a while, drinking our coffee.

"I know that isn't the best story to tell at this hour," she eventually said. "But the reason I tell it is because a better day will come. I must believe that. When we got the guns to Castro today, saw those soldiers, for some reason I knew I could face the chute tonight. It would be my next great picture. Because Fidel—or if not him, then somebody else—is going to make this country whole someday."

She turned to look at me. "I was wrong about you," she said.

Leaning over, she kissed me short and hard on the lips.

"Yes, I was wrong. You know when to help. Even if sometimes you don't know what you're doing."

Our kisses began tentatively, and then the pauses between them became shorter and shorter until we locked, with her stretching out atop me on the couch. She reached out with a free arm and turned off the lamp. Then the only light was from her bedroom, creating wide patches of darkness and reflecting flecks of light against the now-shaded picture frames. A car rolled slowly by outside, its headlights parading across the ceiling from one corner to the other before slipping away for good.

In the shadows, I could see her hands working down the front of her blouse, the fingers deftly guiding the buttons through their holes until the cloth hung free. I slipped both my hands inside, feeling her warm skin, and she began working on the buttons of my shirt.

CHAPTER FOURTEEN

When you have only four teams playing a big-league-style schedule—three games during the week and double-headers every Sunday—ballclubs get to know each other real well. Probably too well. After a while, the little things that can grate on a guy are worked to death.

"Willy is a friend of mine," Cochrane sang in a loud singsong voice, and immediately the rest of us Habana Lions joined in.

"He'll pass out anytime. Tell us, Willy, what honey you disappointed lately? Wake up, silly Willy."

Out on the diamond, Willy Monaghan's head snapped around like somebody had hit him with a rock.

"Knock it off," the Scorpions' shortstop warned.

"Or what are you going to do about it?" Cochrane teased him, moving a step up on the dugout stairs. "You little jerk. I can't tell where your mouth ends and your butt begins. You're one poor excuse for a ballplayer."

Ever since Willy had been sighted one night passed out on the curb outside the Capri with a pleasant-looking whore standing over him, a pained expression on her face, waiting for him to rise from his stupor, he had become a major target of our bench jockeying.

"Wait till you're up, big man," shouted the Scorpions' pitcher, a feisty little guy named Lasorda. "You're going down."

"That's what Willy thought," Cochrane hollered back. "And look what happened to him. As for you, young blood, I'm taking you out of this yard. Mouth off all you want. Enjoy yourself, because you won't be around much longer."

Lasorda scowled and walked off the mound. Up at the plate, Sammy Dion gave us a pleading look.

"Aw, pull your skirt down, Sammy, it ain't gonna hurt," Cochrane said. "Besides, what's he going to gain by beaning you with two outs? Stand in there like a man, will ya?"

Of course, Dion bailed out on Lasorda's next pitch, even though it caught a fat part of the plate. That was strike three and the end of the inning. Disappointed that we couldn't ride Willy for a while, we went out to take our positions for the bottom half of the third inning. Every team finds another team to hate. That's the nature of the game. For us, the ball club that got our blood boiling was the Almendares Scorpions.

This feud went way back, with both clubs nearly seventy-five years old, and it was fueled by our major differences. Our team, the Habana Lions, was pretty much supported by the rich folks, the upper crust. That's why Cuban gentlemen, high rollers like Señor Canillo, enjoyed hanging around with us down at the casinos. Meanwhile, the Scorpions were the favorites of the working class. Whereas our fans sat in the box seats, down so close to the field that they could hear me cursing out our sorry crew of pitchers every time they unraveled, the Scorpions' faithful were in the cheaper seats down the foul lines, and they regularly filled the bleachers beyond the right-field fence.

We wore red and gold; the Scorpions' colors were blue and white. We were a power team; they liked to run. We were affiliated with the Washington Senators and St. Louis Cardinals; they were with the Brooklyn Dodgers. We couldn't be more different, or more ripe for trouble. Taking nothing away from Cienfuegos or Marianao, the league's other two teams, we and Almendares were the top two squads in the Cuban winter ball league.

With two weeks left in the season, we were locked up in another classic pennant race. They were up by four games now, with ten to play. But after pulling out to a nice lead, the Scorpions were a bit nicked up. Conrado Marrero and Vincente López, two of their better pitchers, were out for the rest of the season, while we were healthy and, as Cochrane would say, "ready to make a little trouble for the world."

My buddy had had some good seasons up in the majors, hitting a high-water mark of .310 a couple seasons back with the St. Louis Browns. I hadn't known him then, though he talked about those times so often, I had all the big moments memorized. People liked to hate Chuck because of all his boasting. Still, it was Cochrane who was our leader in the Havana twilight. While I daydreamed about saving my career in the Big Pineapple, he was actually doing it.

The next inning, Francisco Gallardo led off with a sharp single for us. Bunk Johnson, a helluva hitter, followed orders and moved him over to second base with a bunt to the right side. We shook our heads on the bench. Bunk, who was on loan from the Columbus Redbirds of the American Association, could drive the ball when he was given the opportunity. But old Ángel, our manager, was already tightening up, taking the bat out of Bunk's hands. Ángel was playing for one run when we were ready to stomp these Scorpions but good.

Bunk's bunt brought up Cochrane with one out and Gallardo on second. I moved to the on-deck circle, half wishing that Chuck would strike out, leaving the potential RBI to me. I could drive Gallardo in. I just knew it.

"A base hit," Ángel pleaded, his voice ragged from too many years of fine cigars and shouting for no particular reason. "Just a little poke, my friend."

But Cochrane was looking to put Lasorda in his place. He swung from the heels on the first pitch and just missed it, fouling the ball straight back to the screen.

"Time him, babe," I muttered.

Cochrane stepped out of the batter's box and rubbed some dirt on his palms. The umpire, Hermano Rodríguez, waited patiently. He had the reputation for hustling things along. If he'd been doing the game Castro and his bunch had strolled on the field for, there's no way my screwy prospect would have gotten a chance to show his stuff. Still, with Cochrane, Rodríguez bided his time. His face tightened into a scowl as Cochrane stared out at Lasorda. This delay was eating at him, and at the Scorpions' pitcher.

"Get in there," Lasorda snapped.

Cochrane smiled. "That's going to cost ya," he said, stepping back in.

Rodríguez pointed at Lasorda—ready for the next pitch. Lasorda threw a beauty, a nice change-up, and Cochrane swung too early, way out in front.

The Scorpions' bench hooted its approval, with one end of the bench chanting "up" and the other end Cochrane's first name, "Chuck."

Cochrane turned the evil eye on them, looking like he was going to come over and club every one of them individually. The death stare briefly shut them up, and he returned his attention to Lasorda.

"Fastball, change-up," I muttered to myself. "Fastball now?"

That was the logical choice, or maybe a curve. But either way the next pitch had to be off the plate. Still, Lasorda had plenty of spunk. With everybody thinking hard stuff, he came back with the change-up. That would have hung most hitters out to dry. But the way Cochrane was swinging the bat these days, he could do no wrong. He picked up the difference in speed, checked his swing, recocked, and sliced a wicked line drive between the first baseman and the bag. Gallardo scored standing up, and when the dust settled Cochrane was standing on second base, a big grin on his face, and Felipe Guerra, the Scorpions' manager, was on his way out to the mound.

"Felipe, leave him in," Cochrane shouted, nodding at me. "My buddy needs some RBI, too."

But Guerra had seen enough. Lasorda headed to the showers and Agapito Mayor, a hard-throwing Cuban, came into the game. I watched Mayor uncork a few, blistering the catcher's glove. If anything was typical of my season, this was it. Cochrane had gotten lucky off some kid who would never pitch for the Dodgers, while I got to lock horns with another hard-throwing veteran, a guy who'd kicked around as many ball clubs as I had.

Rodríguez impatiently waved me into the batter's box, and I spent a couple seconds digging my spikes in, trying to get comfortable. I must have been a little too diligent with the excavation work, because Mayor buzzed me under the chin with his first pitch, forcing me to fall onto my back to get out of the way.

The Almendares bench was laughing and hooting as I got back to my feet and dusted myself off.

"High and hard inside," I said under my breath. "Now he goes hard away."

And that's just what Mayor did. Despite my being ready, my

bat was too slow and it was all I could do to foul the ba
the right-field line.

Mayor wasted the next one outside, and I barely held up my
swing. Rodríguez thought about it before saying, "Ball two."

I knew Mayor wanted to get me out of the way with this pitch.
He had thrown three straight fastballs and Díaz, his catcher,
didn't have the guts to call for four in a row. Sure enough, here
came the curve. It wasn't Mayor's best pitch, and I took it high to
up the count to three balls and one strike.

Mayor was steaming. We both knew if he had gone with the
fastball, I would be on the bench by now. He didn't want to
walk me. That could put two men on with Ray Katt, a new guy
with good power, in the on-deck circle.

"Take a good look," Cochrane shouted from second base.
"He's got to come to you."

I had a choice: Protect the plate and be ready for anything,
or pick an area and be ready to tee off if Mayor came in there.
Usually I played it safe. That's how I'd hung around for so
many years. But standing there with Cochrane on second base,
the thirty thousand or so going crazy in the ballpark where my
career would have its tombstone, I decided to stop playing
things so safe. I remembered an old-timer once saying, "Select
a box, maybe two by four inches in the strike zone, and if the
ball comes in there—hammer it."

I decided on a small rectangle just above knee level on the
inner half of the plate. Mayor was famous for hard stuff inside.
He would start you off there when he was pressed against the
wall, and then stray toward the outside of the plate only to give
a different look.

Mayor went into his windup, and the ball came flying in with
a little extra. But it shot right toward my imaginary rectangle,

and I'd gotten the head of the bat moving early. The two forces—bat and ball—met with a sweet crack. And, for one of the few times in my career, I knew the ball was out when I hit it.

"Atta baby!" Cochrane shouted from second base, not even bothering to tag up.

In a daze, I started to trot toward first base. When the ball cleared the left-field fence, I flicked my bat away. Head up, I chugged around the bases. I wanted to savor this moment. I wanted to freeze-frame in my mind all those happy people now rising to their feet, so that I could always call them my own. A private daydream that I could conjure up like some magic potion whenever the real world crept too close to my door again. I was rounding third base, shaking Gómez's hand, when I looked up at the pep band of a dozen or more that was in the stands night after night to root us on. Its two tubas and trombone were leading them in some mambo beat that I forever wanted to call my own.

To my surprise, Malena was with them. Wearing a sleeveless top, she was dancing with four other Cuban darlings and blowing kisses my way. Now I didn't care if I never lived another day. I was in heaven. I was certain of it.

Cochrane was waiting at home plate to pound me on the back. His eyes followed mine.

"Your honey," he remarked.

As the music picked up, Malena began to move her hips in time with the music and wave her arms over her head.

"Maybe there's something for going native," Cochrane said as we moved toward the celebration scene in our dugout.

I wasn't in any hurry. She was mouthing the words to the band's frantic song, something about "When will you be mine?"

And when the chorus began with "Now, now, now," those words were punctuated by hard pelvic thrusts and a big smile.

"You're in deeper than I thought," Cochrane said, sitting down next to me on the bench. Both of us slid forward to the edge, taking sly looks underneath the dugout roof in Malena's direction.

"She's still dancing," Cochrane said, much more interested in this play-by-play than anything going on in the game. "Only for you. My God, my God."

CHAPTER FIFTEEN

Malena was the first woman whom I loved to watch sleep. Her forehead glistened with a hint of dampness. Her breasts rose and fell, her breathing deep and soothing. One nipple was exposed that night back at my place in Miramar. The linen bedsheet ran diagonally across her chest, and I pulled it up closer to her chin as the night grew cooler. I remember the breeze coming through the open window, rustling the curtain.

She awoke, looking up at me with those dreamy almond eyes. Then she smiled and reached up, one hand pulling on my shoulder. She laughed a peaceful laugh when I rolled back atop her, surprisingly ready to start again.

When dawn came, we were both asleep, adrift in an ocean of rumpled sheets and wayward pillows. Later I got up quietly, hearing the birds, then the traffic of a new day.

Downstairs, in the kitchen, I laid out a tray with two small cups, a small pitcher of cream, and a sugar bowl. Usually I hated this time. It was too early, and too often I was hungover. Yet that morning the sky was glorious: pinks fading into orange and yellow with hints of the approaching white-brightness of the tropics. I was so caught up in the show that it took the kettle's whistle to bring me back around.

I found what was left of my ground coffee and poured the steaming water through a small wire strainer.

"I like a man who knows his way around a kitchen," she said, entering the room. Her voice was a low purr and she yawned, stretching her arms over her head, looking like an alley cat. She was wearing one of my old jerseys and nothing else.

Malena sat down at the kitchen table. One long bare leg curled up underneath her.

"Coffee's about the limit of my ability," I said.

"Don't be so modest," Malena said, her eyes beginning to come alive. "You have the potential to be a great chef. That's good baseball lingo, isn't it? Potential."

"I've been hearing it all my life," I said, sitting down across from her.

I placed a cup in front of her, and she eyed it like it was a rare treasure. She took a sip and sighed.

"You've outdone yourself," she said. "That's good. It really is."

For the longest while, we simply drank our coffee and looked at each other. The glances became longer and were broken off only when one of us smiled or returned to our coffee. As long as she kept gazing at me like that, I could have made coffee until the cows came home. I was standing up, putting the kettle back on, when my doorbell rang. It was barely nine.

I opened the door to find Castro, dressed in his blue suit and tie.

"I have escaped," he proclaimed. "Now we can continue with our baseball."

From the kitchen, Malena let out a small cry, and Castro strode through the open door with me trailing him. He and Malena met halfway between the kitchen and the front door.

"My Malena," he said, taking her briefly into his arms. "They tried to kill me."

After his hug, Malena retreated to the bedroom. As Castro and I moved toward the kitchen, we heard the shower start to run. Castro stopped, looking back toward the bedroom.

"Yes, you two," he mumbled, like he was mapping something out in his head. "I can see it now."

I started to explain but then caught myself. Why did I have to justify anything to him? Besides, it didn't seem to matter. Soon Castro began talking about his favorite subject—himself.

"Come," he said, brushing past me toward the patio. "It's such a marvelous morning to be alive. We should be out in the sun."

I made up a pitcher of mango juice, with ice and three glasses, and brought it out to him on a bamboo tray.

"Good work," said Castro, pouring himself a long tall one. "You don't know how sweet this tastes after what I've been through."

He sat down at the table. I pushed open the canvas umbrella and pulled a third black iron chair between us. For a moment we both paused, listening for more noise from my bedroom. The water was off, but Malena hadn't reappeared.

Castro set down his glass. His eyes were focused somewhere over my shoulder, out toward the glittering ocean.

"Billy, they tried to kill me," he said in a low voice. "The message you two sent, through the boy. It worked. It saved me."

With that pronouncement, Malena came out onto the patio. My old jersey had been retired. Instead she wore the sleeveless blouse and black slacks I had helped her out of the night before.

"Come, come," Castro said, urging her to sit down with us. "I must tell you both the whole story."

I smiled at her, but she looked away from me.

"I'm sorry I've intruded on your home," Castro said, leaning

forward and touching me on the knee. "But at this r
there is nowhere else for me to go. Nowhere that is safe."

He chuckled to himself and then started rocking slightly in
his chair, like he was getting ready to give a speech. He made us
wait. But, of course, that was the way it always was with him.

Momentous things happen to many people. Hell, I'd been
shot at only a few nights before. But the famous ones are those
who can call attention to themselves in a way that wins us over.
I see now that Castro always had this gift. The last thing I
wanted to be doing on this glorious morning was listening to
him talk about some new adventure. What I should have been
doing was scooping up Malena in both arms and carrying her
back into the bedroom. But Castro had a way of making you
hesitate about what you knew you should be doing. He could
tell a good story, especially if it was about himself, and I've become convinced those are the most dangerous people around.

"What was the boy's name?" he asked Malena.

"Arturo," she replied.

"Yes, yes, Arturo," he began. "Well, after Arturo told me your
story, after he had given me the rifle, I was on guard for anything. Our force was just four cabin cruisers. Not much. But as
we headed out to sea I was eager for anything. I sat in the back
of the boat, in the open air, looking each man in the face, trying
to decide which ones were my enemies. Which ones wanted to
see me killed."

"If you didn't trust them," I interrupted, "why were you
there?"

"Because if I had not been there, I would have been considered a coward."

"Or a fool," I added.

"Billy, sometimes there is very little difference between the
two," Castro said. He refilled his glass and we watched him

quickly drain it. "All right, then. A few miles out to sea, two government boats stopped our fleet. They obviously had been alerted to our movements. We have so many spies in our midst. By the time they got to our boat, the soldiers were laughing at our worthless weapons. They just ordered us back. Their laughter followed us home."

Here Castro stopped again. With angry eyes, he stared at the glass in his hand.

"So much laughter," he said. But then he looked to Malena and me with a faint smile on his face. "As we returned, I saw how things had changed around me. My companions were embarrassed and enraged, too. All promises were off.

"You were right, Malena. If Trujillo could not be killed at this moment in history, then it was back to business as usual. Back to the petty squabbles that constantly divide our ranks. I saw their eyes on me, the faces saying, 'If we cannot kill Trujillo today, why not a rival? Why not get rid of Castro?'

"There were too many for me to kill, so I had to put down that rifle you gave me, Malena. I put it down and jumped over the side."

"But why, Fidel?" Malena asked skeptically. "How could you be so sure they were going to kill you?"

"I just knew."

"But didn't the boat follow you?" I asked. "Try to help you?"

"No, neither of you understand. They wanted to kill me. Once I got away from the boat, I could hear them laughing. They thought I had committed suicide."

"Sounds like they thought you were crazy, Fidel," Malena said.

"Stop it," Castro warned. He stood up and began to pace. "I'm telling you both the truth. For the rest of the morning and into the afternoon, I swam and floated. The only thing keeping me alive was knowing that I was swimming toward Oriente, where I grew up.

"By midafternoon my mind was going. Anytime I saw a dark shadow, I was convinced it was a shark. But mostly it was me and that damn salt water. The taste made me sick—my tongue and lips swelled. When my legs and arms started to tire, I thought of my father. How proud he was of me, especially when I was an athlete. How he smiled when I played baseball, basketball. The land, still so far away from me, became this large smile, my father's smile, and I kept struggling to reach it.

"As the sun set, I was swept ashore on a beach, where a family picnic was ending. It was the Meléndez family. I couldn't believe it. I've known them since I was a boy. They carried me up to their house, fed and clothed me, and then took me to my father's house on the back of their mule.

"I was in and out of consciousness. But when I awoke for good, there was my father. And when I opened my eyes, he smiled the smile I'd seen in the water. We both cried. Then, for some reason, I told him about you, Billy."

"Me?" I said with surprise.

"I told him about our baseball plans," Castro said. "It excited him. For the first time since I was a little boy, I'd made him happy. He was excited about me pitching for the Washington Senators. Can you believe it?"

"How sweet," Malena said, her sarcastic tone returning for the first time.

"Why are you being like this?" Castro asked. "I have escaped our rivals to live another day. I have great plans now. If the world thinks that I am dead, then it is time to reawaken that world. It is time to be cruel to my rivals. Time to deal them a parting shot they will never forget."

"And how do you plan to do that?" Malena said.

"With baseball."

"Baseball?" I said.

"I think poor Billy has about given up on me, haven't you?"
I shrugged.

Castro laughed. "Oh, I like that. I must remember that. Billy, for an American you are a wonder. On the surface, so cynical. Underneath it all, so fragile. Well, you tell that Papa Joe of yours that I will sign tomorrow."

"We can't kid around with Papa Joe anymore," I warned. "He was pretty mad. . . ."

"Billy, I'm totally serious," he answered. "My father would love for me to play in the big leagues."

"But what about our movement?" Malena demanded.

"The two go together, don't you see?" Castro said. "There's no better propaganda than sports. Think of the possibilities if I pitch for the Washington Senators during the summer and return home a hero. I'd be somebody they would all have to listen to. That's a powerful combination, Malena. Remember José Martí spent fourteen years in the United States, laying the foundation for his revolution."

"Martí?"

"Our George Washington," Malena said to me. Then she turned to Castro. "Fidel, I don't know where you get these ideas. We need you here. There is so much work to be done."

"And plenty of capable hands to do it," he said. "Our movement grows every day."

"Stop it," she said. "It goes nowhere without you."

"Hey, hey," I said. "Before you two start tearing into each other again, who needs breakfast? I've got a couple eggs, some fruit."

"Anything you can spare, my friend," Castro said.

"Just more coffee, please," Malena added.

"You bet," I said, heading toward the kitchen.

From the window to the right of the stove, I could see them, still arguing. But I was happy. Maybe things were falling into line for me.

Feeling inspired, I diced a green pepper into the scrambled eggs. Deciding a tomato would finish things off nicely, I ducked outside to the row of plants that grew along the side of the house. After latching on to a nice red one, I was heading back inside when the word *"extranjero"* got my attention. Castro had called me that. And he was giving Malena a hard time about being seen with me, for having inappropriate feelings toward me. After all I was only an *extranjero*. An American at that.

To her credit, Malena gave him both barrels back.

"You have no right to criticize my personal life," she said. "It's none of your business."

"I only want you to be happy," he replied, and I could feel myself growing angry. I fired the tomato off across the lawn toward my neighbor's mansion.

"Billy?" Castro said. "Are you here?"

I didn't reply, storming back into the kitchen.

The eggs could have used a few more minutes, but I didn't care. I shoveled them onto a plate and brought them out to the patio.

"Ahhh," Castro said. "I'm so hungry."

He offered Malena a forkful, but she waved him away. She looked like she was about to cry.

"Let's take a walk," I told her.

She nodded, and Castro watched us stroll toward the gardens that bordered the estate.

"He had no right to call you that," I said when we were out of earshot.

"So, you eavesdrop, too," she replied. Her face had gone

hard, like the whole world was against her. "You're as bad as he is."

"That's not true," I replied, trying to put my arm around her. She turned away.

"Don't. Not with him here."

"So what if he is here?"

"Because he's right. Can't you see?" she said. Tears were welling up in her eyes. "How can I criticize him and his baseball when I'm with an American? Who am I to talk?"

"I'm sorry. I'm not asking you to decide between this cause of yours and me. I don't care about your politics."

"Then you don't care about me."

"That's not true. You know that. Don't mix me up with him, or with kids who shoot at other kids with guns, or with protesters who love to break up baseball games. I only care about you. OK?"

She didn't answer. In silence, we walked past the four rows of palm trees Señor Canillo had told me he'd planted when he first bought this house.

"Will you dance for me again? Tonight?"

She shook her head. "I must work. I need to photograph a businessman. He'll only do it at night, with the casino and hotel lights as background. His idea, not mine."

"You're not an *extrajero*," I offered.

She laughed, a cross between a gasp and a cry.

"Of course I am," she said, turning toward me, the tears welling up again. "Don't you see?"

CHAPTER SIXTEEN

Cassy and I follow Eván through the streets of Old Havana. We have decided to spend the day sight-seeing, with her as our guide.

As we walk I look at the dilapidated buildings and cannot believe what Castro has done to the city I loved. While he remains the most famous person I have ever known, I'm in no hurry to see him again. In rising to power, I realize, he cast away everything that makes a person human. He has scarred his people forever.

"Fidel declared that Havana was evil," she tells Cassy, "and he's done his best to, how do you say, let it go to hell."

It took me years to realize that Malena was right about me and Castro. Both of us were so determined to be heroes—me with baseball and him with revolution—that we were destined to make a mess of everything.

Heroism to Malena wasn't about scoring the winning run with a ballpark of people looking on, or igniting a revolution that scorches a nation as it carries you to the presidency. No, her brand of heroism was about doing the small things, day after day after day, that can heal a people and hold a country together.

The low, odd-shaped buildings of Old Havana form an ugly lair now, spreading out in front of us down to the Malecón breakwater. Most buildings stand unpainted. Many of the columns have been eaten away by the salt air, down to metal skeletons of rebar.

Nowhere is there any hint of past happiness. There are no longer any of those strange, gorgeous places where the shops and apartments used to cluster like barnacles, so close to the ocean's edge that in rough weather this section of Havana would be engulfed in its own private downpour. The waves crashing against the Malecón breakwater would scatter ocean spray into the air, and on many a night when Cochrane and I passed along this stretch, our cab was forced to turn its wipers on.

I begin to tell the girls that story. About what it was like to ride around Havana in the wee hours of the night when this city was the most decadent, glorious destination in the world. When there was always another party to go to and a cheap ride waiting to take you there. When the lights never went off and the laughter, no matter how sinful it may have been, echoed through these streets, making your pulse race and spreading a smile across your face.

On evenings that lasted until dawn, Cochrane and I would sometimes head to Cárdenas, on the outskirts of Havana. There we would watch the overnight ferry from Key West unload. The cars would spill down the ramp, everything from wood-paneled Mercury station wagons to Hupmobile Skylarks to Chrysler Town and Country convertibles, until it seemed as if the entire world was coming to this island.

At the bottom of the ramp, their horns blaring in the dawn twilight, most of them made a beeline for the casinos and the hotels, heading up the Malecón, eager to be gathered into a city that promised always to bare its soul.

I almost returned to Cuba aboard the overnight ferry in the summer of 1953. I drove from West Palm Beach, whose class B team had given me my unconditional release, down to Key West. I walked out onto the pier, wanting to sail again and make amends for everything. But I didn't. For you see, that day I had also learned Malena was dead.

A newspaper clipping Lola had sent me from Havana caught up with me in West Palm Beach. It told how a revolutionary group led by Castro had attacked an army barracks near Santiago, a place called Moncada. Castro had told his followers to "take the sky by surprise" in their predawn raid. Instead his entire force was eventually captured or killed.

At the bottom of the clipping was a list of dead, compiled after interviews with the military and interrogations of the captured Fidelistas. Three names from the bottom I read Malena Fonseca.

When I read that, I felt like my heart had stopped, but stupidly, stubbornly, it went on. I spent the rest of the day numbly packing, trying not to think but still wondering how much time faded dreams can take up.

That night on the Key West pier, I tore the clipping into pieces and cast them upon the rough waters separating me from Cuba. Then I turned for home and what I believed was my last chance at any redemption. I was ready to marry Laurie Anne Summers, if she would still have me, and get on with my life.

I return from my daydreams to see Eván looking back at me, a faint smile coming over her face.

"We're almost at the Malecón," she says, and in a few blocks we reach the famous breakwater and turn right, heading toward the harbor, following the tourist trail from decades before.

I tell myself to slow down. I fear that my mind is running

away with me. But then I look at her again and, in my heart, something tells me what I fear the most: that I am her father.

But then I repeat the truth as I know it: Malena Fonseca died in 1953 at Moncada. In her letters she never mentioned a child. If anything, Malena teased me for staying in touch with her. Any money I sent to her went to the revolution. "Go back to your baseball," she wrote to me weeks before Moncada. "That is your first love." And how those words stung, because I wanted to prove to her that it wasn't so. But Malena never gave me the chance.

Eván brings us to the front of a three-story marble building with a wide staircase leading up from the sidewalk.

"The old presidential palace," I say.

"You have a good memory, Señor Billy," she comments, nodding at a bronze sign anchored to the left side of the doorway. "But as you can see, it's been renamed."

"Museum of Martyrs?" says Cassy.

"I've never been inside, myself," Eván says. "But people in Santa Clara tell me there's plenty we will be interested in."

I pay the admission for all of us and we enter. In front of us, taking up much of the front foyer, are life-size statues of Castro and Che Guevara.

"Should we kneel or simply bow in their presence?" Eván wonders aloud, and Cassy begins to giggle.

The disturbance brings over one of the tour guides. She is a compact woman with a face furrowed like a field. I guess that she is about my age, seventy or so. She wears a freshly ironed but worn white dress with a nameplate positioned directly above the breast pocket. González, it reads.

"Where are you from?" she demands.

I hesitate before answering. "The United States."

"Not Canada? Well, then I will give you a personal tour."

"We're fine on our own," Eván says, towering over the woman. But the guide isn't intimidated.

"You aren't a Yanqui, my girl," she says, glaring up at her.

"That's right. I'm as Cuban as you."

"Is that so? But what do you know of the revolution? You're too young."

"My mother *was* the revolution," Eván says.

The guide laughs and waves her hand in front of her face, dismissive of such talk. "Don't be silly, child," she says. "Come. All of you. When will you ever receive an invitation like this?"

She begins heading up a staircase, and Cassy and I fall in behind her, with Eván bringing up the rear. She offers whispered translations of González's remarks to Cassy.

"We recently opened a new wing," González says. "It is about the origins of the revolution. Everyone should see it. Outsiders need to understand that our desire to govern our own affairs goes back longer than any of you know."

On the second floor we enter a room with several glass counters and showcases. Black-and-white photographs hang down from the ceiling and cover much of the walls.

"These pictures were recently rediscovered," Gonzalez says, "They reveal an extraordinary aspect of the revolution's past. You see, by 1950 Fidel had decided that Cuba's political system had no basic integrity. To make real progress, he decided, force must be used. In the countryside, he began forming small revolutionary groups, or cells, to overthrow the corrupt system."

González stops and points at a model of a small house under glass on a table in the center of the room.

"In July of 1953 he was ready. Fidel assembled his revolutionaries at a farmhouse outside of Santiago. For a week his loyal followers gathered. They came as separate groups. None of them knew each other."

"Why was that?" asks Cassy.

"For security reasons," Eván answers, then she adds in Spanish, "Batista's secret police, the SIM, were everywhere. Nobody was safe, so any operation had to be carefully planned."

González looks at her with a combination of surprise and newfound respect. "I wish more people your age knew these stories," she says. "For you are the children of the revolution."

"Don't be sentimental," Eván replies, smiling at the guide, trying to egg her on. But González returns, matter-of-factly, to her story of the past.

"Early in the morning of July twenty-sixth, 1953, Fidel and his forces struck Santiago," she says. "Before dawn, in a half dozen cars, they set out to forcefully take the headquarters of Infantry Regiment One."

González points to a photograph of an ugly stone fortress, almost medieval in design, that takes up much of the near wall.

"Moncada," she says, with contempt in her voice. "Fidel had studied the barracks' layout and security for months. He knew the fort could be rushed through the number three gate. It was a bold plan. It would have worked with the proper support—"

"You're being too kind," Eván interrupts. "His strategy was foolhardy at best."

"Don't be this way," González says. "You cannot judge his actions many years later, picking away at them like a vulture or jackal, saying this was wrong and this was right. This is our history. History can be neither wrong nor right. It can only be."

The guide stops a moment, trying to gather herself. I half expect Eván to jump in again, but she waits, as if she almost feels sorry for the guide.

"It was carnival time in Santiago," González says. "Many of the soldiers at Moncada were away on weekend passes. With dancing and music in the streets day and night, Fidel had some of his supporters move among the masses dressed in fiesta costumes. Still, his main force was the car caravan coming from the farmhouse. But too many of them became lost or were delayed along the way. What was drawn up as a well-coordinated attack on Moncada fell into disarray in the heat of combat. In the end, Fidel was lucky to escape."

González then points to the far wall. "As you can see, others weren't as fortunate."

We look past her outstretched arm to photographs of bloody faces, corpses spread across a white tiled floor, their spilled blood pooling in small puddles around the bodies.

"God," exclaims Cassy, "that's terrible."

"They tortured any Fidelista they got their hands on," González says. "They went as far as to take out eyes, beat people into unconsciousness with rifle butts, shoot them in the back of the head. These photographs helped awaken a nation. They were taken and then spirited from the scene by a young woman photographer. The story is that she hid the photographs in her . . . what do you call it in English?" The guide's hand moves nervously across the center of her chest.

"Her bra?" asks Cassy, and the guide nods.

"Without these pictures," González continues, "I believe there wouldn't have been a revolution. These pictures shocked our country."

"Who took them?" says Eván, suddenly more interested.

Gonzalez stares up at the ceiling. "Oh, I cannot believe I've forgotten. This is embarrassing."

"There's a small plaque over here," Cassy says.

We move away from the guide and I crouch down, reading the short inscription aloud. " 'Photographs by Malena Fonseca. The revolution's true patriot, 1923–1959.'" I look up at Evangelina. "In 1959? How can that be? She died here—at Moncada."

Eván shakes her head. "No, Billy, she didn't die a martyr's death. That's another myth Fidel built up around her. You'll find that the truth about my mother is much more complicated."

"But why didn't she tell me?" I continue, my voice beginning to break. "She knew where I was. I would have come back."

"Perhaps she knew that you had started a new life," Eván says, turning from me to Cassy.

González rejoins us, an incredulous look on her face. She stands over me as I sink to my knees in front of the plaque.

"I could have saved her," I say. "But I didn't even know she was alive."

■ ■ ■

"Sometimes I wonder if my mother's soul ever came to rest," Eván says. "To me, it feels like it is still up there, lost and alone."

She and Cassy are talking on the hotel balcony overlooking the street. Below them music echoes up among the buildings, occasionally carrying a shout or piece of conversation with it. It is two in the morning. We are to tour the country tomorrow, bright and early. Evanglina has more to show us. Thanks to U.S. dollars, it has been all arranged. Tonight Eván is staying with us. I paid the night clerk a hefty amount to look the other way. The whole world is built upon bribes down here.

"How can you know about somebody's soul?" I hear Cassy ask her.

"I have my ways," Eván tells her.

The two of them grow quiet, listening to Havana's cries and laughter.

In my bedroom, I also listen to the sounds of the night. I

want to go out to the balcony and explain everything to them. But how? For an old man like me, with another journey starting in the morning, sleep and drink are fast making a prisoner of my best intentions. How to explain to them that when you leave somebody you love, your only choice is to start again? How to tell them that when this happens, you are desperate to remake the world into something that promises to be less painful than the one you left behind?

On this night I wonder whether, if I had believed more in Malena Fonseca, more in our love, I would have somehow known she had escaped at Moncada. Known that she had run and faded into this land, the way she had so many times before. Instead of tearing up that newspaper clipping and scattering it on the black water along the Key West pier, I would have made the overnight passage again, this time to rescue her. Instead, I became the one who needed rescuing. I'm not sure I can forgive myself now for outliving her. I suppose I needed more time to repay her for all she'd done for me.

After Moncada, I married Laurie, a pretty girl from Middleport three years my junior. She taught me a lot about forgiveness, and much more, over the years. She was already two months pregnant with our oldest, Danny, when we went to the altar that fall. At the time I wasn't certain if that was the only reason she'd agreed to marry me. But as time went on, I knew that it was far more than that.

I returned to make a home in the cold land where I grew up. I took over my father's farm, and I was there to bury him when first he and then, sixteen months later, my mother died. They were laid to rest, side by side, in the Methodist cemetery a few miles outside of town. Laurie was buried there as well. My plot is right next to hers.

Decisions were made. When the farm went bust, I became the gym teacher at the high school, and I lived as honorably as I could.

So, now what do I do about this girl who has appeared in my life? How could I not have known about her? Am I such a fool?

To say that Eván is mine is to admit that my entire life has been a lie. I want to go out onto the balcony and try and explain this to them. But I am old. Sleep, drink, and, ultimately, fear are clouding my thoughts once more.

Too soon I feel myself drifting off. I begin to dream of white beaches where the water envelops me with the feel of light silk. As I wade farther out into the turquoise waters, I hear music and laughter. The music builds, its bass line as steady as the surf itself, and I lie back in the water, feeling the tide begin to carry me out as I peer up at the small clouds being blown by a soft breeze over the horizon toward the open sea.

CHAPTER SEVENTEEN

Castro signed a professional contract with the Washington Senators the same afternoon he returned from his great adventure, right there in Papa Joe's suite at the Hotel Nacional. While his signature assured me of an immediate future in baseball, I couldn't wait to get the proceedings over with.

I hated to admit it, but I was jealous of him and Malena. Of the power that he had over her.

Castro kept his promise, making me his personal coach. He signed with a flourish. His right hand hung in the air for a moment, like he had just finished playing the piano to a standing ovation. Papa Joe deftly slid the two-sheet contract out of sight and placed it in a thick file folder labeled New Recruits. The folder then was returned to the top drawer of his wooden file cabinet.

"Well, that's that." Papa Joe beamed.

"That's that," repeated Castro, who had pocketed the Mont Blanc pen Papa Joe had handed to him to sign with.

"The organization would like you to work out with Billy for the next ten days," Papa Joe advised. "You're due at the Senators' camp on February seventeenth. I'll go ahead and book you both seats on the late-afternoon flight to Miami the day before."

Castro nodded. "For me and Billy."

"As the contract indicates, Billy is your personal coach," Papa Joe continued. "Still, once you're in camp, we would like you to utilize the other excellent pitching instructors within our system, too. Besides, I have plans for Billy. Once he's back in the States, I'll need him to make the rounds. Some special assignments for me."

Despite my recent hot streak, my dramatic homer against Almendares, the Senators had no playing job waiting for me, not even anything to compete for, once spring training began. I was to deliver Castro and then wait and see what Papa Joe had in store for me. From the way he was letting Castro down easy about me not being with him every step of the way, I expected to hear a similar speech about my future as a scout sometime down the line.

"We'll do good work before I leave," Castro promised. "If it's all right with Billy, I could stay at his flat."

Papa Joe raised his eyebrows and looked over at me.

"I like that idea," he said. "What do you say, Billy? From what I hear, you've got plenty of room out there in Miramar."

"I don't know . . . ," I began. After what Castro had called Malena, I wanted nothing to do with him. I didn't trust him. I couldn't decide how serious he was about baseball as opposed to politics. Besides, a man's home is supposed to be his castle. The last thing I wanted was Castro and any of his buddies underfoot, with all their silly schemes about how to overthrow the government.

"Billy, it'd make a lot of sense," Papa Joe said. "It would be easier to keep an eye on our new prospect that way."

"I'll think about it," I said, hoping the issue would be forgotten.

"Good, good," Papa Joe said.

I started to head toward the door.

"Stick around just a minute, will ya, Billy?" Papa Joe called. "Well, Fidel," he said, shaking Castro's hand one last time, "I won't begrudge any celebrating tonight. But tomorrow it's back to the training table. All right?"

Castro couldn't stop smiling. He was wearing the same blue suit that he had worn that first night at the revolutionary club. On the way out, he stopped in front of me.

"Thanks, my friend," Castro said, holding out his hand.

When I went to take it, he pulled me close, burying his head briefly atop my shoulder. "I'll make this worth your while," he whispered before letting me go.

I nodded as he moved past me, closing the door behind him.

Papa Joe had his back to me, looking out at the city and the ocean. "You don't seem very happy," he said.

"I'm not, I guess," I replied.

"Why is that?"

"Mmmm, maybe it's because he's on his way to the majors, while my career has landed in the ditch," I said. "That's how I see this blessed event of him signing on the dotted line."

"You shouldn't take things too much to heart," Papa Joe cautioned. "Cochrane says you think too much, and he's right. Too much thinking is trouble for a ballplayer." He sat down at his desk and opened the lid of a new box of cigars. "Everything depends upon how you look at things," he added.

His mahogany desktop was so polished its surface reflected the hot afternoon sun nearly as well as did the blue ocean beyond his window. It was the same blinding light, the kind of light that gets in a guy's eyes. Makes you oblivious to things that are right there in front of you.

He held out a cigar and I reached for it. Rolling it with my fingers, I studied the beauty. A Mineros—sold only on the island. One of the best cigars there was. I brought it to my mouth and bit off a small slice of the tip.

"Attaboy," Papa Joe said, holding up his office lighter, a miniature version of the Hotel Nacional itself.

"You should celebrate, too," he said. "You played this Castro kid well. A couple times I thought he'd jumped the line on you. I'm impressed with how you handled it. You've got a nice future on this side of the business."

I listened to his crap until the cigar was halfway gone. Then I also headed for the door.

"Don't be a stranger," Papa Joe said as I opened the door.

"Sure," I replied.

Outside, sitting on the stairs, was Castro.

"Hello, Billy," he said. After smiling and laughing in Papa Joe's office, he had a sorrowful look on his face. I started to move past him.

"Please sit with me, Billy," he begged. "I should be so happy, but I'm not."

I stood over him, wanting to bring my foot down on his precious fingers.

"Don't believe Papa Joe's baloney in there," I grumbled. "After what you told Malena, I can't stand the sight of you right now."

"I know, I know," he began. "Sometimes I get too swept up in my big ideas. I don't realize what I'm doing."

"I love her," I said.

He stared at me in disbelief.

"No . . . ," he said, standing up.

He was a head taller than me. Still, I was hoping he would start something so I could take a couple swings at him.

"And I want you to stay away from her," I warned.

"Billy, you don't understand. We are *compañeros*—for life. You and me. Me and her. Each in our own way—"

I cut him off, jabbing a finger into his chest. "Don't give me any of your big talk. I'm sick of it."

He stood there as I taunted him, flecks of my spit catching in the silly beard he had started growing while training for the Dominican "invasion."

"I don't know what kind of hold you have over her," I said.

"We are partners in a great cause," he said. "Just as you and I are."

"No way," I answered. "Understand? No fucking way." I took my key ring out of my pocket and peeled the house key off the metal band. "You need a place to stay? Fine and dandy. It's yours," I said, dropping the key at his feet. "Be quiet and stay out of my way until our plane leaves next week."

I left.

Señor Canillo's office was up the street from the Hotel Capri. I went there for another house key. Canillo was out, but his secretary, a pleasant thing, recognized me, even though I had long forgotten her name. She handed over a new key, no questions asked.

"So what is Señor Canillo up to today?" I asked, making small talk.

"Business." She smiled.

There were still five hours before game time, so I took a cab crosstown to Malena's apartment. She wasn't there.

"The *señorita* has to make a living," an old lady called out from an open window on the first floor. "She left hours ago."

It was Malena's landlady, and she invited me in for a cup of coffee.

"My Malena works very hard," she said after I sat down in

her parlor. "I keep one eye on her. Do what I can. I worry about such a nice-looking girl. Out day and night. Always with her cameras. When Malena first moved in, two years ago this spring, I'll admit I wondered about her work, being gone at all hours . . . it gets a woman of my upbringing to thinking, if you know what I mean. Thinking about how she did earn her money. But then she showed me her pictures. So beautiful. Like her, I decided. One doesn't create such art by luck. No, one must work very hard. That's when I decided that I should be honored to share a roof with such an artist."

"*Señora?*" I interrupted.

"García," she replied. "My family and Malena's family go back three generations. We both came over within a year of each other from Spain. We are the nobles. My, how things have changed. Now all the rich people live in Miramar, not Havana. There's no respect anymore for what was built here, the struggles people had to go through. And for what? For this system where everybody has their hands in somebody else's pockets."

I tried to steer the conversation back to Malena.

"Any idea when she'll be back?"

Señora García shook her head. "She left with her cameras. That could mean an hour or a week. She said something about doing a portrait. That was music to my ears. God knows, the girl needs the money. And she does such beautiful portraits of businessmen. I think that's good. It keeps her in the right circles. Keeps her with the people who can help her make ends meet."

She rubbed her gnarled index finger and thumb together. "If you want my opinion," she said, lowering her voice, "she spends too much time on things that aren't worth her while."

"She pays her rent?"

"Who are you to ask such a question?"

"I'm a friend of hers. Billy Bryan."

"Let's leave it, Señor Bryan, that our families go way back, like I said. We have an understanding. I know when to look the other way when she falls behind in things like the rent. Sometimes what's important to one person is overlooked by another."

Her black eyes were on me as I took another sip of her coffee.

"How much is Malena behind in her rent?" I said.

Her right hand waved in the air as she answered, "Fifty, sixty pesos. No more than that. I will see the money. I have no doubt about that. But when one runs a business, like I do, one appreciates being paid on time. I couldn't help but notice you coming out of her apartment the other morning. Such a confident young man. An American."

I reached into my pocket and pulled out my wallet, watching her eyes grow larger. I laid a U.S. $20 bill in the middle of the cherrywood coffee table.

"Will this cover it?"

"*Sí, sí,*" she replied hurriedly.

In one motion, Señora García neatly folded the bill in half and slid it down the front of her loose blouse.

CHAPTER EIGHTEEN

When I arrived at the ballpark that afternoon, I discovered that I had been benched. Hilly Hanson, a nice enough kid from Beaumont, Texas, was penciled into my spot behind the plate. The Cardinals had sent him to Havana for a little seasoning before the spring training camps opened. I realized he could use some at-bats, but that didn't mean he had any right to mine.

"I don't want to hear it," Ángel said when I walked into his office.

"But Papa Joe said that I'd be in the lineup until the end of the season," I said.

"Well, my friend, that was last week. Now the Cardinals want Hanson out there. What can I do? My hands are tied."

We lost, 5–2, to Marianao, and I never got in the game. Neither Malena nor Castro was in the stands.

"You stag tonight?" Cochrane said as we filed through the tunnel back to the clubhouse.

I nodded.

"Well, partner, why don't you join me? It'll be like old times."

Cochrane had gone three for four and driven in both our runs. Some guys hang their heads after their team loses and they have done well. To his credit, Cochrane wasn't like that. He was honest enough to be happy, ready to celebrate, even though we had suffered a good ass-whipping.

"What's the schedule?"

"A Havana doubleheader?"

"I don't know."

"Oh, c'mon, bud. I didn't see your honey in the stands tonight. What have you got to lose?"

"Well . . ."

"Trust me," Cochrane said. "It will be just what the doctor ordered."

After a shower and shave, the two of us caught a cab toward Old Havana. By day the city was like a kid's rainbow: the hot sun shining down on a world of smiles, flowers, and ice cream. By midafternoon the whole place simply became too hot, and the stores and restaurants closed until the dinner hour. At such times you holed up, waiting for the night, because that's what anybody with money or class did. And the wait was always worth it. Soon after the blazing orange sun set, the wind would shift, coming in off the sea. The air would become misty with fog. Angel halos formed around the metal streetlamps topped by glass globes. That is the way it was on this night as Cochrane and I barreled toward Old Havana.

Our first destination, the Shanghai Theater, was in Barrio Chino, Havana's Chinatown. From the high ground outside the ballpark, we were able to see all the way down to that section of town. As the crow flies, it seemed to be a clear shot. But once we were rolling, the cabbie chattering excitedly about a game we had just lost, the clear view soon disappeared. The narrow alleyways and small blocks of white-columned storefronts and apartment buildings seemed to turn back on themselves, like so many dogs chasing their tails. The blocks alternated between apartment buildings and taverns and stores. We flashed by the Blue Moon Tavern, its crescent-shaped front window lighting the street like a bit of heaven that had fallen to earth. Had we been more flush, we might have begun the evening there. The Blue Moon's owner was Rudy Bradshaw, a Jamaican who loved baseball more than we did. But our tab was growing a bit long to press our luck there tonight.

We stopped, waiting for a light to change, a few blocks down from the Blue Moon. A half dozen whores were walking on the opposite side of the street. They were specimens of Cuban beauty—*mulatta* and *negra* honeys with asses that rolled and wagged as they walked. None of us said a word, and the driver was still gazing longingly in their direction when the light changed. A blast from a car behind us brought us all out of our respective daydreams. "*Los prietas son muy grandes atrás*," the driver said. "The dark ones have large behinds."

"Ain't it the truth," replied Cochrane.

I laughed. "Chuck, since when did you know that much Spanish?"

"Hey, Billy boy, when it comes to women I know the language no matter what land I'm in."

The street changed to cobblestone, the steady *clunk-clunk* bringing us back to life. When the taxi pulled up in front of our destination, Cochrane was ready, pressing a couple bucks into the cabbie's hand before he could start pleading about his poor grandmother in the interior, or his brother who had lost a finger in the last sugarcane harvest. But I was feeling more generous. I gave him a dollar bill, telling the cabbie to spend it on a big-ass whore.

He gave me a puzzled look. "They only want Americans," he said.

Inside the Shanghai, a bluish haze hung over the hot room. Beads of sweat glistened on foreheads, and I suddenly wanted to be back in my cool flat in Miramar, waiting for my Malena.

Up on the Shanghai stage, two figures in black hoods led a girl in a short white dress, a would-be vestal virgin, out to a red pillar and secured her to it with handcuffs. The music was sup-plied by a four-man band—a wailing saxophone and three bongos. The sax soared high and low, with the bongos plod-ding in a slow backbeat.

When the "virgin" was secured, two other women in black robes brought a tall black man, wearing a full-length red cape, out in front of the girl and flung him to the floor. He hit with a thud on the wooden stage, and the crowd, standing room only, laughed approvingly.

With what appeared to be a great deal of exertion, the guy they called Superman slowly stood with his back to the crowd, the bongos picking up speed, now in time with his every move. "Now you'll see why they call him Superman," somebody shouted. Swaying along with the music, he spread his arms wide, the red cape extending from either limb, creating a shadow that fell far back into the crowd.

Then he started moving toward the so-called virgin.

As the lights dimmed, Chuck moved closer toward the stage. He couldn't help himself. Meanwhile, I hung near the door, feeling the cool air blowing in off the street. Closing my eyes, I listened to the bongos and soaring sax. The music somehow rode above the laughter and whistles and shouts accompanying Superman's performance.

When I opened my eyes again, it was like I was seeing the whole scene in a different way. There were many women in attendance, too. Most were showgirls from the classy hotels whose shifts were over. They giggled at the Shanghai's main attraction and their dates' reaction to Superman. These women had been here before, had spent their off hours drinking and whispering in their benefactor's ear about how nice it would be to have a suite at the Nacional, how this show was nothing compared to what the two of them could do.

As Superman finished with the virgin, he and the music fed off each other, both going faster and faster. The room held its breath, everyone involved in one collective screw. The faces of the men and women were the same: a nervous tongue perhaps moistening dry lips, here and there a head drawn down into the shoulders, as if the rhetoric from a well-disciplined childhood was waiting for this sin to end, so that the necessary guilt could flood in like alcohol sanitizing a paper cut.

Few turned away. The crowd watched as the virgin suddenly opened her eyes wide. They watched as the four in black hoods, their bodies pulsating in time with the frantic music, closed in from either side. They watched as Superman arched his back and gasped.

When the music ended, the houselights at the Shanghai briefly went out, and when they came back up the stage was empty.

"I can never get enough of that show," Cochrane said when he rejoined me. "That's something you'll tell them about back home and they'll never believe you."

After another drink, we were back outside, in another cab. When we pulled up in front of 32 West Cabal in Old Havana, I couldn't believe what I'd gotten myself into. Even though we hadn't been here together in a long while, the madam greeted us with smiles and hugs at the door. Her face was covered with pancake makeup and her mouth was outlined with bright red lipstick. She gave us both big smacks on the cheek, pulling us close with both hands. The whole operation had the delicacy of branding cattle. Cochrane had two distinct lip marks on his cheek, and I knew I was sporting the same thing.

Cochrane bargained a price while keeping hold of my shoulder. As we walked farther into the place, the pounding mambo music grew louder. We stood near the bar and watched a line of honeys, all shapes and sizes, parade past us. Farther up, on a darkened stage, there were more, wrapping themselves around golden bars that ran all the way up to the ceiling. Some were kicking their legs up in time with the music. All of them were naked, expect for a small patch of rhinestone cloth between their legs and pasties stuck to their breasts.

"Anything we want," Cochrane shouted above the din, rubbing his hands together.

He waved one girl out of the crowd that had gathered in a half circle around us. She was kind of plain, with thick, coarse black skin and dark, rough hair. Her eyes were more alive than most, and she kept wetting her lips with her tongue. She was big-boned and plump, the kind Cochrane wouldn't be reluctant doing anything with. He yelled for me to hurry and pick one, too. When I put my hand up to my ear, like I couldn't hear him, or didn't want to hear him, he went ahead and selected one for me.

Lost back in the crowd was a small, sweet thing with red fingernails and breasts the size of my palms. Cochrane nodded to the madam, who still hovered by our side, and then the girls led us by the hand upstairs—the big one with Cochrane, the small one with me.

The girl held my hand as we headed toward the back, passing other rooms where laughter and groans and sweet whispers echoed into the hallway. I slowed and finally stopped. Still holding my fingertips, the girl looked back at me. She smiled, only her eyes and bright teeth clearly visible in the shadows.

I shook my head and turned to leave. But she grasped my hand tighter, pulling me slightly in the direction that Cochrane and the other girl had gone.

I brought her hand to my lips and kissed it. Her grip slipped away, and she followed the others down the half-lit hallway.

Downstairs I ordered a gin and tonic and went outside to a street table. The madam gave me a curious look and hurried over.

"You no like?" she said. "Plenty more available. You choose again."

I shook my head, and she went back inside.

A thunderstorm was coming in off the ocean and the street traffic was moving spasmodically, everybody trying to get home before the whole thing really got going. The storm, though, was moving faster than anybody expected, and soon the wind was gusting, announcing its arrival. With a flash of lightning and a good crack of thunder, the skies opened with a pelting rain. The human world tried to wedge itself underneath the stone archways and the cloth canopies along the main street. The umbrella at my table swayed dangerously in the wind and then fell over. Back inside, a couple of girls stared out at me, their faces pressing against the glass. I ignored them, staying where I was in spite of the weather. The water dripped down the end of my nose and quickly seeped through the shoulder seams of my sports jacket. Easing my chair back against the brothel wall, I had a bird's-eye view of the water coming down as a sheet, overflowing the gutters, falling as a torrent just beyond my table. Only when the storm blew over and I was soaked to the bone did I get up to leave.

In the cab I gave Malena's address. Thunder could still be

heard in the distance. At her place I rang the doorbell, hearing it echo through her apartment. I could picture the photos on the wall, the rooms, the couch. I had decided this was where I wanted to be. With her and only her.

I knocked again. Nobody came to the door.

I couldn't believe it. It was almost one in the morning. Where was she?

I pounded on the door again, this time with a closed fist. The only one who stirred was Señora García. Her parlor light came on and she peered at me through her lace curtains. In the shadows, she looked like a crazy witch. She pulled her door open a crack, enough so I could make out a worn blue satin robe and her hair pulled back from her face with pins and rubber bands.

"Señor Bryan," she said in a questioning voice. "It is late."

"Where's Malena?"

"I don't know. Please go home. I'll tell her you called again."

The fear in her voice made me angrier. I hated this whole crazy world, where nothing ever added up to what it should be. No matter how hard I tried to believe, things always fell apart on me.

"Where is she? I must see her. Tonight."

"Please go," she begged.

Her door showed only a sliver of light now, narrow enough for her to close it if I tried to force myself in.

"Open her door," I ordered. "I paid the rent."

"Go. Now," she replied. "Or I'll call the police."

With that she closed her door and bolted it.

I sat on the porch step, feeling Señora García's eyes on me. I grew cold and began to shiver. Only then did I leave.

■　■　■

My apartment back in Miramar was empty. By the door there was a manila envelope and a smaller white envelope. I took them to the kitchen table. In the distance, I could hear huge breakers crashing on the beach.

Inside the manila envelope there was a newspaper, a broadsheet, the kind where the ink comes off on your fingers. By the back door light, I was able to make out a couple of stories about the university law school. Then I saw the photograph. It was Arturo, the kid Malena and I had talked to at Holguín. With it was a story about how he had helped save Castro's life. How Castro had swum back to shore, escaping his assassins. How Castro was back in the political picture. There was nothing about his signing a baseball contract with the Washington Senators.

Inside the other envelope was an invitation to a party honoring local artists. It was the following night, at a house nearby in Miramar.

Holding up the photo of the kid from Holguín and the invitation, I smiled in spite of myself. Maybe things weren't as bad as I made them out to be.

CHAPTER NINETEEN

I dug my tux out of the closet. Only in Cuba would I need such a thing.

I tried to sneak it into the clubhouse. But as soon as I walked in, half the team saw me with the coal-black formal draped over my shoulder.

"Where's the wedding?" shouted pitcher Jackie Collum.

"You'd be surprised," replied Cochrane. "Our boy Billy is in love."

I'd arrived at the ballpark not expecting to play. My game plan was to sit on the bench until the late innings, duck into the clubhouse, and leave as soon as the last out was made. But our manager, old Ángel, appeared to be finally showing some balls. No matter what the powers on high had told him about Hanson, he had me back in the starting lineup.

I was putting on my uniform when Cochrane ambled over.

"You left me creaking in the knees," he said.

"It wasn't my style last night," I said.

"It sure used to be," Cochrane said, fingering the tux hanging in my stall. "So where you off to in the monkey suit?"

"An art show."

"Really. With your honey?"

h."

"Sounds like you need a chaperon. Before you do something foolish."

"Tag along. I don't care."

Cochrane whistled softly to himself. "I can't get a good read on you anymore, bud. One day you've gone native, the next high society."

"It doesn't matter," I said. "One day I'm out of the lineup, the next day I'm in. I'm slipping through the cracks. I can't count on ball anymore. That shakes a fella up."

Cochrane leaned in close. "You ain't washed up. You know it. I know it," he whispered. "You're just getting swept under the rug. It happens to everybody sometime. The trick is to take it out on the other team. That's how you prove to all these sorry fuckers that you can still play."

With that something clicked inside my head. For the first time in quite a while I felt myself loosen up about this impossible situation I found myself in. Papa Joe and the others wanted me to fail. They expected it. Until this point, I had been accommodating them by winding myself up tighter and tighter, allowing the pressure they heaped on me to totally derail me.

Cochrane *had* always been able to read me like a book. When he admitted, at least in part, that he shared some of the same fears, the same worries, that I had been carrying around like the weight of the world, it freed me up somehow. I wasn't alone. And if I was being drummed out of baseball, it would be done on my terms and in my way. I began grinning like an idiot—excited about playing just for the fun of it.

"There you go," Cochrane said, watching me. "Forget everything else. Just play the game."

And so we did.

Between us, Cochrane and I went six for eight, with five RBI.

Yet what felt really good was how we kept Skipper Charles, our rookie pitcher, from blowing the game in the ninth inning. With men on first and second, one out, Cochrane and I had a little heart-to-heart with Skipper on the mound.

"You're being a pussy with your slider," Cochrane said, never one to mince words. "No more free passes to first. You've issued your last walk of the night, understand?"

The rookie glared over at me and then to the dugout. Ángel sat there, spitting tobacco. He knew we were better than him when it came to talking a young pitcher down to earth. I stared at Skipper, suddenly wondering if he was old enough to shave. All these kids climbing into my game.

"Give me the slider once," I told him. "A good one. No dicking around. Then you come right back with it a second time. Got it?"

Wide-eyed Skipper said, "Not twice in a row. Not the same pitch. That's Dunbar up there. He'll clobber it."

Cochrane grinned. "The hell he will. Damn, you make these Cienfuegos guys out to be some kind of fucking gods. Listen to your catcher, partner. He's the best friend you've got. And if I see you shake him off, just once, I'm coming over here and ramming this glove where the sun don't shine. Do I make myself clear?"

Skipper nodded.

"This man here," Cochrane said, pointing his first-baseman's glove at me, "he knows more about baseball than the rest of this team combined. Why don't you do yourself a favor and listen to him."

"Two sliders," I said. "I'm going to signal everything else. That son of a bitch of theirs on second base steals signs. Throw the slider, whatever I show you."

"Now let's pat the good boy on the butt," Cochrane said,

tapping Skipper's behind once. "Make all the world think we believe in our sweet rookie so much."

With that the mound conference was over. Barney Dunbar was up for the Elephants. He had had one good season with the Red Sox a couple years back, poking what would have been fly-outs in any other park off Fenway's Green Monster. Since then he had been traded to the New York Yankees, where he hadn't done much at all.

Paddy Padden, the umpire, met me halfway back to the plate.

"I gave you enough time to settle the affairs of the world out there," he said.

"And I appreciate it," I replied.

"What are you going to try?"

"The best-laid plans of mice and men often go haywire on the gutlessness of a young pitcher."

"Oh, this should be good," Paddy said, pulling his mask back down over his face. "Can't let things take their course, can you, Bryan?"

"Just call a strike a strike, OK?" I said.

"I'd be honored to."

Skipper's first slider was weak. Hardly any movement on it. Still, Dunbar was expecting something else and took it for a strike. I could have made a fortune in the majors if I had been lucky enough to see a few more of those sorry pitches when I was at the plate myself.

Skipper looked downright pale when I nodded for the slider again. This one was higher-quality, and Dunbar tried his best. Yet I knew by the sound of his bat hitting the ball, a dull thud instead of a sharp crack, that we were in business. The ball went like a magnet to Vern Bennett, our second baseman, who flipped to Sammy Dion, covering second, who then threw on to Cochrane at first base. Bam-bam-bam. Double play. Game over. Baseball's such an easy game when it's played right.

From the smile on Skipper's face, you would have thought he'd just learned how to piss standing up. Cochrane and I took one look at Dunbar's stunned expression and broke up laughing.

■　■　■

The party in Miramar was at a house that looked like it had dropped out of the movie magazines. The outside was white stucco with patches of red brick simply for show. After coming up a horseshoe-shaped driveway, we arrived at a wide porch with red carpet and daintily dressed butlers fluttering about like bees around a hive.

"With what you're wearing," Cochrane chuckled, "you could always find work here."

We followed the red carpet up to the front door, which had a crystal chandelier hanging over the outside porch. Inside I handed the invitation to another uniformed guy, who announced my name "and guest" to the crowded room. Nobody even looked over to give us the time of day.

"There wasn't any need for that," Cochrane told him. "Isn't it obvious? This crowd loves us!"

The main floor was swarming with people. They moved in a slow-paced dance along the white walls, closely examining the paintings and photographs like they were searching for hidden treasure. A wide staircase, this one carpeted in dark green, led up to a second story, where a balcony overlooked the first level. Up there, we saw more people.

"I need a drink," Cochrane announced, and he strode into the crowd, taking the last three champagne glasses from a passing tray.

"Here," he said, thrusting one out to me. "This piss-water will hold us until I find the real bar."

"I'm going to take a look around."

"That's it. Leave me in my hour of need."

I started for the stairs. Photographs also lined the walls here, like silent sentries to the hubbub. Farther away from the front door, people seemed to decide not to make such a show of being interested in all this art. Every now and then somebody would turn and give a framed work a glance and then move along—determined to make it to the next clump of people and the next tray of cocktails.

As I got to the top of the stairs, I saw several of Malena's photos—a shot of the Havana harbor with the waves crashing against the breakwater and, just a little farther, my favorite, the boy and the herd of horses.

I looked around for Cochrane. I wanted to show him this. But he was nowhere to be seen.

I moved closer to the photograph, getting so close that for a second the noisy party around me didn't exist anymore. It was just me and that kid, both of us with the same resigned look on our faces. Together I could see us trying to gather all those horses into line and never being quite able to pull it off.

"You made it," said a voice behind me.

I turned to find Malena smiling at me.

"Where were you last night?" I said.

"Don't start, Billy. I'm here tonight, aren't I?"

She came toward me and kissed me on the cheek. With that my anger disappeared, no matter how hard I tried to hang on to it.

"I was afraid that my invitation was too much of a mystery," she said.

"I may be a ballplayer, but I'm not stupid."

She was wearing black slacks, a dark jacket, and a white blouse that was unbuttoned at the collar. From a distance, we made a nice-looking couple.

"Some of your friends are here," she said. "Papa Joe is downstairs. In that white suit, he looks like a big white whale plowing through an ocean of people."

"Now, that would make a good picture, huh?"

She smiled again. "Oh, Billy . . ."

I waited for more. Maybe a simple thank-you for paying her rent. Maybe an apology for leaving me wondering about her whereabouts. Instead she looped her arm in mine and said, "Come, there's a person you should meet," and she led the way back downstairs.

"We've been working on this show for months," Malena said excitedly as we descended. "I cannot believe how many people showed up."

On the main level, on the other side of the large ballroom, stood a taller woman with piercing green eyes and thin lips. Her long reddish brown hair was pulled back from her tanned face into a wavy ponytail that flowed down past her shoulders. She was older than Malena, probably in her late thirties. She wore a long flowing skirt with specks of color scattered throughout it. It was one of those gowns that is meant to look like something from the country, from the people, but it had to have cost a small fortune.

"That's who you have to meet," said Malena. "Her name is Señora Sánchez. She goes to baseball games. She says she's seen you play."

We started to make our way across the crowded room, stopping every couple feet for somebody else to congratulate Malena. Halfway to Sánchez, we came upon Cochrane and Papa Joe, who were hooked up in a heated argument.

"He says you helped him sign Castro," Cochrane said to me.

"The driving force," said Papa Joe.

"I don't believe it," Cochrane said. "Since when did you start working both sides of the street?"

"Since Papa Joe said my days as a ballplayer are numbered," I replied.

Cochrane reached over Malena's head to latch on to another champagne glass. "Never did find any beer in this place," he grumbled. With his other hand, he took the tray and held it down to her.

"Forgive my manners, darling," he said to her. "You look like you could use a sprinkle."

Malena nodded, taking the glass.

That done, Cochrane glared back at Papa Joe. "It seems to me my buddy's getting jacked around here. Jacked around but good."

"It was his idea to scout," Papa Joe protested. His voice was a bit panicked. "Tell him, Billy."

Malena sipped her champagne and watched us.

"Papa Joe said the Senators don't have a spot for me on their spring roster," I said.

"But that's no reason to climb into bed with a guy like Castro," Cochrane interrupted. "Papa Joe tells me you're baby-sitting him, making sure he reaches spring camp. How can you lower yourself to that? You're a ballplayer, partner."

"And what's wrong with Castro?" Malena asked.

"Begging your pardon, *señorita*," Cochrane said. "But I've got friends over at the American embassy. They tell me he's everything that's wrong with this country. I hear he bad-mouths the U.S. of A. Now, I know you and him are tight. Frankly, I can't figure out what the three of you have going. That's none of my business, I guess. The bottom line is that maybe Billy here can still play ball. Maybe old Papa Joe isn't sticking by my buddy. Doing him right."

Malena said, "Señor Cochrane, you appear to be a person who enjoys Cuba—"

"You bet I do."

"As long as its people know their place."

"Hey, I didn't say that."

"Let one of our athletes make it in your major leagues and that's somehow not right."

"Bullshit," snapped Cochrane. "I've played ball with plenty of Latin boys. Hell, the big leagues are filling up with them, whether I like it or not."

"And what's wrong with that?" she said. "Maybe we're simply better at playing your games."

Cochrane turned toward me. "You've got a real lulu here, bud. I hope she acts better in the sack than she does in public."

With that Malena fired what was left of her champagne into Cochrane's face. A good bit caught him in the eyes, and he began to roll around in the crowd, bouncing off bodies like a big bear.

"God damn bitch," he yelled. "My eyes are my life! I can't hit what I can't see."

Papa Joe got out his handkerchief and tried dabbing at Cochrane's eyes. For his trouble, Cochrane mistakenly punched him in the jaw. The two of them sprawled backward into a pack of Cuban socialites.

Malena took me by the arm and we escaped to a balcony off the ballroom, which overlooked the ocean.

"Don't be mad at me," she said.

"He had it coming," I replied.

We stood there in silence, looking out at the water. When we returned to the ballroom, Cochrane and Papa Joe were gone.

The hostess, Señora Sánchez, was wearing a brave smile, but her face clouded over when she saw us. Quickly she made her way through the crowd to confront us.

She smiled briefly at Malena and then turned her daggerlike green eyes at me.

"Your friend was very drunk," she said.

I apologized. "Sometimes he gets carried away."

"Nothing is harmed," she said. "Except my reputation."

"I'm sorry," I replied, trying to sound genuine. "I hope you'll let me stay."

Malena chimed in. "Naty, you'll find that Billy Bryan is a very different kind of baseball player."

Sánchez bit her lower lip, still deciding my immediate future.

"As long as he stays with you, Malena," she said. "I won't allow this reception to turn into a circus." Then she paused before adding, "Besides, I hear we have a mutual friend in Fidel Castro."

"You know him?" I said.

"But of course." She smiled. "Please, come with me—both of you. I noticed you were admiring my view of the ocean. But did you really see it?"

We followed her back out to the balcony.

"I've done so much to the house's interior," she said. "But this is still my favorite place in the house."

"It is beautiful," I agreed. From our vantage point, we could see the lights of Miramar melting into the dark waters of the Caribbean.

"I came into money at an early age," Sánchez said. "Many people talk about marrying into wealth. I was more fortunate. I was born into it and then made a good match that brought me even more. My husband was older. He died a few years back. Once he was gone, I decided to see if there's more to life than making smaller nest eggs into bigger ones. If there's more for a woman of my position to do than refurnish a beautiful home. That's why our mutual friend excites me so. If the people in that room only knew."

She strode out to the edge of the balcony.

"Your photos of a few days ago, from Holguín, were superb," she told Malena.

"Thank you," said Malena.

"I'm told that's just the beginning," Sánchez added. "Our mutual friend has left Havana."

"Left?" I said. "Again?"

"What do you mean?" said Malena, latching on to my hand.

"Oh, I see I know something that not even his most trusted friends have been told yet," Sánchez teased. "Oh, maybe I should have kept quiet."

"Where is he?" Malena said.

"Hush, dear," Sánchez warned. "Even my walls have ears. That's why we are out here to discuss such matters. From what I understand, our mutual friend has gone to Manzanillo. Part of his new plan. I see now how his mind works. He expected you two to be here tonight. That I would tell you and you would help him. He's a genius. The way he protects all of us from knowing too much."

"What's in Manzanillo?" I asked.

"The Demajagua bell," Malena said, rapidly putting things together.

"Very good," Sánchez said. "Señor Bryan, it is a bell that tolls for Cuba. Much like the Liberty Bell in your country. Our corrupt leaders asked the people of Manzanillo to deliver it to them as a vindication of their rule. The people of Demajagua refused. Our friend has gone there to bring it to Havana as a symbol of our side's righteousness."

She looked from Malena to me. "I see I've done my job," she said. "To tell you, so you could act. Now, if you'll pardon me, I need to return to my guests."

After she left, Malena stood there, looking out at the blackness. "I can't believe Fidel. Why didn't he tell me about this? Why did he need to involve her? Sometimes I don't even know what he's thinking anymore."

All I could think of was that Papa Joe wouldn't be any too pleased that our boy had once again flown the coop. The funny thing was, I was starting not to care.

CHAPTER TWENTY

Looking back on it, I see now that Castro was a person who was comfortable being many things to many different people.

To Papa Joe, Castro would always be an exceptional pitching prospect. To Señor Canillo, he was a dangerous revolutionary. To Señora Sánchez, he was a dash of excitement—something her money couldn't buy. To a boy like Arturo, Castro was as heroic as someone out of an adventure tale—the chosen one who could lead any army to victory. To Malena, who saw his blemishes better than anybody, he remained her country's best hope for a brighter future.

Now, I don't want to come across like I was smarter than everybody else. God knows I was as smitten by his charms as anybody. But, even back then, I couldn't help feeling that something was terribly wrong. I scoured the local newspapers, reading where Castro said something one day, only to contradict himself a few days later. I began to realize that he was as sloppy as he was smart. He left a topsy-turvy world in his wake and didn't care if he smashed up people and alliances, as long as it benefited the common good. And, of course, he was the only judge of what that common good should be.

Castro was a hurricane unto himself. When I first met him,

that side of him seemed refreshing, almost funny in a strange kind of way. But after he returned from his swim with the sharks, the storm around him grew in force. And even though I'd like to believe that most of us knew better, we kept following him no matter how crazy it all became.

Malena and I left the next morning, an off day for the Lions. Once more Malena was headed into the countryside to document our hero's struggle.

I accompanied her because I loved her. I was beginning not to care whether Castro caught that plane Papa Joe had booked us both on. No, I went because Malena needed me. For the first time in my life, I felt it was important to back somebody else up. Somebody who wasn't in uniform and playing on the same side of the ball field as me.

I had rented a car, a Nash 600 four-door. I was taking charge, at least a little bit, and Malena didn't mind at all. If anything, she seemed to enjoy it.

We passed by Cienfuegos, the backwater city that was the home of the Elephants, on the way to Manzanillo. After seeing the place firsthand, the flies as relentless as the heat, I understood why the Elephants played most of their games in Havana. You could die from playing ball in those parts.

By midafternoon we arrived at the farmhouse on the outskirts of town, where Señora Sánchez had told us Castro would be. And sure enough, there he was—playing baseball.

"Billy, look," my pitching prospect cried from atop a newly formed pile of topsoil and clay. The mound was the color of dried blood and looked about as steady as quicksand. A stick served as the pitching rubber. "And you thought I wouldn't have time to practice."

I didn't answer. This wasn't baseball. It was another of his shows.

One of Castro's men handed me an old catcher's mitt. I recognized the third baseman, Arturo, the kid from Holguín. He winked at me and then shrugged. Like the rest of the infield players, Arturo was playing barehanded. Only Castro and I had gloves.

Incredibly, even under these conditions, Castro's stuff was pretty good. His curve was as sharp as it had been when he made a believer out of Papa Joe at the stadium.

The infield was no more than a beaten-down patch in a field of waist-high grass. One of Castro's boys had a bat, and he tried hitting grounders to the motley crew of fielders. After a couple balls took some crazy bounces, jamming a finger or two or clunking off a shoulder, most of the players edged slowly over to the side, out of play, where they were able to light a cigarette and talk comfortably among themselves.

Arturo hung in there, though. He caught one ball in the forearm, then gamely went after it and threw to first base. However, the next grounder smacked him high in the chest, a couple inches shy of his Adam's apple. He went down in a heap, falling backward on his ass. A couple of his buddies hurried over and pulled him back onto his feet. He was red in the face, about the same color as the dirt, and was having trouble breathing. Once he could walk, they helped him over to the sidelines and safety.

Castro never looked back, continuing to pitch.

"This is stupid," I called out to him, whipping the ball back as hard as I could.

Sweat ran down my spine, making a sponge out of my shirt. There was nothing to be gained by this. Castro was in good shape. All he was doing was showing off for his *amigos*.

"I've had it," I said, setting down the antique catcher's mitt on the tin plate that passed for home plate. "Castro, call me when you've got a real game going."

Castro came running off the mound. Despite the heat, he hadn't broken a sweat.

"No, no, Billy," he said in a hushed tone. "We'll play. I promised them."

I shrugged him off. "I'm sick and tired of your silly tricks."

Beyond him I saw that the knot of men had stepped in a little closer, curious about what we were arguing over.

"You're embarrassing me," Castro pleaded.

His pouting face put me over the edge.

"I don't care if you're embarrassed," I snapped. "Look at them out there. You call them ballplayers? You call this baseball? Like I said, it's just another one of your tricks."

"Please?" Castro said. "Just for a little while."

"Screw you," I said, moving past him.

Malena was sitting in the shade. One camera was in pieces in front of her, laid out on a red scarf. Without looking at me, she cleaned the lens and mechanical innards with a white cloth.

"C'mon, we're going back to Havana," I said.

"So you finally told Fidel off," she said.

"That's right," I said, standing over her. "Now let's clean up and get out of here."

"Why should I go?"

"For Christ's sake," I said. "The only reason I'm out here is because of you."

She looked up at me and smiled. "I know. But that doesn't mean I have to do everything you say."

My shirt was completely soaked through. I was hot and tired and angry. I stared up at the baby blue sky, hanging over us without a cloud in sight.

For some strange reason I started thinking about the last time I'd been this mad about anything. It had been six years earlier, that afternoon at the draft board back home in Middle-

port. The only other time I had gotten close to being in anybody's army.

"This is nuts," I told Malena, nodding at Castro and his boys
in the field. "That isn't baseball."

"I didn't realize that baseball wasn't like ice cream," she said.
"That it didn't come in many flavors—vanilla, chocolate. No
variety in your world, Billy."

"So what?" I shouted to the sky, hoping that a big storm
would roll in out of nowhere and wash Manzanillo right off
the map.

"I think you've been out in the sun too long," Malena advised. "You should take better care of yourself. You know something, Billy? You're beginning to sound more like a stupid
Yanqui every day."

"Well, good. Because that's what I am," I said. "Listen, because I'm only going to explain this once. Baseball is what I do
for a living. It's the only thing I know. And parading around in
the sun without a clue about what the hell you're doing is not
baseball. It's just something you do to show off to what's got to
be the sorriest bunch of revolutionaries I've ever seen."

Malena laughed. "I thought you said you didn't know anything about revolution or politics."

"You're right, I don't. But I know baseball."

"Billy—"

"And that's not baseball," I repeated, yelling loud enough to
drown out her gibberish. "Baseball isn't about politics. Hell,
half the ballplayers I know can't spell *politics*."

"That's why you're so different," Malena said. "For some reason, we thought you could."

"All right, let's talk politics, revolution, coups," I said. "When
are you people going to wake up and face the fact that the
world doesn't work that way? You live your life controlling

things that you can control. Like pushing the ball to the right side with a man on first. Like trying to drive the ball deep enough so a man can tag up and move over with less than two out. Like talking a young pitcher through the first time in his life that he can't simply blow the ball by hitters. Don't talk to me about politics. It's out there, somewhere. I can't see it, taste it, fight it. Every country's run by faceless crooks. Work your ass off to get them out, and some more will just take their place. Why waste the time? You're right, life isn't baseball. In baseball you can win. Sometimes."

"You done?" Malena suggested.

"Maybe I am," I said.

She began to gather her camera gear and carefully place it back in her bag. "Then I guess we can go."

Castro was back on the mound, with Arturo as his catcher. The boy was using the old glove. He made a stab at a ball in the dirt but missed it miserably. The ball rolled into the high grass, and when we left them, Castro was leading his men into the shoulder-high grass, searching for the ball so the game could go on.

"We'll be in Havana in two days," Castro shouted at us. "Tell our friends to make ready."

Malena waved good-bye and I led the way back to the car. Soon we were on the main road, going home.

"I never liked uniforms," I told her. "At least not military ones."

"Why? Because of the war?"

"It's because I wasn't in the war. I never got the chance."

"You were lucky, then," she said.

"Not really."

I pulled the car over to the side of the road and turned off the ignition. Trees loomed over us and the land was quiet. The only sound was the ticking of the cooling engine.

"Let me tell you something I've never told anybody else," I said. "I wanted to fight. The day after Pearl Harbor was attacked, I went to the recruiting office. I had three of my friends with me.

"Together we filled out the forms, took the pledge, got in line for the physical. When it came to my turn, the doctor really looked over my back. He examined both knees and traced my spine with his finger. I'll never forget that old bony finger running down my back.

"He decided that I couldn't be in the army. My spine was too much out of whack. He took a bunch of measurements and found out that my left leg was a quarter inch shorter than my right. The gist of it all is I flunked my physical. The best athlete in my high school, lettered in baseball, football, and basketball, and they wouldn't take me into their stupid war."

Malena held her camera bag with both hands. "And what happened to your friends?"

"They died. John, Randy, Warren. They all ended up getting shipped to Italy. None of them came back."

I started up the car and eased it back onto the road.

"Santa Clara is not too far away," said Malena. "I know a good place for a drink."

She directed me up a narrow street. Chickens scattered in front of us as we pulled up in front of a small cantina. It had two wooden tables and a half dozen bamboo chairs scattered across a stone patio. A small man with a black beard, which had seen so much attention it shone, came out at the sound of the car. Even walking over toward us, he couldn't keep his fingers off his face, playing with the curly ends of his mustache.

"Malena," he shouted. "Malena Fonseca."

She walked over to him, and he wiped his hands on his stained apron before giving her a bear hug.

"Let her up for air," I said in English.

"Stop it," Malena said, and the guy drew back.

"No, no," Malena said. "Not you."

In Spanish, she told the innkeeper, "My friend can be very jealous."

The guy shot me a wary look, like I might slug him right then and there.

"This is my good friend Bernardino," she told me. "He is Señora García's son."

"Señora García is a fine lady," I told him in Spanish. "I'm happy to know her."

Sensing things were fine between us, Bernardino led the way into his cantina. He seated us at the only table in the place. He brought over a couple chairs, then a graying tablecloth and several glasses of beer.

I looked across at Malena. I had never known a woman like her. One minute I'd be ready to walk out on her; the next I'd stand on my head to see her smile. Around her I wasn't a baseball catcher anymore, the one who calls the pitches and then sits back to direct the action. With her I was out front—rubbed raw and often ready to explode.

"Castro will forgive you," she said to me, nodding at Bernardino for another round. I could tell Bernardino was in awe of her beauty. He scrambled to his feet and headed for more refreshments.

"I don't care about Castro," I said.

"Castro has a big heart." She was a good half glass ahead of me on the beer.

"He must be big elsewhere to keep all his women in line," I

said, wanting to annoy her. "You. Señora Sánchez. How many others does this old boy string along?"

Her face clouded over again.

"I don't love Fidel," she said.

"Right."

"It's true. It's safe to say that Naty doesn't, either. Castro may be the most unromantic man in the world. He just doesn't think that way."

"What are you saying?"

She thanked Bernardino when he brought over two more glasses of beer.

"Have you ever seen Castro dance?" Malena asked.

I shook my head. "I've never had the honor."

"I have, and he can't," Malena replied. "When was the last time you saw a Cuban who couldn't dance? Didn't love to? Around women Fidel is so shy he can't talk sometimes. It took him months to work up the courage to say hello to me."

"So what's the attraction? And don't start in about revolution and all that crap."

Malena took another long swallow of her beer.

"The attraction is that I'm as good as any man in his eyes," she said. "How many men can I say that about? Can I say it about you?"

I didn't answer.

"When I come into a room, Fidel doesn't immediately size up my ass or my breasts. Fidel sees a photographer. Somebody who doesn't like many of the things that are happening in this country. He sees somebody who can help him. Somebody who shares many of the same beliefs. It's refreshing, understand?"

"And when you want something else besides political talk?" I asked, smiling.

"Then at such times I'd wish the man I was with would stop nursing his beer."

When we had drained our glasses, she took my hand and we walked past a smiling Bernardino and up the stairs.

"I've been thinking about how to bring you here for some time," she said. "Since that first day, when you came to hear Castro, I wondered why you dared move out of your cozy world. Were you that adventuresome, or simply that foolish? Sometimes I worry that you can't take the punishment."

Her taunting got to me. When she opened the door to the small room with a bed and little else, I grabbed her around the waist and kissed her hard. She only smiled dreamily, which made me want even more to show her that I was everything her pal Castro wasn't.

CHAPTER TWENTY-ONE

Eván argues with the cabbie as we drive through the streets of Havana, across the Almendares River, up into Miramar, heading west out of town.

"This is where I used to live," I tell the two of them, pointing down one of the boulevards that lead to the beach.

"It's still mostly for tourists, foreigners," she says before returning to her running debate with the cabbie. He recommends another route out of town, but she won't hear of it. It's as if she has always dreamed of having a cab at her disposal. She and the cabbie launch into another argument about directions and routes. He calls her a stupid country girl, and she tells him to shut up and watch the road.

Cassy has fallen asleep. Her shoulder bounces slightly against mine. I reach over with my left arm, pulling her close to me. This one is my daughter, I tell myself. I don't need another.

Cassy was waiting for me when I awoke this morning. While Evangelina slept on the rollaway bed in her room, the two of us went down to breakfast.

"She says she is my half sister, your daughter," Cassy told me.

"The math works out. She says she was born in 1948. That was less than a year after you left."

"That's so long ago," I said. Both of us drank our coffee and nibbled on fruit while the waiters huddled by the door to the kitchen.

I tell myself that it was Cassy who was insistent about coming here. After she had found the scrapbook in the attic, saw that photograph in *Fidel,* there was no stopping my youngest child. She is the one who has brought this upon us.

"So, Dad, what are we going to do about Evangelina?" Cassy asked me at breakfast.

"Do? What should we do?"

"I mean, look how she lives. Tomorrow, when we go into the country, she'll be in the same dress and broken sandals that she wore today. She says she teaches school, but is that enough to earn a decent living down here? I don't know how she's getting by."

"So what are you suggesting? Simple charity?"

"Dad, why are you being like this? We should help her somehow. I mean, after all, she could be family, blood."

"Blood?" I answered, angered by the very use of the word. "Blood is not a reason," I told my Cassy. "After all these years, we're supposed to help somebody who has fallen out of the clouds and into our lives? What if she is as fickle as her mother? Do you know how much money I sent her? And for what? To find out that she lived on after the world thought she was dead. That *maybe,* and I emphasize *maybe,* she and I had a child, who now, miracle of miracles, appears out of the blue."

"But Dad, we need to do something."

"Cass, honey, I feel like I wasted too much of my life trying to find out where I should be. When I married your mother, I knew that was where my duty, my obligation, was. The way I see it, I don't think my place was ever here, in Cuba."

I looked up at the restaurant's stained-glass windows. The bright light was already streaming in.

"Hon," I said, trying one last time to explain, "I'm not going to live two lives again. When I married your mother, I closed the door on this place. Maybe she is family—blood, as you say. But is that reason enough to move heaven and earth? I don't think so."

I replay this conversation in my head as the city streets straighten out, angling off toward the vast green lands of the country. This woman named Eván and the cabbie are still debating alternative routes, but their squabbles have become nothing more than background noise to me.

I look out the window and realize that I have forgotten how overwhelming the land here can be. Across the way comes the gray smoke from the sugarcane harvest. As we draw closer, I see the men with their machetes, easily thirty or more. Their knife edges gleam as their arms stretch briefly toward the sun before coming down, breaking off the stalks as close to the ground as possible. That's where the sweetest sugar lies.

The road has become as straight as a line drawn with a ruler, and the cabbie barely slows down as we speed through one small village after another, scattering chickens in our wake. Occasionally we pass small lines of people along the shoulder. They are lining up for the bus that may come in an hour, or maybe not for another day. I glance back, through the cracked rear window, as we pass another line and I see a couple young bucks flip off our passing car with raised middle fingers. I don't want to be stranded out here. A lot of anger still remains in this land.

The countryside unfolds in stages before us. The cab's city engine whines as it chugs up a series of small hills, and at the top of the last rise we begin to slow.

"Trouble?" I wonder aloud.

"No," the cabbie says. "She says we are here."

"What's here?" I ask.

"The next stop in our journey," says Eván, pointing to the left-hand side of the road.

Cassy stirs beside me. With an exhausted sigh, the cabbie pulls over.

In front of us are giant concrete blocks. Each is twice as big as the vehicle in height and width.

"For Moncada?" the cabbie asks.

"Very good." Evangelina smiles, and suddenly, it seems, we are all friends. "Yes, in honor of Moncada."

We get out, and farther up the road I see that there are more places like this one, areas where the sugarcane and grass have been clipped away and more large concrete blocks piled up toward the heavens. I look back at the spot where we have stopped. There are three large stones. Each has a name and dates on it. It is then I see that the top one reads "Malena Fonseca, 1923–1959."

"It's her," Cassy says.

"Well, a memorial to her," Eván says. "Her real resting place is back in Havana."

"We must see it," Cassy says.

"We will. Later."

"She was at Moncada?" asks the cabbie. "She was one of them?"

"Yes, and if the world was just, she would have died there. Like so many of her friends," Eván says. "But come, I'm getting ahead of myself. Please, let's sit in the shade."

The cabbie hesitates.

"You too," she says. "For this story, you can be family, too."

We sit down in a half circle in the shade of the giant concrete blocks. The air is quiet and sticky. Eván reaches into her knapsack and pulls out a bottle of homemade wine and plastic cups stolen from the hotel.

"This story is the closest I come to going to church," Eván says. "So this will be our holy wine."

She hands around the cups while I uncork the bottle and pour for everyone.

"The assault on Moncada worked for only one person," she begins. "That was Castro. Our Fidel. Attacking the government barracks in Santiago was supposed to prod the people, tell them that the revolution was at hand and have them rise up and crush the government. It was supposed to be so easy. But Castro's plans rarely work as envisioned, and they often hurt friends more than foes."

Eván stops, looking out over the green fields, and we wait for her to continue. She wipes her reddening eyes with the back of her hand.

"This is when you don't know whom to believe," Eván says. "Where is the difference between the story and the legend that has grown up around it? All I know is what my family has told me. My mother had her camera. Her precious Leica. Remember, it was carnival time. She was one of those in the crowd, moving before dawn through the crowded streets toward the Moncada fortress. I'm told she wore a gold-colored mask and a cap decorated with long feathers. She was supposed to be a peacock among all the other costumed revelers. She was one of the few who reached Moncada in time. So many of the others got lost or became cowards. Too many ran when the shots began.

"But my mother stayed. She did her job. She took the pictures we saw yesterday. She got them back to Havana. A woman who looked like a party girl, overlooked and yet brave amid the killing.

"Our Fidel has always been lucky, hasn't he?" she says, turning to the cabbie, who nods reluctantly. "Instead of being killed or tortured or beaten, he was sent to prison, the Isle of Pines. That's where he gathered his followers—always so eager to begin again.

"But the attack on Moncada killed something inside my mother. She was never the same. One of my earliest memories is of her returning from there. She didn't smile, even when she hugged me. It was if she had seen something so terrible that it drained the happiness right out of her. When Fidel returned and began his revolution in the mountains, she didn't join him. There were orders, then pleading letters from him. But she never responded. Not even when he and Che swept down to capture Havana years later.

"When I was growing up, some whispered that she had lost heart. Instead, at Moncada, I think she saw how awful, how bloody, it would always be as long as our Fidel was in charge."

Eván stops, and we sip our wine. A slight breeze ruffles the leaves in the tops of the trees.

"You will find this odd," she says. "My mother never wanted to be remembered for her role at Moncada. She wanted to forget about it. Never wanted to see those terrible pictures again. But Fidel wants people never to forget, especially if it helps him and his cause in some way. He insisted that she be included among the Moncada dead, honored with these huge blocks of stone. He insisted on this even though she died years later. I remember coming here with our family for the ceremony.

"It has only been in recent months that I've realized how adept Fidel is at using the dead. With my mother, Camilo Cienfuegos, Che—he mines our memory of them. He makes sure they are never forgotten, and because he does this so well, he always hangs on to power."

CHAPTER TWENTY-TWO

That night as I slept in the cantina I dreamed of snow. The kind that falls thick over a couple days, piling up alongside the country roads where I grew up.

When I was a kid, most families hunkered down when a full-fledged blizzard roared in off Lake Ontario. Everybody's cellars were stocked with jars of cherry preserves, Indian corn, green beans—canned in the last days of fall, just for nights like this one. In the houses across the flat farmland where I was raised, the fireplaces were roaring, maybe a guitar or fiddle taken down off the wall, and these household parties, glowing ebbs of light in a nightmare of weather, kept burning into the wee hours.

In our family, after my mother and sisters had gone to bed, I would wait to hear my father still up and about. When I heard him pulling on his rubber boots lined with gray felt, I would scramble to get into my long underwear, then corduroy pants and a thick wool sweater, so I could go with him. He would be waiting for me at the foot of the stairs. Without saying a word, he would size me up and then nod. I had passed inspection. Before anybody else woke up, we hurried out to the barn.

My dad kept the tractor in fine running condition for nights like this. With him astride the wide spongy seat, revving the pedal accelerator, I would swing open the barn door. As the tractor puttered out into the blizzard, Dad would offer me a hand, pulling me up alongside him.

Out in the wind, the snowflakes flew horizontally and I hung on for dear life as Dad gunned the engine. Back then, when I was maybe ten years old, I imagined that all those flecks of white, dancing in the light of our lone headlight, were knights or cowboys or Indians. Time after time they charged down at us. But we were huge and mighty and could take whatever the world dished out.

It was easy to imagine myself as a hero back then. You think it and somehow you become it. That's the magic of being a child. In my daydream of long ago, nothing held me back. Nobody told me I wasn't good enough to play or man enough to fight. The world was as it should be—all spread out in front of you, waiting to see what you can bring to it. I remember laughing at all that snow flying in my face. Laughing at how fair and reasonable the whole proposition of being alive promised to be.

When I awoke at the cantina, Malena was downstairs, having a cup of coffee at the bar. It was getting dark outside, but the air was still hot and sticky. Those cold north winds that my father battled every winter for fun would never be felt down here. I decided that was too bad. This country could use a good blizzard every once in a while.

The more Malena showed me, the more I became convinced that Cuba was so far gone, so corrupt, that it needed to start over. Anybody could see that down here—if they cared enough to open their eyes. Many were desperate for any kind of change.

Still, of all the leaders I read about in the papers, I wondered if Castro was the one to head this revolution. He sure thought so. Malena, Señora Sánchez, Arturo, and a whole lot of other people had bought into the bargain as well. But, more and more, I couldn't see it. Castro was only one man. What if he couldn't deliver on what he had promised? What if he had no intention of doing so in the first place?

To believe too much in anybody, in anything, was to end up bitter and brokenhearted. I had learned that as well as anybody. It seemed foolish, at least to me, to put all one's faith in just one person.

I sat down next to Malena, and Bernardino set a small cup of *café cubano* in front of me. It was deliciously sweet, and I nodded in appreciation to Bernardino.

"Bernardino was telling me that Castro will get the bell," she said.

"Of course. Our boy gets anything he wants. He's blessed." I looked out at the darkening sky. "So I guess there's no use in us going back into the jungle," I said.

"No, Fidel will be in Havana in two days, three days at the most."

"So what do we do?"

Malena smiled. "We can go home."

"But what if I need to give my prospect another pitching lesson?"

"You never give up, do you, Billy?"

I finished the last of the coffee. "I'm not as big a fool as you think I am," I said. "I can see he's slipping away from me."

"And what are you going to do about it?"

"Maybe start believing in things closer at hand. Like you. Me. Us."

I laid a U.S. $10 bill on the bar. Bernardino's eyes lit up. His mouth protested, but the García in him didn't put up much of a fight about taking the money.

For the next few days it was as I had hoped—just Malena and me. She came to my games, becoming our good-luck charm as we drew within two games of Almendares for first place.

I came through with a game-winning double against Marianao, but at the Cardinals' insistence, Hanson was again getting most of the starts behind the plate. Still, with a week left in the season, we had four games left. We would play Cienfuegos and a rematch with Marianao, then two games with Almendares over the last weekend. Then it was over. Castro and I were scheduled to fly to Miami the afternoon after the last game of the season.

We didn't talk about me leaving. She knew all about it but didn't bring it up. If anything, that made me appreciate her even more. Outside of going to the ballpark and out for dinner afterward, we stayed at my place. We slept, arms around each other, until late morning. Hand in hand we took long walks on the beach and looked out across the water toward the States. How I wished I could reach across the water and simply yank the southern tip of Florida closer to us, make it something that could be seen from Havana instead of a place that was out there somewhere, clouded over by too many miles of water and ocean fog to be real. When something becomes visible, it's less dangerous. I'm sure of that. But left in the mind's eye only, it can play tricks on you, lie to you, and its power can grow all out of proportion.

I mentioned the plane trip to Miami only once.

"You could come with me," I offered one night as we lay in my bed, watching the ceiling fan spin above us.

"You know I have work here," she said, as if I had somehow insulted her.

"I'll be back next season," I said.

She didn't say much. But later, softer, she replied, "I know you'll come back."

So that's where we left things: hung like a coat on a rusty peg.

Malena sat in Papa Joe's box seats, and sometimes Papa Joe joined her. She was actually civil toward him. He told her about the game's finer points, and when the Lions came out from the dugout to loosen up, she rose and cheered like a schoolgirl when she saw me. It was hours before game time. The gates were barely open, but it felt good to have a one-person ovation in a sea of empty green seats. Cochrane saw her and kept his wisecracks to himself. It was noticeable even to him that we had a good thing going.

"You going to take her with you?" he asked as we started to throw one night.

"I don't know what to do with her," I said.

"Well, if I were you," he said, pausing, "I'd figure something out."

As a team, we were on a roll. We beat Cienfuegos and then Marianao; Almendares got fat on the last-place Tigers before we did. But then Almendares was shocked by Cienfuegos, losing 6–3. God, for a night we were big Elephants fans. Heading into the final weekend, we were only a game out of first place. And one Ángel González, like anybody who has ever managed a ball club, decided he was going to do whatever it took to win.

Two days before the first Almendares game, we had a workout at the stadium. Afterward he called me into the three-by-five-foot rat hole that passed for his office.

"Hilly's a bit nicked. Bad foot," he said. His wooden desk was buried in old box scores, lineup cards, scouting reports, and other pieces of paper. The far leg of the desk was stained with tobacco juice, where he had tried for the green steel wastepaper basket and usually missed. "Remember when he got drilled with that foul ball?"

I didn't remember the kid getting hurt, but I nodded.

"Hilly has a great future," González continued. He loved saying Hanson's first name. "I don't want to endanger that. That's what I told the bosses this morning. I told them I've got to rest him. I have no other choice. So that leaves you to start both games against Almendares. You understand what I'm saying."

"Perfectly." I smiled. My manager had finally recognized that I was the best man for the job.

That night I took Malena down to Old Havana and we found a quiet café up a narrow cobblestone street near the cathedral. It was a leisurely meal, and we did justice to a good bottle of wine. Well after midnight, we took a cab back to her place. When we came to her front door, I sensed something was wrong. I almost told the driver to keep going to my place, hoping we could escape from this, but by then she had already seen the note stuck to her door. Castro was scheduled to arrive early the next morning at the Havana train station, with the famous bell in tow.

Upstairs, I didn't rate a second glance. She scurried about—changing her clothes, readying her camera gear—in preparation for the big event. I sat on the couch, watching this woman who never needed sleep when it came to revolution. A couple times I tried to grab her by the leg as she raced by. But she wasn't in the mood.

"Billy, stop it," she warned. "There's too much to do."

So I fell back on the couch, imagining she was undressed and on top of me.

"You must know the history," she said, darting back and

forth in front of me. "This is a stroke of genius on Castro's part. He would have told you all about this the other day if you'd had the courtesy to stay with him. The Demajagua bell was first rung in 1868, as any Cuban schoolboy knows."

I gazed at her with tired eyes. Where did she find the energy?

"The people who house the bell are strong, far wiser than many in this country," she said. "Their mayor is a Communist, did you know that? When we toll the bell, who knows what force it will have. Castro's plan is that when the people hear it ring, they will rise as one and descend on the presidential palace, demanding his resignation. Fidel would have told you that if . . ."

In the middle of another lesson about Cuban history, I fell asleep on the couch and dreamed again of snow.

CHAPTER TWENTY-THREE

Castro returned home a real hero, arriving at the Havana train station the next morning with the bell. His gang of supporters swarmed toward the train, enough of them to lift the three-hundred-pound bell from a railroad car to the backseat of a Packard convertible. Dressed in his dark suit and prep school necktie, Castro climbed in beside his prized possession. With his pitching arm around the bell, the short trip to the university began. We followed on Malena's motorcycle, this time without the sidecar. I was on the back, my arms around her waist. She darted up the side streets, pulling ahead for another camera shot, as people lining the route poured off the sidewalk, touching the bell for luck.

At the university, Malena found an open window on the second floor in the Gallery of Martyrs, where the bell was to be kept overnight. The vantage point offered a nice view of the plaza below. The square- and diamond-shaped patterns in the stone stairs and landings were soon covered by people as Castro and the bell arrived.

Standing in the candy red convertible, using the bell for support, Castro addressed the crowd.

"Soon we cast off our shackles!" he declared, and the crowd roared its approval.

Tapping the bell with his palm, he said, "The liberators of yesterday have faith in the student youth of today. They know we will continue their labor for this nation's independence.

"This struggle we have inherited with open hearts. Soon we will challenge the puppets in government with all our might."

With that he jumped down from the car and began directing the movement of the bell up the plaza and into the Gallery of Martyrs.

Malena and I scrambled down a back stairway to Castro and the bell. The Gallery of Martyrs was like the inside of a tomb—dark and mysterious. There were stairs and corridors leading every which way. Castro had decided that the bell should be placed in the room next to the office of the chancellor. There it would remain overnight until the great antigovernment demonstration planned for the next evening. Castro was positioning his guards in strategic spots when we found him.

"My friends," he said when he saw us. "You are here."

Malena stepped forward to take his picture, and Castro instinctively flopped a paw back on the glorious bell. After Malena's lens recorded the moment for all time, he hugged both of us. Our argument in the countryside was never mentioned. We were all *amigos*-in-arms again in Castro's eyes.

His men carried the bell inside the office. Malena took a final shot of it before the door was closed and bolted. Castro directed three of his men with shotguns to guard the entrance. One of them was Arturo, the kid from Holguín.

"Here you will stay for the night," he told them. The sentries were at attention, eyes front. "Be vigilant. Tomorrow we present the bell of independence to our people."

There were plenty of Castro's supporters milling around, but

few of them were armed. He positioned the ones with any kind
of weapon up and down the hallway leading to the office. But
he was clearly worried about his lack of firepower.

"We need more," he said. "Where are the guns we were
promised?"

"El Extraño has plenty of guns," Malena volunteered.

"I don't know," Castro said. "El Extraño? I need to go begging to him?"

El Extraño meant "the strange one." All I knew about him
was that he was one of the gangsters, probably the most powerful one, in Havana. With the campus grounds being off-limits
to the city police and state security, the gangsters made their
headquarters in this part of the city.

Pacing back and forth in front of the office door, Castro
studied his meager troops.

"I barely have enough to patrol a hallway. How can I overthrow a government?" he muttered under his breath. Then he
looked at Malena. "This El Extraño," he said. "You know him?"

"I photographed him last year," she replied.

"Do you trust him?"

"No. But do you have any choice?"

Castro looked around him again, taking a deep breath.

"You're right. You can take me to him?"

She nodded.

The three of us left the Gallery of Martyrs, walking away
from the plaza, into the honeycomb of streets where Malena
and I had been shot at only weeks before. Castro reached into
his suit pocket, fingering his revolver. And Malena took her
firearm, a new derringer, fully out of her camera bag.

A few blocks away we stopped in front of a black door to
what once had been a stunning house. It was three stories high,
with a stone terrace leading from the street. Ten years earlier it

could have hosted a party as elegant as the one at Señora Sánchez's, but now every window was shielded with black curtains, and newspaper replaced the panes that had been broken. The exterior paint was peeling badly. The tall hedges that cut it off from the houses on either side were overgrown. Barbed wire, strung along the top of the hedges, glistened in the afternoon sun.

We walked up to the front door. Malena raised the tarnished gold knocker, which was in the shape of a lion's head, and let it fall against the black door with a thud. Eyes appeared in a peephole. Malena spoke hurriedly. Then the small opening slammed shut and we heard nothing for a while.

"Well, maybe we go?" Castro said.

"Not yet," Malena said.

Soon we heard the bolt and then the lock loosen, and the door opened to receive us. The only light inside the house came from candles in wrought-iron holders that lined the hallway. We followed somebody dressed in black until we came to a large room with sheets covering all the pieces of furniture except a golden throne. On it, surrounded by red-and-white flags and bathed in shadows, sat Jesús Gonzáles Lartas, aka El Extraño.

Castro smoothed the front of his suit and approached the throne. El Extraño sat silently while Castro told him about his momentous plans for the following day: how the liberty bell would ring in a new age for Cuba, but how that brighter tomorrow was in peril if he didn't have support, more guns, to protect his treasure through the night. When Castro was finished, there was silence. His face half hidden in the shadows, El Extraño appeared angry, like a vengeful god. He gestured to the sentry at the door to come to the side of his throne. A conversation of whispers took place between them, and I saw Castro leaning closer, trying to catch a hint of what was going on.

"El Extraño wants to know," the sentry said, "aren't you the boy who came to Havana and immediately opposed him?"

"That's true," Castro said. "But as you say, I was a boy then. I didn't know El Extraño had such power. I was a fool."

Getting down on one knee, Castro continued. "I beg for El Extraño's help. We've had our differences. I was young. But we need to put such disagreements behind us. For the good of the country, we need to stand together. I need your weapons to hold the bell."

The sentry started back to the throne, but a thunderous voice spoke from the shadows.

"And what do I get in return?" demanded El Extraño. "Besides the satisfaction of bringing a boy to his knees."

Slightly embarrassed, Castro got back to his feet.

"You will have a country without a dictator," Castro said. "A land where people have opportunity. A country with more freedom for individuals like yourself."

El Extraño was silent, as if he was trying to imagine such a place.

"Why is this bell so important, boy?" he asked.

"Because it's a symbol of a better day. We ring it and its music captivates our people. Once we ring it, there's no turning back. Not after they've heard it."

"And if I give you guns," El Extraño said, "you must promise to sing the praises of El Extraño, too."

Castro hesitated. "The only things that should be spoken of now are the government's cruelties and how we must join together against such tyranny."

"You are still a boy," El Extraño sneered. "The guns you beg for are no more than pennies in my rich purse. But even if I give them to you, they will do you no good. You remain a boy who lacks a basic understanding of how the world works."

With that El Extraño waved his hand, like he was brushing away a fly. Another sentry appeared out of the shadows and began ushering us toward the door.

"I need those guns tonight," said Castro as El Extraño's man pushed him away with the butt of a rifle better than any the student revolutionaries possessed. "Tomorrow is too late."

"Pray for my kindness," El Extraño said, laughing. "Pray, boy."

Walking back toward the campus, Castro said, "I don't know why I bothered. That animal will support us only if we win. We lose, and he'll just feast with the others on our bones."

Back at the Gallery of Martyrs, surrounded by his people, Castro brightened. He had his guards open the door to the office, and once he saw the bell, glowing bronze in the dying sunlight, he again was talking and scheming.

I interrupted him to say good-bye. It was time for me to leave for the ballpark. The first big game with Almendares was that night.

"So we all have chances for glory," he told me. "Billy, these are exciting times. I wish I could see you play tonight."

I didn't care if Castro came. I was hoping Malena would be there. Yet she was on the stairs above us, taking more pictures. I waved, and all I got was a blown kiss in return. She didn't come down to see me off.

"After tomorrow, when I present the bell, things will change in Cuba," Castro said. "The people will rise, take things into their own hands. They won't need people like me to show them the way. They will see the path and rush down it.

"This is the last piece of work I must do before I go with

you. In America, I will be the new champion for Cuba. I can bring home money for our freedom efforts. I can be somebody our struggling nation, reborn after throwing away the dictator's yoke, can turn to."

"All I know is that you've got a pretty mean curveball," I said.

Castro broke into a hearty laugh that began deep in his belly and bubbled out, fast and easy, like champagne from a bottle.

"We have our disagreements, you and me," he said. "But our future, Billy. Ah, it holds so much promise."

CHAPTER TWENTY-FOUR

I t rained again that night.

A steady downpour stopped play for good after we batted in the bottom of the sixth inning. Despite the protests from the Scorpions' bench, we won, 3–1, tying Almendares for first place with one game left to play.

My hit became the game winner. A little bleeder chop, hit the opposite way to right field, just past Avelino Canizares, their second baseman. It came with two outs, the bases jammed, and because of the three-two count everybody was running. In the box score the next day it would look as good as a line drive off the outfield wall.

"Your luck's turned," Cochrane said as we waited in the dugout for the umpires to call the game. "I figure I'm jumping aboard the bandwagon."

Afterward Ángel went a little overboard with his postgame pep talk. After years of trying, he was like an old dog that had found the scent. Unfortunately, his enthusiasm wasn't actually contagious.

"This don't mean a blessed thing if we don't win tomorrow," he said, standing in the middle of the clubhouse. All of us tried to look humble and determined. "We caught a break tonight.

Now we've got them by the balls, boys. Tomorrow let's squeeze. Hard."

I focused on my bare feet. My soggy shoes had been the only part of my equipment I had gotten off before our manager had burst in on us. I looked hard at my toes, trying to tune old Ángel out, trying not to laugh at his attempts to get us juiced up for the next day's game, the last one of the season.

Cochrane wasn't as lucky. He started to giggle, and that got Bennett going; the merriment quickly spread through the room in an undercurrent of stifled gasps and heads buried in hands and towels. Ángel really thought he was getting through to us until Spider Jorgensen muttered, "Save some for tomorrow's speech, Skip? Please, you're killing me."

With that Ángel retreated into his office to spit more tobacco juice in the direction of his wastepaper basket. As soon as he shut the door, the room burst into peals of laughter.

"Hey, hey," Cochrane said, the tears running down his face. "Let's win it for the old fuck. How can't we after that sorry show?"

After I changed, I took a cab back to the university. In the wake of the storm, a mist was coming in off the ocean, and along with it government troops had arrived aboard long-bed truck carriers. Their grim faces appeared out of the gray fog, smoking cigarettes, questioning with rapid-fire authority. Most had machine guns, the strap hanging loosely around their shoulder, one finger on the safety.

As soon as I got out of the cab, one of the soldiers demanded, "Who are you?"

"American. A tourist," I replied in English. "The casinos tapped me out. I'm walking to clear my head."

He translated for those around him, and the soldiers had a good laugh at my expense. The officer waved me past, and

I walked up the plaza's stone steps to the campus. Despite this show of force on the streets below, the rules about the university—no outside interference—still were in effect. The soldiers were lined up across the street, but they hadn't come any nearer. When I got closer to the Gallery of Martyrs, the mist engulfed them. Yet there was no mistaking that they were still out there. Every now and then you could hear a barked order, the smack of boot heels on the wet pavement; the sounds echoed through the university plaza. The night felt like ghosts were riding the wind, waiting for the right time to appear.

Inside the gallery, the air stank of cheap cigarettes. To my surprise, I was able to walk right in, where the world was abuzz with confusion and fear. Everybody was talking, but nobody was in charge. Castro was nowhere to be seen. Somebody said El Extraño hadn't come through and he was still hustling up more firepower.

With Castro away, nobody had thought to rotate or replace people. Arturo and the other two guards were still outside the office that housed the bell. They were bleary-eyed and looking a little scared. One of the kid revolutionaries glared at me, but Arturo settled him down.

"When's Castro coming back?" I asked.

"Soon, I hope," Arturo said. "But nobody knows."

"The woman go with him?"

There was a long pause. The schoolboy sentries looked at each other, not knowing how to answer.

"The photographer lady, you mean," said Arturo finally.

"Of course that's who I mean," I said, trying to get to the point. "Guys like you wouldn't forget her. Tight ass, nice lips. Remember?"

They all grinned for a second before regaining their composure.

"Señor Bryan, she's not here," Arturo said.

"So she's with Castro?"

"I don't think so."

I shook my head. "I don't believe this. Either she's with Castro or she's here somewhere. I know her."

The taller guard took a step toward me. His fingertips danced on the barrel of his shotgun. He looked like he enjoyed shooting things for kicks.

"How does a Yanqui know so much about such a woman?" he wondered aloud. "Look around. Do you see her? No, I didn't think so. Now, why don't you go home?"

Arturo leaned his shotgun against the wall, next to the door, and came over to talk to me.

"You must pardon them," he explained. "Everyone here is on edge." He looked back at the other two. "Stay there and keep your eyes open," he told them. "I'll deal with this."

Arturo and I walked a short ways down the hallway. The office was still in view. Arturo was tired, but he still wasn't missing a thing. He seemed to be the kind of kid who could stay fully alert until he dropped. Full speed or neutral—he had no middle gears.

He fished a bent cigarette out of his front shirt pocket. Despite the rain and mist outside, it remained hot in here. Above us were several stairways and people coming and going, making plenty of noise. He leaned forward and I lit his cigarette with my lighter. He took a deep breath of smoke and tried to relax.

"How many soldiers are out there?" Arturo asked.

"Plenty of them. But they're not allowed up here, right?"

"Those are the rules," he said. "All over the island people know this campus has its own ways. It's off-limits to the authorities. Always."

Arturo was saying these words like he was trying to convince himself.

"So how long has Castro been gone?"

"Hours," he said. "Without him, people get nervous. No-body's in charge. Nothing gets done."

"Like somebody relieving you guys?"

"We won't give up our guns, so we can't be relieved," he said. "We'll stay until we get more weapons. But we won't give up our guns. I'd rather be tired and armed than defenseless and asleep."

"But why not get some rest? You said the campus is off-limits."

"Lionel and I got to talking," Arturo said. "He's the short one over there. We agreed that in this kind of weather things can happen. People can lose their bearings. Or later can say they did."

Our talk had moved entirely into Spanish. At first he had dropped in a few words, testing me. I went along with him.

"So how does an American know our tongue?" Arturo asked.

I told him about growing up on my dad's farm. How I played ball with the migrant kids whose parents worked in my father's tomato fields. How I had lived with Oscar and his family.

"We are crazy for the game," Arturo said. "Perhaps it is best that you think about your baseball now. My suggestion to you, my friend, is to get your rest. You have a big game tomor-row, right? Almendares? See, I know. I'm a big fan. It's in our blood."

"But the woman?"

"Your lady friend? Funny that she would not tell you of her plans." He looked over at his rifle and then back to me. "She's safe," he said in a low voice. "You can believe me. Everybody knows something is going to happen tonight. She has readied herself in her own way."

"Take me to her," I ordered.

Arturo sighed. "I'm sorry, my friend, I don't have that authority."

We stood there for a moment, not knowing what to say.

"I've seen you play," Arturo finally said. "I remember now. I was at a game early in the season. Before Christmas. You blocked the plate on Demerdal. The big one with Cienfuegos."

For an instant that whole painful moment flashed back to me. The bastard had run me over. I had had no choice but to stand my ground with him bearing down on me. The collision had sent me sprawling, but somehow I had hung on to the ball.

"I see you remember," Arturo said.

"How can you forget something like that?" I joked.

"That's right, how can you forget?"

I watched him drop his cigarette to the floor and grind it out with the heel of his boot.

"Who are your friends?" I asked, not ready to leave.

"The taller one is Larrando. He and Lionel are brothers. New to our cause."

I nodded at their unsmiling faces.

"You remember the night Castro came out to pitch at the stadium? They say they were with him. They still talk about it. You caught him, right?"

"That's right."

"You would think they would remember that. It's funny. You know what they talk about the most from that night?"

"What?"

"Not Castro," Arturo said. "Not you. They remember the field. The grass. How it smelled. How it was so well taken care of it was spongy. They say you could feel it bounce when you walked on it. They remember that like it was yesterday."

He started to take another cigarette out of his pocket, but

then paused, putting it back. "I must save this," Arturo said. "I think it's going to be a long night." Then he looked at me. "Billy Bryan, I don't know where you fit into this. On the ball field, I know your place. Here? Your lady friend gave us orders not to be disturbed. Only a few of us know of her whereabouts."

"So take me there."

"I can't help thinking of that play of yours, the one with De-merdal. I'm a big fan of yours. I bet you didn't know that. You showed such courage that night, standing there, knowing you would be hit like that. I can't help but think maybe you made that play because you didn't know what the pain would be. Maybe you had made that play a hundred times, but you seem like a man who can forget. I think that's good. If you did remember, you wouldn't be able to make that play again. Your body might try, but your brain won't work that way again."

"Where is she?" I shouted at him.

Across the room Lionel and Larrando came to attention, ready to step in.

Arturo smiled.

"Stop it," he said, like he was talking to a baby. "Sometimes it's best not to know everything. Like your play with Demerdal. Maybe this is such a time, too. Without Castro here, I cannot be telling secrets. I must be a good soldier. I'm sorry. But think of how it is for me. You will understand."

With that he returned to his post by the office door. There were more men above me, taking up positions in the shadows. I walked up past them, all the way to the roof.

There was one guard, with an old rifle, on duty up here. He eyed me for a minute and then let me stay. I moved over toward the edge and looked down across the plaza, in the direction of the grand hotels and casinos. The wind was picking up, blowing much of the ocean mist away. From my vantage point, the long-bed carriers of the government soldiers could be seen for a moment or two, then they disappeared as another patch of fog blanketed them. On the plaza below me, there were no large groups of people. Only one or two hurried by at a time. Some were actual students, heading to the library or home to study. Others were revolutionaries, hoping to overthrow their government before the weekend was over. I looked down at the plaza, lost in my thoughts, until I saw Castro and Malena move out from the shadows and start across the plaza. They moved like they were excited and happy to be with each other. Castro looped his arm around her shoulders and pulled Malena close to him as they continued to walk away from me. I watched as she clung briefly to his chest. When she did pull away, she laughed, a lovely sound that echoed into the air. Then the mist covered them over and I couldn't see them anymore.

Back downstairs, I found Arturo.

"Where did they go?" I demanded.

"My friend Billy, I have no rank in this new army. What are Castro and your lady friend up to? I don't know. I don't want to know."

Outside I started walking in the direction in which they had gone. But after a short while, I stopped and began looking for a cab. I was tired of chasing after them.

I decided that on this night I would turn back the clock instead. After Ángel's silly speech, Cochrane had suggested partying at the famed Tropicana. My teammates were there, and on this gray night I suddenly wanted to be in their company one last time.

■　■　■

Cochrane loved to sit down front, and no matter how big the crowd, he would tip the hostess enough so that he was in the front row. That's where I found him, Skipper Charles, Sammy Dion, and Bunk Johnson on this night. They were ringside, right where the stage lipped out, reaching as far as architecture would allow into the crowd.

Any visitor to the Tropicana was first awed by the glittering costumes of rhinestones, the way the spotlights, coming from three sides, embraced all the beautiful bodies, reflecting the hot white light back into the audience in maddening flecks. And down close, where we were, one could witness the most beautiful women in the world—white, black, brown—from almost every possible angle. They hovered above you like angels from any schoolboy's dream. Despite the relentless music, driving them to perform, they smiled throughout, maintaining perfect posture—back straight, tits out front, ass pulsating—as they went through an exhausting series of leg kicks, body twists, and dance moves in which one after another leaned out over the edge, defying gravity, their eyes locking on yours, giving the illusion for a second or two that any of them was attainable.

Then they peeled back and more beautiful angels took their turns in the bright spotlight. New costumes faded in and out of the glare as quickly as the newest row of dancers. Towering headdresses of feathers and sparkles gave way to flashy G-strings, followed by dancers whose breasts were covered only by small pasties over the nipples. Wave after wave appeared. Some walked down staircases next to the palm trees that flanked the stage. Others rode swings rigged to an elaborate series of wires and safety lines.

"Gorgeous," Cochrane marveled, and soon he was on his feet, with the rest of us following his lead. All of us were simply happy to be captivated by this forty-five-minute performance devoted to every form of female beauty that God had ever created. This was no simple strip show. In fact, the girls never dropped a stitch of clothing. Instead it was their stunning beauty and the sheer numbers that elevated the whole performance. The Tropicana, like Cuba itself, embraced lust so well.

Later the MCs, dressed in their white tuxes, were as smart-ass as anybody found in the New York clubs. They were good, prodding us with jokes and insults. But here they knew they would never be the main act. We waited them out, laughing at many of the things they said. Then came the finale. It seemed like every girl who had been out earlier returned, taking one last turn on the stage.

You tried to memorize a particular smile, a beloved face, the shape of a breast, the way a particular leg sloped so nicely up to firm buttocks, and then, before you could do anything about it, the angels in rhinestones disappeared. Another show at the Tropicana was over.

CHAPTER TWENTY-FIVE

From the Tropicana, it was on to the Capri. Lola was at Señor Canillo's table, as was Papa Joe. Canillo had a bottle of champagne on ice beside him.

I ordered a rum and Coke, and Canillo congratulated me on my game-winning hit.

"I'm no expert," he said, "but you've picked your game up a notch or two. Am I not right?"

"Billy has come to grips with age," said Papa Joe from the far end of the table. He was half in the bag. "It's something that snags all of us sometime. Last year Billy would have pulled that same ball and grounded to short. Now he goes with the pitch, hits it the opposite way. And what do you know? Success. If only we knew what to do when we were young enough to do it."

"I'll drink to that," Cochrane said, raising his glass.

Canillo smiled. "I'm going to miss you ballplayers. It's always such a long summer without you."

"Such talk," Lola said. "Can't we find something more pleasant?"

"Agreed," Canillo said, raising his glass. Everyone else at the table followed his lead.

"To our lady," he said, nodding at Lola. "Who is as beautiful as she is intelligent. She's correct. Let us remember only the good times—like tonight."

"Hear, hear," Cochrane answered.

All of the men briefly stood, their glasses coming together with a soft tinkle in front of Lola's beaming face. Afterward Papa Joe fell back into his chair and drained the remaining drops of champagne straight from the bottle.

"On that note, gentlemen and most beautiful lady, I must go," said Canillo.

"So soon?" said Cochrane. "What are we to do without our leader, our benefactor?"

"Don't worry, Charles. I'll still pick up the tab."

Cochrane smiled sheepishly. "You know that's not what I meant," he said. "C'mon, sir, the night's still young. Hell, we're all here and we've got our last game tomorrow."

"I'm sorry," Canillo said. "But every now and then one has pressing business that must be attended to. Unfortunately that rare occurrence has happened on this memorable night."

Everybody moved uneasily in their chairs until Canillo waved the waiter over and settled the table's tab. Then there were smiles all around and Cochrane, Skipper, and finally I shook Canillo's hand, saying good night. Normally he loved such attention, but on this evening he couldn't wait to get away.

Canillo hurried out with two of his henchmen bracketing him like bookends. I watched them go. Near the front door to the Capri, I saw Canillo rudely push a tuxedoed gentleman out of his way. When the guy started to protest, Canillo snapped his fingers, and one of his thugs grabbed the guy by the lapels and threw him into a small crowd near the coatroom. I couldn't believe it. I had never seen Canillo lose his temper before.

I moved down next to Papa Joe. "Everything looks good for

the day after tomorrow," I said. "Castro threw the other day. He looked pretty good."

Papa Joe stared at me. "You don't have to lie, Billy. You've done a helluva job, a helluva job, regardless of what happens."

When Cochrane and Lola got up to dance, I watched them enviously. Once again my buddy had things falling into line when he needed them the most. When I closed my eyes, I saw Malena and Castro hurrying across the plaza. After I finished my drink, I got up to leave.

"Share a cab?" said Skipper. He was our starting pitcher for the final game against Almendares. "I should be heading home soon, too, I guess. God knows what I'll do when I get there. I can't sleep."

"I think I'm going to walk a bit," I said, trying to put him off.

Skipper nodded. "Oh, OK. Well, I better save my legs."

"My legs were shot a long time ago," I said. "Walking in the rain helps shake loose the cobwebs."

Outside it wasn't windy anymore, and the ocean fog had settled in thick and low for the night. Near the campus, most of the soldiers had left. Two military jeeps sped away as I came up the hill from the casinos to the stone stairs and the plaza. As I got closer I heard the yells and commotion, and I ran the rest of the way to the Gallery of Martyrs. Inside there were arguments and finger pointing. Everybody was trying to talk at once. I moved past the first group of Castro's people down the hallway toward the office where they'd put the bell.

Arturo was still at his post. He was in a sitting position, his back slumped against the wall next to the door. He still held his precious shotgun in both hands. His mouth was open, drool running from one corner. In the center of his forehead was a neat bullet hole and a steady trickle of blood.

I couldn't believe it. The kid was dead. The boy who had

shown more responsibility than anybody around him had been left to bear the brunt of the madness and hatred. I found myself still staring at Arturo, clenching and reclenching my fists, when a hand reached from behind me and closed the boy's lifeless eyes. It was Castro.

"I underestimated those who oppose us," Castro said. "The other two. That Lionel and Larrando. They were with the government."

The office door was open. The bell was gone.

I immediately thought of Malena, and Castro read my mind.

"I sent her home," he said. "She holds the key for finding out who did this."

"What do you mean? She was with you. I saw you together."

"She was—earlier," Castro said. "But when this happened, she was already hidden away. Ready for such a crime. When they came, she took pictures of it all. She went home to develop them."

"And you let her go?"

"What's the problem, my friend?"

"Don't you get it?" I said. "Whoever did this knows all of us. They know where she lives. They'll be there next."

I started running out of the building. Behind me, Castro barked a few orders and then joined me. Together we raced across the plaza, and I hailed a cab a few blocks from the neon lights of the casinos.

"San Martín Terrace," I told the driver.

"Number fifty-five," Castro added. "Hurry."

I pulled a wad of money from my pants pocket and peeled off a few U.S. bills.

"Earn this," I said, watching the driver's eyes grow wide.

We flew up Caledo Boulevard, two lanes going in each direction. Our driver was heavy on the accelerator and the horn, and we rolled from one lane to the other as if we were a small boat caught far out on a rough sea. Pulling up in front of Malena's flat, Castro opened the door while the cab was still coming to a stop. I handed the driver more money.

Castro had a key. I followed him inside, locking the knob and pulling the dead bolt into position behind me.

Castro called for her as we ran up the stairs to her second-story flat.

"Yes," came a voice from the back.

"The darkroom," Castro told me.

He led the way through the kitchen, ducking through a series of black curtains. I had never been back here before.

"Careful," Malena warned as we broke in on her. "I'm printing."

She stood in front of a machine with a bellows, a lens, and a board base. In back of her were three trays, with eight-by-eleven pieces of paper floating in each. On a line along the back wall, hung with clothespins, were finished shots drying.

"Who did it?" Castro asked her.

"I don't know. Not yet," she replied, pushing at the several prints in the first tray. "Something should show up in this batch."

"We don't have time," I said. "Those soldiers could be here any minute."

"Start gathering up the pictures," Castro ordered. "We cannot leave anything."

Malena dried her hands with a rag.

Calmly she said, "Billy, hand me those," pointing to the photographs on the clothesline. She reached into a cabinet, pulled out a small backpack, and began loading it up.

"The soldiers aren't at the university anymore?" she asked.

I couldn't believe how cool under pressure she was.

"No," Castro said.

There was a noise down on the street, and Castro ran to the front window.

"Stay behind the shade," Malena told him.

I stood behind her and we watched the vague outlines begin to appear on the paper in the first tray.

"This is a new solution of developer," she said. "It'll only take a couple minutes to see what we have."

Castro was back, wild-eyed. "It's them. They're at Señora García's door. They'll be here next. Let's go."

"Wait," Malena said, her eyes still studying the tray.

He joined us, and together we peered down into the developer soup.

"I was in a small room above the chancellor's office," she said. "There was a window to shoot through. They came through the back. There wasn't enough protection there."

"We didn't have the guns," Castro said. "We were watching all those soldiers across the street. How was I to know they'd attack there?"

"I know," Malena said quietly. "I know."

In the solution, faces were becoming clearer. There were three men getting out of a car. The first two had revolvers in both hands. The last one was behind them. He was pointing and talking.

"That's in the courtyard next door," Castro said. "They came onto university property."

"Only one car," said Malena. "With plenty of weapons and a plan. People already on the inside for them."

Downstairs there was a heavy knock on Malena's door.

Castro blew out a long breath.

"One's Cruz," he said. "Head of the secret police. The one next to him is one of his assistants, maybe Pino. The one in back? I don't know. . . ."

There was another knock on the door—louder this time.

"Wait, I see now," Castro said. "Don't you recognize him, Billy?"

"Yes," Malena exclaimed. "I should have known."

Then it all came into focus for me. The person in the background, calling the shots, was my landlord—Señor Canillo.

Castro yanked the remaining prints from their trays and wrapped them in a towel. "Follow me," he said, taking Malena by the hand, with me trailing. We ran back through the apartment to her bedroom.

"The fire escape," Castro ordered. "You can reach it from your window."

He propped open her bedroom window and leaned out with one hand. "Do as I do," he said, and he reached until he caught the railing with one hand, then jumped to a landing a few feet below.

"I can't," Malena said.

"*Now,*" Castro ordered.

With that she jumped down to him. Then I leaped to the landing, with both of them steadying me before I rolled over. Back inside we heard them breaking down the door. It sounded like they were using an ax.

■   ■   ■

Castro soon left us, returning to campus. I accompanied Malena to a small flat on the top floor of the Hotel Pasaje, a few blocks from the waterfront. Throughout the night, the bell atop Havana's cathedral tolled once on the hour.

Malena told me that in the old days, the bell announced

the end of the working day. After it sounded, the gate to Old
Havana closed until morning. The gate was gone, as was the
stone wall that had once surrounded the old part of the city,
but the streets remained as narrow and as twisted as anything I
imagined back in ancient Spain. In the darkness, the smaller
trawlers and tugboats docked alongside the long stone piers
that flanked the narrow harbor. The oceangoing freighters were
anchored out in the bay. A revolving searchlight at El Morro,
the old Spanish stone fort, spun through our world like a
distant comet, illuminating the area with a brief flash of light
every fifteen seconds.

The bedroom overlooked a main boulevard and had several
escape routes. There was a small crawlway in the far corner of
the room, in back of the door. From there one could quickly
reach the roof and run to safety. Also there was a back staircase
at the end of the hallway that led to the alley in back of King
Salmon's store. From there, one could duck into the store, hiding amidst the racks of linen goods and dyed cloth, or run
thirty feet until the alleyway split off into the barrios near the
harbor. Most of the storefronts along the Calle de Bolivia were
sheltered by columns and archways. In the rain, one could walk
the length of the street, from the waterfront almost to central
Havana, where the casinos were, and never get wet.

"Havana is the city of columns," Malena told me as we gazed
down upon the street. "I've hidden in this flat before. It is a
good place. I'd like to think that it is lucky."

She stopped, looking up and down the street. But all was
quiet.

"Once, last year, I was staying here," she added. "I was coming back from somewhere, just crossing the street, when I
heard a shout. Usually, during the day, such loud sounds are
lost in the noise. But this time the street was stone still. No kids

playing by the foundation, the merchants inside their stores. I ran back into the shadows of the columns.

"The shout had come from up the street, near King Salmon's. A man was in a dark Buick, while two others slowly walked past the storefronts, shielding their eyes so they could peer inside. I ran to the end of the street, believing I heard the old woman that managed the flower store whispering for me to go faster. I turned the corner and ran until I reached the harbor, losing myself in the outdoor markets and the ships off-loading their treasures."

She put her arms around me, and I smelled a hint of jasmine and dust.

Her fingers unbuttoned my shirt and her palms began to slide inside the fabric, drawing across my chest. I turned toward her, and she settled onto her knees. With both hands she began to unzip my fly.

"If they find us tonight," she whispered, "we will kill them."

CHAPTER TWENTY-SIX

The biggest game of the season and my mind was elsewhere. Malena and I had been safe from the secret police and soldiers, and Castro found us in the morning. He told us that his big rally would still be that night. He had decided to go ahead without the famed bell.

Malena accompanied me to the ballpark before walking on to the university. Even though I wanted her to stay out of it, she insisted on being with Castro and the others now.

"They have no evidence to detain me," she said. "Once I reach the campus, they cannot arrest me with so many of our people around."

The prints, without a fixer bath, had faded to black in the morning sunlight. The negatives were in my athletic bag.

"Wish me luck," I said at the clubhouse door.

"Yes, win," she said, like it was an afterthought instead of the game to decide everything. "Play well."

The clubhouse was a morgue, the quietest it had been all season. Even Cochrane sat in front of his locker, slowly putting on his equipment, staring into space like the rest of them. Years later most of us would look back on this game and probably shrug it off as a battle for first place in a league long since forgotten. Athletes tell themselves they live in the present, focusing on the game at hand, yet what really fuels us is fear. Fear of being the guy who screws up and costs the team the game. Fear about carrying that with you for the rest of your days. Victories can be forgotten, but losses you directly caused—by a dropped ball, freezing on a fastball down the middle, being thrown out at the plate—those stay with a guy forever.

I sat down, trying to focus on the good things that could happen. I imagined myself swinging for the fence and the ball carrying, carrying, still carrying like a rocket well into the seats. But really, all I could think of was Arturo's face. That dazed look of death.

I wanted to talk about it, but I didn't dare. Not even to Cochrane or Oscar. In this world, I had no idea anymore who were my friends and who were my enemies. My only choice was to keep it bottled up inside. If I hadn't met Castro or Malena, I could have sat there and concentrated on a ball game and built it into the biggest thing in my world. But Arturo was dead. I had seen his body. There was nothing I could do to make that memory go away, no matter how well I played that day. No matter how well I played ever again.

The big game took place under a cloudless sky, with a pink-orange sun setting beyond the tall buildings downtown. The grass was freshly cut, and as I stepped onto it, it felt forgiving. I wondered if Arturo would be buried back in Holguín.

Skipper Charles, our starting pitcher on this day, had the best stuff on the club—major-league potential. Yet the way he alibied and complained, you would have thought he'd never gotten a batter out in his life. He was back at it now. When I caught him before the game, down in the bullpen, he was belly-aching about his fastball, even though it had plenty of giddyap.

The slider, his best pitch, was breaking great, but I knew he would have to be coaxed into throwing it again.

Later, as we walked up the right-field line toward our dugout, it was all I could do to convince him that he could get anybody out.

"Hector Mesa," I said, starting at the top of the Almendares batting order.

"He's tough," Skipper babbled. "Can't give him anything too fat to hit. Maybe pitch him away. Maybe he'll fish for it—"

"But he can't handle anything hard inside," I reminded him. "Let's push him in there."

"I don't know," said Skipper. "I guess."

"Canizares," I said, moving on to the number two hitter.

When Skipper didn't say a word, I went ahead with our scouting report.

"Start him off with the slider. He can't handle it. None of them can, if you bear down."

"But won't they be looking for it?" Skipper interrupted. His eyes were wide, holding too much fear. "You know, in a big game like this? They've scouted me. They know my tendencies. It's not like we're strangers anymore. Why don't we throw them completely off balance? Do everything backward? Instead of coming inside, we go away. Change-ups. Off-speed stuff."

"That's not your strength," I said. "Skip, let me do the thinking, OK? Whatever I signal, you throw. Put yourself in my hands. You're making this into too much of a big deal."

"That's easy for you to say," Skipper said. "They told me a couple days ago I would get a shot with the Senators this year. Everybody's watching me. I've got a good chance, they said so."

I wanted to deck him. "Relax," I growled. "Shut up and let me do the thinking for both of us."

I walked down to the end of the dugout, where Cochrane was checking the bat rack.

"I'm going to need a little help with Skip again," I said in a low voice. "The kid's as nervous as a bridegroom. He's got this notion that his entire career hinges on this one game."

"Maybe it does," Cochrane said, pulling out a bat and tapping it against the wooden rack, checking for cracks.

"The last time this guy fell apart you helped out," I reminded him.

"Partner, I've got my own act to shore up, if you catch my drift," Cochrane said. "Skipper thinks he's coming into a big-league spot? Well, ain't that great. Me? I'm fighting for a job. You may have a nice deal lined up with Papa Joe at the end of the season, scouting or whatever. Babe, I'm on the edge. Papa Joe told me so last night. Said a good game puts me a long ways down the road toward a job waiting for me in Florida."

I gave up. If everybody was covering their ass, I would too.

We were the home team, so Almendares had first ups. Throwing nothing but weak stuff, Skipper walked Mesa and Canizares on a combined ten pitches. The Scorpions had the heart of their order—Rickert, Caswell, and Morgan—coming up with ducks on the pond.

"Tell him I'll give him anything close," Raúl Atan, the umpire, whispered as I started out to the mound. I began to give the good news to Skipper, that the ump was ready to give him the benefit of the doubt for a while, but my pitcher wasn't listening. I waved at Cochrane, and he reluctantly came over. Ángel wandered out from the dugout because he seemed to have nothing else to do.

"Get somebody warming up fast," I told Ángel, meeting the manager in between the dugout and the mound.

"Can't do that," Ángel said. "Washington has people here. They want him to play. If I had my way, the whole pen would be up by now."

I shook my head. This was nuts. The only thing I could do was try to bring Skipper back to the land of the living.

"Remember when Cochrane and I browbeat you through that game a while back?" I asked.

Skipper smiled weakly. "Best performance of my life."

"You remember what the sky looked like that day? The hours before you shut them down?"

"Sky blue."

"A lot like it was today, wouldn't you say?"

Cochrane snickered. "Listen to this."

"Shut up," I snapped, then turned my attention back to Skipper. "Remember how it was hot that day, too? A lot like this one was. A bit of a breeze coming in off the ocean."

I motioned with my mitt at the row of palm trees beyond the left-field fence, and to my surprise Skipper, Cochrane, and Ángel followed my arm. "Remember how it rattled the leaves in those trees over there? Remember, Skipper?"

"I think so," our starting pitcher said, apparently becoming a little curious about what I was up to.

"Remember how you were unhittable that day?"

Cochrane raised an eyebrow.

"Skipper, I've got a confession to make," I continued. "That was the best game I've ever seen by a young pitcher. I mean it. You were great. I'm not going to ream you out today. Because you and I know you're better than that. You're a young guy who's going to be a great pro. A young guy to be reckoned with. Years from now the rest of us here will be talking about how we once played with old Skip in Cuba."

Atan was walking out from home plate to break things up.

"In a minute the ump's going to tell me to shut up," I said. "But I want you to know something, Skip. You're the best. I've been around a long time. Maybe too long. But you've got the goods. So why keep it a secret from these assholes? Mow them down."

Raúl joined us.

"That's it, gentlemen," he said.

Skipper turned and walked away from us, gazing out at the dark outline of the palm trees past the left-field fence.

Cochrane brushed past me, heading back toward first base.

"Five bucks says that sweet-talking doesn't do any good," he said.

Ángel gave me a puzzled look. "If it works, I'll be kicking myself for not taking notes," he said.

I walked with Atan back to home plate.

"You got your slider eyes on?" I asked.

Out of the corner of his mouth, he said, "Wide open, Billy."

The Scorpions' Rick Rickert stepped into the batter's box. He was a big right-handed hitter who could turn on the ball real quick. As he dug in, I signaled for a slider; Skipper simply nodded and went into his delivery. The ball came in with half as much spin as I'd have liked. Rolling way to the outside, it hit the dirt and bounced away from me. On all fours, I lunged for the ball but missed it. By the time I came up with it, the runners had moved up to second and third.

"Ball one," Atan said with disgust.

I fired the ball back at Skipper's head. Now we had two men in scoring position, none out. Skipper caught my bullet with a flick of his glove, called time, and walked back off the mound for more soul-searching.

I started to go out to him, but Atan stopped me.

"You've had your say," he said. "Let's play ball."

Rickert grinned at me. "This is getting good."

The more a pitcher is struggling, the more time he takes between pitches. It's a basic law of baseball. By the time Skipper got back to the pitching rubber, Rickert was practically drooling for his next pitch.

I signaled for the slider again. This one had a better break, and it barely caught the outside of the plate.

"Strike one," Raúl cried, and the way the crowd went crazy for a simple strike, you would have thought we'd won game seven of the World Series. Rickert wasn't happy with the call. He glared back at Raúl and then pawed at the dirt with one shoe. When he finally stepped back in, Skipper tried to power a fastball by him. Rickert was ready, but thank God he swung underneath it. The way the ball jumped off the bat, I thought it would be deep enough to score Mesa from third. But with the breeze blowing in, it was too shallow. The Scorpions had their runners hold. There was one out.

Frankie Caswell was the next batter. He was left-handed and a natural home-run hitter. Skipper's slider would come right into his wheelhouse. If he threw it too flat, we would be down 3–0 in a hurry.

I crouched closer to the ground, hoping Skipper would hit my glove, staying away from Caswell's power. The danger was that if he threw it too low and another ball got away from me, we would hand them another run.

Skipper's first slider hit a good foot in front of the plate and bounced left. I rolled toward it, feeling it catch me first in the chest and then slide down my torso. If Mesa had been running, he would have been safe easy. But Bobby Hughes, the Scorpions' third-base coach, was playing things safe. He smelled a big inning and didn't want to take any chances.

When I finally came up with the ball, Mesa was still on third, straining at Hughes's orders like a wild dog.

"Nice stop," Raúl said.

The near tragedy had shaken up Skipper. His eyes were becoming large and wild again. He had run halfway down from the mound to cover the plate.

"Another pitch?" he said to me. "We'll go with something else."

I shrugged, knowing there was no way we could back out of this masterpiece now. We would stick with the slider, passed ball or no, because Caswell would definitely be looking for a fastball.

When I signaled for another slider, Skipper looked a little pale, but he nodded and went into his delivery. The pitch was a tad high. Still, the baseball gods were smiling on us. Caswell was so jazzed up for a fastball that he was way out in front of the ball. He lined it toward third base. Diving to his left, Spider Jorgensen snared the drive before it hit the ground, and then, on all fours, beat Mesa back to the bag for the double play. Skipper had to be the luckiest arm I'd ever seen. Somehow he had escaped the top of the first without allowing a run.

From then on, old Skipper became Cy Young. A real machine out there. I would flash the signal and he would simply nod and throw for my mitt. Now he was working like his car was double-parked outside. The infield was on their toes, able to go that extra foot in either direction for the ball.

Skipper got nicked for a hit in the third inning, and that was just as well. I didn't want him fretting about any no-hitter. It was better to keep such worldly things from the young boy's mind. A nice, well-pitched ball game was all we needed here.

Skipper kept rolling along, which was good, seeing as we

weren't coming any closer to getting any runs on the board, either. We left two men on in the fourth inning. I did us no good with a towering pop-up in foul territory down the third-base line. We left another base runner stranded at third in the next inning when Jorgensen lined into a double play with Cochrane standing in the on-deck circle.

"We're jinxed today," Cochrane said.

Heading into our at-bats in the seventh, we were still locked in a scoreless tie. I was first up. The heart of the order had had a miserable day. Cochrane's opposite-field single in the first inning was the only damage. Freddy Martin, the starting pitcher for Almendares, was cruising along, matching goose eggs with Skipper. When I stepped into the batter's box, I had no idea what to expect from him. He was a lanky right-hander who delivered the ball somewhere between sidearm and three-quarters—making it easy to lose the pitch in his uniform or the background of the outfield grandstand. He had kept me off balance pretty good. My first at-bat, he got away with a fastball right down the middle for strike three. The pitch had been set up nicely with a couple curves on the outside edge. My second time, he busted me in on the hands. I turned on the heat well enough but hit the ball off the handle, shooting it into the air beyond third base. This time around, I was guessing that he would go outside early, so I focused on a small square of space on the outer half of the plate.

However, Martin crossed me up again. He came back with the fastball inside and I was out on a limb, my body leaning, looking for slow stuff away. I couldn't get out of the way of his bullet. The ball caught me on the upper arm, right below the shoulder. Any higher, with the way I hunched my neck and back at the plate, and the ball would have gotten me in the head. For a second I couldn't feel any sensation in my fingers. Then it all came back, like somebody had plugged me into a wall socket. A weird tingling ran up and down my arm. In pain, I got back up on my feet—no way this clown was going to get his jollies by watching me wriggle on the ground—and I started stumbling toward first base.

Allie Hacker, our first-base coach, hurried down the line to put an arm around me.

"Nice play," Martin taunted me from the mound. "That's the only way you were getting on and you know it."

I yelled back, and Atan ran out to make sure nothing more developed. I got to first base and stood there, still hurting. My arm had started to stiffen and I shook it, wondering if I had broken anything.

Hacker tapped me on the back.

"You've done your part," he said. "Take a break."

I looked over to our dugout to see Hilly Hanson coming out to take my place. At first I didn't get it. But when the rookie came up to me, grinning his ass off, it dawned on me that I was leaving. I'd played my last game for this season—maybe forever.

Head down, I brushed past Hanson, wanting to shove his pretty face into the ground, and jogged over to our bench. I got a good round of applause.

Oscar put down a decent enough bunt to move Hanson over to second. We had the lead run in scoring position with one out. Bobby Haas, an old warhorse, was our next batter, and he promptly hit a ground ball to the right side, moving Hanson easily to third. Canizares, their second baseman, bobbled the ball, so now we were really in business. Runners on first and third, still one out.

Ángel took a long look down the bench, thinking about a pinchhitter, but with a resigned look on his face he told Skipper to go ahead and bat. Frankly, I couldn't remember the last time one of our pitchers had gotten a base hit. But the way Skipper was slinging, Ángel was going to ride him into the ground.

Everyone in the league knew Skipper swung the bat like a girl, though, and so Martin had a smirk on his face when his opposite number came up to the plate.

He threw a half-assed curve over the plate, and Skipper missed it by a mile. Then he buzzed him a little tight with a fastball—not too far inside, because Martin might face the same treatment if he was still around to bat later in the game.

Pitchers are arrogant animals, sometimes too much so. That's what happened to Martin with his next pitch. He tried to simply throw the ball by Skipper. But anybody who is playing at this level has some degree of talent. Sure enough, Skipper made him pay for being so high and mighty. He got enough of Martin's heat to pop the ball up and deep to right field. As the ball began to come down, we knew that Hanson would be tagging up and heading for home.

Rickert, their right fielder, backpedaled and then came in, catching the ball in stride and throwing hard for the plate. As soon as the ball hit Rickert's glove, Hanson was off, and at first I thought he would make it.

Rickert's throw was a little up the line, but Hanson was too slow. By the time he went into his slide, Díaz had been able to snag Rickert's throw on one hop and lunge back toward the plate. The Almendares catcher clipped Hanson on the shoulder before both of them tumbled across the plate in a heap.

"Out," screamed Atan, and the crowd groaned.

"I don't believe it," Cochrane said.

Hanson tried to hurry off the field. Yet before he crawled out of sight, the crowd had decided upon his punishment—one that warmed my heart.

"Bo-lo, Bo-lo," they began to chant—louder with each repetition. We hadn't scored, but there wasn't a happier person on God's green earth than me.

CHAPTER *TWENTY-SEVEN*

Papa Joe's door was open, and at first I thought this was going to be easy.

He was sitting on his red leather chair, with his back to the door, gazing out at the lights of the Malecón and the star-filled sky hanging over the Straits of Florida. The only signs of life were the light of his desk lamp and the slow curl of cigar smoke building above his head.

"Who's there?" he said. His voice was soft, and he didn't bother to turn around.

"Billy Bryan," I said.

There was a long pause, and finally he answered, "Isn't it a nice evening, Billy? How appropriate for your last one in Havana."

He slowly swiveled around in that big chair of his. He looked like he hadn't slept in days. Eyes ringed like a raccoon's with circles of fatigue stared back at me.

"I never get any sleep when the season ends down here," he grumbled. "It's the nature of the beast."

He slid an envelope across the desk. "Your plane tickets," he said. "As promised, two for Miami."

"Thanks," I said. "You know, this will be the first time I've ever flown out of here. I've always had to take the ferryboat home. I'm always broke."

"Lucky you," Papa Joe said.

He took a couple more puffs, and then set the cigar down in a golden ashtray on his desk.

"Here, sit down, my boy," he said. "Tell me, how is Castro?"

"I'm hopeful."

"Sure you are." Papa Joe smiled. "So, everything is coming together for you, then. Your team wins the championship. That Cochrane is something, isn't he? Hitting a two-run shot after Hanson gets thrown out at the plate. You should be proud, Billy. You're on a winner for the second year in a row."

I didn't feel much like a winner.

"I've got a little story to tell you before I go," I told Papa Joe.

"That's what this time of the year is for," he said. "Stories. Wrapping things up."

I began, "The other night, up on the campus, a kid was shot and killed."

Papa Joe's face held no expression.

I continued, "Our good friend Señor Canillo was behind it."

"Billy, be careful—"

I cut him off. "Then the authorities went after my girl and Castro. We were lucky to get away. You knew about this, didn't you?"

Papa Joe sighed and looked at the ceiling. "I'm just a peddler of baseball flesh, my boy. I'm not interested in politics. You know that."

"Do I? Nobody's as cozy as you and Canillo. The way you were half in the tank the other night, you knew. I'm sure of it."

Papa Joe took his cigar from the ashtray and turned away from me, returning his gaze to the glowing Malecón.

"Billy, I don't know where you get your wild ideas," he said. "Cochrane was right about you. You're in too deep with the local culture down here. That's not healthy. You need to remember where you come from, who your friends are."

I stood up. "Now that I've got Castro's plane ticket, I want his contract, too."

"Why?" Papa Joe said, turning back toward me.

"It's too dangerous in your hands. Castro thinks playing ball can make you a hero. I know that's not true. You slip that contract to Canillo, and maybe it puts Castro in a delicate spot. You know, they could blackmail him with that. Claim he's nothing but a goofy ballplayer."

"My, my, the thoughts that are spinning around in that head of yours. Billy, you're beginning to sound like a budding revolutionary yourself." He blew out a puff of smoke and smiled. "I'm just an old man. How am I going to stop you? You know where the contracts are."

"The gun in your bottom drawer," I said. "The one next to the bourbon. Put it up on the desk, so I can see it."

"I see I have let you get too close to me," Papa Joe said.

His weapon was a silver Colt. He stood up and put it at the far corner of his huge polished desk, well beyond the ashtray.

Sitting back down, he said, "Billy . . ." and then no more.

I kept an eye on him as I moved toward the filing cabinet. The door was unlocked. When I pulled it open, Castro's contract was the first among those for the new recruits.

"Your friendship with Castro has a price tag," warned Papa Joe. "Take that agreement and our relationship is over. I'll never recommend you for another job. If I can help it, your baseball career will be over. Think about it. Do you really feel like throwing it all away for somebody like Castro?"

I took a deep breath and then picked up the contract. It was two pages, with the additional clause naming me as Castro's private coach. I folded it in half and held it by my side.

"He would have been a helluva player," I said.

"And you would have been a helluva scout, a good organization man," Papa Joe said.

I slipped the contract inside my blazer pocket.

"May you rot in hell," I said, hurrying for the door.

In a whisper, Papa Joe answered, "Amen."

∎ ∎ ∎

It was dark by the time I returned to campus. A huge crowd had completely filled the plaza beneath the Gallery of Martyrs. The black mass of people hung like a boulder on a cliff, ready to roll down the hill and smash the casinos and their blinking neon into so many pieces. Fires had been set in metal drums throughout the plaza, and in the flickering light the young faces appeared ancient and angry.

As I moved through the crowd I heard talk about a march on the presidential palace that night. These were mad people. Mad to be saved. Mad to make everything perfect. Up at the microphone in front of them was Castro—the one who fueled their blaze of insanity. He spoke as passionately as I'd ever heard him, swinging his fist in time with his words as he spoke about the cherished bell and its disappearance.

"It stood for all we fight for," he said. "An injustice that we will not allow to stand. This deception cuts deep. We know for certain that the government was behind it. They have betrayed us all."

The crowd let out a loud cheer, different from anything I had ever heard at the ballpark. It was a low growl, without any real enthusiasm—the sound of impatience and desperation.

"I have a confession to make," Castro said, dropping his voice. The mass hushed each other to listen. "I thought this would be easier. I didn't realize that this government was evil to the bone. I thought that they would recognize our efforts. Work with us. But this Grau, and Batista, the one who hides in Miami—they have forgotten us, forgotten their people. Instead of a helping hand, we have been cast into the darkness."

Now his voice started to rise in anger. "I was a fool to think it would be any different. That this struggle wouldn't require my full attention. But now I pledge to you—" Here the crowd again grew quiet. "—that I will not rest until this government falls."

Castro raised both fists to chest level and shook them. "I will swing these weapons until I have no more strength. Together let us march on their palace of corruption. Let us together strike another blow."

With that he jumped down from the podium, locking arms with those in the front row. Slowly the crowd began to move as one, down into the city streets below the campus.

I ran around one flank and elbowed my way up to him. I got within a couple bodies of Castro but no closer.

"Fidel," I shouted, and he turned to see me. He looked like a man strapped to the front car of a roller coaster headed downhill.

"Billy," he said.

"You had the best curveball I've ever seen," I said.

He nodded. "You'll preserve that part of me. Tell them about how I could play. It would make my father proud."

I was swept back a few rows, and my pitching prospect was soon out of sight. I let the crowd push by me on either side, try-ing to ride the current of people to the edge of things, to a place where I could catch myself. At last I was alone, standing next to one of the metal drums, its insides hot with flame and ash. I watched the crowd go, following Castro to the presidential palace. I took the contract out of my pocket and held it over the fire. The flame caught one end, and I kept my grip on the paper until I felt the heat on my fingers. Then I dropped what was left into the drum and watched it quickly burn. My grand scheme for staying in this game the rest of my life was officially history.

CHAPTER TWENTY-EIGHT

The air is so still that I can hear the camel trucks throttling down to negotiate the traffic circle around José Martí Plaza and the national library, almost a quarter mile away. On this trip I have told myself to stay open to anything, with little success. When Eván pointed to a camel truck earlier this afternoon, joking that we could ride one of those along Zapata Boulevard up from the hotel, I drew the line. No way was I setting foot on a bus that looks like a dungeon on wheels, able to cram five hundred people aboard at a single time. So, with no cabs to be found, we walked, arriving at Colón Cemetery just before seven, closing time.

With the gates closing for the night, we have hunkered down amidst the tombstones, waiting for complete darkness. We are near La Milagrosa's grave, a lucky place for an evening like this, Eván tells us. We are biding our time reading the small plaques of wood and clay that the pilgrims have left. "Thanks because you let my son go to the States," reads one. "Thanks for our new house," says another. "Thanks for any miracle you can spare" is my favorite.

The noise of the main gate slamming shut for the night echoes up from the guard station and curator's house. The three of us move farther back under the branches of a squat laurel tree.

"Stay still and we'll be OK here," Eván whispers. "The guards are scared of La Milagrosa and her magic. They won't come down here unless they have to."

"Who was she?" Cassy whispers.

"She and her child died in 1914. They were from a good family and were buried here. The story I was told was that somebody visiting another grave stopped by La Milagrosa's to admire the statue of her, holding her baby. He said a prayer, asking for something good to come into his life, and such a thing happened. Over the years the word grew that La Milagrosa could bestow miracles. Now people bring the plaques you see and place them on her crypt, praying for the best."

"Do you believe it?"

"I don't know. Why not? What would you ask for, Cassy?"

"That you could visit us in America."

"Now, that would be a miracle, wouldn't it?"

"But I thought people were leaving here all the time," I say, "coming to the States. South Florida is still filling up with Cuban immigrants. You see reports about it on the news."

"Anybody who leaves here has family in the United States," says Eván. "Family that will declare that they want them. Will back up those words with money."

"Money," I repeat, with disgust.

"Yes, Billy. It takes a lot of money to get out of Cuba."

I nod. "This sounds familiar. Did you know I sent your mother a fair bit of change over the years? Money that I shouldn't have been giving away?"

"She always spoke warmly of you. If it will ease your mind, your money went to good causes."

"Like the revolution and Fidel?"

"No, you'd be surprised. Some of it did go to Fidel. But some of it went to me. Getting me the best teachers. Making sure I had clothes and shoes."

"That's good, then," I tell her. "But I wish your mother had used it to get out."

I don't like this anger that exists between us. But I've been down this road before: throwing money into Cuba and having it never bear any fruit for me.

"What did you say we are doing here?" asks Cassy, eager to change the subject. "Something called Santería."

"That's right," Eván replies. "It means 'cult of the gods.' It's a blend of African and Cuban faiths."

"Are you some sort of priestess or something?"

"No, Cassy," she says, the laughter rumbling outward like breakers at the beach. "All I know about Santería is what an old aunt taught me a long time ago. She believed in all the descendants of Santería. That the wife of Christ was Odudua, the goddess of the underworld. She told me sailors turned to somebody called Yemaya for protection." Eván laughs again. "I'm not an expert in anything, especially Santería. But it's like the whites say down here: '*Yo no creo pero lo repeto*—I do not believe, but I repeat the ritual.' "

She pauses, turning her gaze back to me. "There is much holding the three of us together. Perhaps we will never understand it. But it seems to me that we are all trying to reach an understanding with the past. That's never easy. So I steal a little from my memory, take a little advice from my friends—who, like my old aunt, really believe. Maybe it will help us. Maybe it is a better way to tell the stories that run through all of us. Maybe we can find an ending in this night."

Eván glances down toward the guardhouse. "Come. It is time. We have waited long enough."

We follow her in a zigzag pattern through the tombstones, away from La Milagrosa, toward the far corner of the cemetery. Two paved roads, in straight lines, enter Colón from the four sides, crossing at the cemetery's heart, where the most gaudy tombs and crypts, many with life-size statues and angels, are erected. The three of us cross the asphalt road, our shoes clattering under the darkening sky. We're making too much noise, I think. What would they sentence us to for being here in this graveyard at this hour? I try to focus on Eván's bulky frame, her dress flowing back in the wind as she runs, and I tell myself to move faster, go with her. This is not a place I want to be lost in. For at my age, I have more in common with the dead than with these two women I chase with all my strength.

Cassy has caught up to Eván and follows her like she is her twin. Their images appear to accelerate away from me, flickering in and out of the glow of the streetlights. I am beginning to lose them. No, not now. Not now, I say to myself, repeating this plea until it becomes a prayer, the only force that keeps my aging body moving forward through the honored dead that surround me. I think again of Laurie and hope that somehow, though our bodies are literally hundreds of miles apart, she will reach out to guide me.

"Dad, in here," Cassy says as she pulls me by the arm back into their midst. And for a few precious moments I feel her fingertips on my skin. My breath is frantic, and I wipe away the cold sweat from above my eyes, feeling what it is like to still be alive.

"Dad, you OK?"

"Fine. I'm fine."

Eván, who has sat down across from me, leans over and briefly runs her hand through my thinning gray hair. I look up into her face, feeling like I have known her my entire life.

From her small knapsack, Eván pulls out a slender candle, wedges it into the ground between us, and lights the wick with a wooden match.

"Won't they see us?" Cassy says.

"Believe you are safe and you are," Eván replies. "They won't come. Not now. What goes on out here in the night frightens them too much."

She reaches into her pack and brings forth a small pack of papers and letters held together by a rubber band.

"My mother's grave," she begins, and then stops, nodding at Cassy. "It is right behind me."

She turns and runs her hands across the dark marble chamber. Beyond her fingers I am able to make out "Malena Fonseca, 1923–1959. A true messenger of the people and the revolution."

After so many years, the past and I have caught up with each other.

"Growing up, my girlfriends and I used to tell each other that we had family in the United States," Eván says. "There is no better thing to brag about than that."

She turns to Cassy. "So when your letters arrived, I couldn't believe it. How precious a dream, you understand? But when the second letter arrived, that's when I decided that if you ever came to visit me, we would do this. The three of us."

Eván unfolds a yellowing piece of paper from the small stack she has taken out of her knapsack.

"From my mother's diary," she explains, and then begins to read. " 'October fifteenth, 1958. The sun shines as brightly as ever, but I cannot raise my eyes to it. I fear for this land. Fidel will be its new king. I have no doubt of that now.

" 'I recently returned from a short trip to the east, where he carries on the battle. He wanted me to stay. I couldn't. The peasants will support him to the end. I'm sure of it. And with their support goes any chance that somebody else, somebody with a better heart, will step forward.

" 'Fidel has a way about him. Everything works out, but only for him. I have seen it happen to our friends and now his growing army. I don't know if I can watch it happen to my country as well.

" 'Fidel told me Che will take Santa Clara by Christmas. I believe him. How I wish it weren't so.' "

Eván stops reading and then holds the paper over the flame. The paper soon catches, and as it burns she holds it over the grave site, letting the ashes fall on the marble tomb.

"Rest, my mother," Eván says, her eyes closed and her voice low. "Rest."

When she is finished, Eván pulls out a smaller piece of paper, ragged at the edges, that appears to have been torn from a larger volume.

"Now, Billy Bryan, you must read this," she says, holding it out to me. I take it from her and in the poor light try to decipher it. Cassy leans closer to me, ready to help.

" 'December first, 1958. I find myself dreaming of Billy Bryan. He probably thinks I'm dead. In the confusion of Moncada, I was listed as such. Not one of those to go with Fidel to prison.

" 'That was more than four years ago. Have I been that sick in the head? That depressed by the situation to allow this much time to slip past without contacting him somehow? I tell myself that I have let it be this way for my daughter, Evangelina. It is better for me and her if the authorities think I'm truly dead. That's what I tell myself.

" 'Still, I miss him. With each passing day, I seal myself more up in this country and its fate with Fidel. But sometimes my mind runs away with me. I wonder what Billy would say if I appeared at his door, with Evangelina in tow. He has returned to his land of ice and snow. A place that when he talked about it sounded like it belonged in a fairy tale.' "

My hands are shaking by the time I finish. I turn to Cassy, the one from my world. The one who made me smile the most over the last forty years. But then I look at Eván, unable to fathom how this could have happened.

Eván takes the candle from the ground and holds it out to me. "Burn the words. Burn the past," she urges me. "Take away her pain. Take away yours."

I do as she tells me, holding the edge of the paper over the flame, surprised by how quickly it catches. I follow her example, letting the paper burn down before setting what's left upon Malena's vault.

"And now this," says Eván, holding out a faded newspaper clipping to Cassy. "Both of you. Please look at it."

A photo shows the celebration in downtown Havana as Castro and his troops roll into the capital, waving at the throng from atop tanks. It is dated January 8, 1959.

When we are finished, Cassy returns it to Eván, who burns this as well.

The last piece of paper has an official-looking letterhead. "The Department of State," it reads in Spanish.

" 'January twenty-first, 1959,' " Eván begins, but she sighs and wipes her eyes with the back of her hand. "I'm sorry. I can't. Will you?" she asks me.

I take the typed letter from her.

"A friend in the government gave me this a year or so ago," Eván says. "Ever since, I've prayed that you two would come."

I begin. " 'Report on Malena Fonseca. The subject has been under surveillance for three weeks. On the night in question, she left her apartment accompanied by her ten-year-old daughter. They had several bags with them and traveled by cab to the airport.

" 'When she attempted to board the last flight that evening to Miami, authorities interceded as ordered by President Castro.

" 'Señora Fonseca resisted arrest and, in the ensuing altercation, she took out a gun and threatened to shoot if not allowed to board the plane.

" 'An airport guard tried to subdue Malena Fonseca, but the subject saw him and turned to fire. When she did so, we also opened fire.

" 'Malena Fonseca was pronounced dead at the university hospital at eleven o'clock in the evening. The child has been placed with family in Santa Clara.' "

There is no noise coming from the guardhouse. Except for a lone light burning in the lower window of the stone building, there is no other sign of life. The night sky has turned a milky blue, vaporous and ghostly.

Eván takes the document from my trembling fingers and begins to burn it like the others.

"Now she is free," she says. "Let us pray that we are all free of the past as well."

I move my mouth as though to speak, but no words will come. I sit with my head buried in my hands, shamed by my loss of faith.

A s was Castro's style, he couldn't leave well enough alone. He wanted it all—and all at once.

The support he received that night more than forty-five years ago, when I saw him for the last time, should have been victory enough and a reason to fight another day. It was apparent that Castro was the new leader among the students and fast becoming the voice of the people as well.

When the demonstrators reached the palace, Castro and the students were able to surround it. Their numbers had swelled that much. They waved their signs. They chanted their slogans. Some threw rocks, with the world's news cameras recording the moment. Yes, it was a good beginning, and that was all it had to be. The only one who couldn't live with that was Castro. He actually thought he could begin and end his revolution in one day.

He decided to rush the palace, and many of his new converts blindly followed. The troops, sitting in their nests of sandbags and bullets, were waiting for them—delighted by the turn of events. They must have smiled when the order came to open fire. Their machine guns tore through the crowd like knives—

of light and pain—turning Castro's joyous victory into a bloody standoff. The government remained the powerful one, an elephant swatting at a pesky fly. Instead of pictures of angry faces shouting for a new regime, Castro's supporters were shown weeping over their dead. With one mistake, his cause had gone from being worldwide headlines to a small box on the back pages, from stirring news to simply more trouble in Cuba. More of the same. Trouble that had been stopped, with the government still in charge.

"He took us right into them!" Malena said. "No thought of the consequences. How many people died? I don't know. Many. Too many. Not one needed to. We just had to walk away. We'd made our point."

I was quiet. It hurt to be leaving this way. Everything was falling apart.

"Where's Castro now?" I asked.

Malena shook her head. "I don't know. I don't care."

I tried to laugh. "Until a couple days ago, he was coming with me tomorrow, on the plane to Miami."

"If you think that's still going to happen, then you're a bigger fool than he is," Malena snapped.

"I know that," I replied, a bit angry with her. "I went to Papa Joe. I got Castro's contract tonight."

"And what did you do with it?"

"I burned it. It's gone. Castro will never have to worry about that part of his life again."

"How noble of you, Billy."

She was mocking me. I was getting madder, rising to the bait.

"You threw away what you wanted," Malena said. "You men are all the same."

"I thought you'd be happy. Castro's all yours. He's one hun-

dred percent rebel, right? You told me that the first night we met."

"Billy, you're too kind," she sneered. "So understanding for an American."

"What's the problem?" I asked. "It's the way you wanted it, right? He's here. He's staying. I'm leaving—"

Tears began to well up in her eyes.

"Yes, it's perfect," she said. "You've done so much thinking. How good of you. Everybody's thinking and scheming," she said, her voice growing shaky. "You go. Leave us with this man, no, this child. Castro is going to drag us to the top of the hill or kill us one by one in the process. You're smart to get out. Americans always are. There isn't any middle ground here anymore. Things have become too dangerous."

We were at my apartment in Miramar. I walked across the room and stared out the full-length windows to the patio and the dark sea beyond. She remained on the couch, bent over at the waist, crying harder. On the kitchen table were the airline tickets. I picked them up.

"You don't have to put up with this," I said, returning to her. I held out the tickets. "You can come with me. There's no names on these. We can write yours in. No problem. If Castro's so crazy, why stay? Come with me."

Malena's face was wet with tears.

"I'm serious," I said. "Let's get out of here. The two of us."

"No, it's not that easy," she said. Then she buried her face in her hands and started to cry again.

■ ■ ■

Later that night, in my bed, she said, "Won't they be waiting for me at the airport?"

"If you have a ticket and are going on an American plane, I don't see how they can stop us," I said. "At the airport, I'll write in your name. If anybody messes with us, I'll call the U.S. embassy. That should make them think."

"You would, too," she said.

"You bet I would," I replied. "Let me take care of everything."

"But what about my pictures? The ones from the night Canillo and the others took the bell? Those must come with me. People must see them. They'll at least search me, looking for them."

I was quiet, thinking of a way to make this all work. In the old days, I traveled with my own stash of bats—thirty-two-ounce beauties, their handles sticky from so many passes of the pine tar rag. When I was younger, I carried that bat bag, its long handle looped over one shoulder, to every new town into which baseball took me. After all, these were the tools of my trade. Players didn't leave such important things to the equipment goons. What did they know about bats? A quality ballplayer took care of his own. As my career leveled off, though, I didn't have my bats with me all the time. I stopped working through my stroke in front of the bedroom mirror every night.

So it took me a while to find a bat in this house, and the one I did locate was Cochrane's. It was from one of the first days of the winter ball season. He had stayed with me until Canillo fixed him up with a place of his own. Cochrane's bats had a good-sized barrel, probably better suited for this job than my skinnier ones.

"How's this going to help?" Malena asked. She had followed me on my search through the house.

"Wait," I replied. "You'll see."

In a storage room off the kitchen, there was a small workbench. I placed the bat, head up, in a vise and located the corkscrew drill. After carefully lining things up, I burrowed with the drill lengthwise down into the barrel wood. I went two and a half inches before pulling the drill back out, blowing the wood dust onto the floor.

"Now that I think about it, I should have done this more often," I said. "I had one of my best years using a corked bat. See, you dig out a bit of the barrel and load it up with cork, maybe a golf ball—something light, something with pop. Then you've got the same bat area but a lighter head. You can really turn on the ball. Problem is, you break this sucker open, the cork goes flying, and the whole world knows that you've been—"

"Cheating," Malena put in.

"That's right," I said.

With the hole finished, I smoothed down the opening with a bit of sandpaper.

"OK, get me the negatives."

She returned with a small strip wrapped in waxed paper.

"These are the best ones," she said.

Using the border between two shots as a crease, I carefully doubled the strip over. Her negative slid nicely into the hole at the top end of the bat.

"Now we seal it shut," I said.

In a drawer were a number of slices of wooden dowel. This was one of the advantages of being in the same place year after year down here: I never forgot my address, and everything I needed was here, somewhere. The chips looked like wooden pennies. I pulled the drawer out; laying it on the worktable, we both hunted through it until she found one that fit perfectly into the hole. With a light touch of wood glue, the opening was closed over. Once the glue dried, it received a light sanding and a brush of varnish. Unless somebody knew where to look, it appeared to be a regular bat.

"I'll find another and put them both in the bag," I explained. "I'll personally carry it on the plane."

She smiled. "Yes, this will work."

CHAPTER THIRTY

Malena left my place early the next morning, saying she would meet me at the airport by three in the afternoon. I spent the rest of the morning packing my gear. The other players had their stuff forwarded directly on to whatever spring training camp they were bound for. But seeing as I didn't have any idea where I was going, I put my parents' address on the wardrobe and two cardboard boxes. I had nowhere left to go but home to upstate New York.

When I finished packing, I rang Malena's flat. Castro answered.

"She's not here," he explained. "The scum beat me to her. I just walked in. You should see this place. They tore it apart."

"What are you talking about?"

"The word on the street was they were going to pick her up today," Castro replied. "They know she has the pictures of them."

"Where did they take her?"

"Probably the main police station. The one in Habana Vieja."

"I'll meet you there."

"But Billy, you don't understand. We can't go there—"

"In ten minutes?"

There was silence at the other end.

"In ten minutes," I repeated.

"All right," Castro replied. "Ten minutes."

He was waiting when my cab pulled up in front of the gray stone building with no windows a few blocks from where the Malecón ends on the east end of town. Castro fell in beside me as I walked up the stairs toward the main door.

"Billy, we need to talk this over," Castro said, pulling at my sleeve. "Plan our attack."

I shrugged him off and kept walking toward the door.

"Where's your balls, Fidel?" I asked. "Aren't you the guy who got a lot of people hurt last night? Aren't you the guy who left a young kid guarding that stupid bell of yours? It seems to me that you have a lot of courage when somebody else's life is on the line."

"You don't know these animals," he said.

"Sure I do. One of them is my landlord, right? Besides, I don't care anymore. They have her. There must be something we can do."

We reached the front door. It was black steel, thick enough to stop bullets. I pushed it open and we entered a dark chamber with a lone desk and one uniformed man across the way. The clock on the wall read a few minutes before noon. I had my bat bag and valise. I could have left for the airport at any time— be free and clear. But I had decided I wasn't going to leave without her.

Approaching the desk, I took the solid bat out of the bag. The guard was just looking up at us when I rapped it hard across his tabletop.

"Listen good," I told him in Spanish. "I want to see your boss, right now. Understand? Tell him a crazy American is looking for a little batting practice."

The guy sprang to life, jabbering to somebody over the intercom.

"He's going to throw us in jail," Castro whispered.

"If he tries, it'll become an international incident," I said. "I guarantee it."

I brought the bat up again, ready to deliver another strike atop the desk. But the guard shook his head.

"Wait, wait," he begged.

We heard a door somewhere back in the shadows open and men rustle out like bats exiting a cave. Castro was looking around, ready to run.

"I never saw you use your bat with such fury on the diamond," said a familiar voice. Stepping into the light was Señor Canillo.

"And I never knew where you really worked," I said.

"Billy, there are many things you don't know about me," he said. Canillo nodded at Castro. "You're nervous without your rabble, aren't you, little man?"

Castro started to say something but caught himself.

"Where is she?" I said.

"How would you say it?" Canillo mused. "I know. She is as safe as if she was in the arms of Jesus."

"I want her."

"Billy, you should know by now that I never give anything away. Except my money when I pick up the tab for you ballplayers at the Capri."

I was quiet, unsure how to reply.

"Maybe a trade?" Canillo said. "A beautiful young girl for a low-life revolutionary."

Castro glared at me. "You've set me up!" he exclaimed.

"No," I said to both of them. "I'm leaving you two to fight that out among yourselves at another time. Not now." I focused on Canillo. "Release Malena to me and she's out of your hair forever," I said. "I'm taking her with me on the Miami flight this afternoon."

"How did a baseball player become so rich all of a sudden?" Canillo wondered. "Any ballplayer I know is taking the overnight ferry. Like any other tourist with empty pockets."

I reached into the inside pocket of my blazer.

"Two first-class tickets to Miami," I said. "In fact, I'll even let you write in the names, Señor Canillo."

Canillo examined the plane tickets.

"Legitimate," he said. "From your Papa Joe?"

"A going-away present," I said. "For services rendered."

Canillo nodded, glancing at Castro. "Your Papa Joe is a generous old fool. I see he pays in full even when the results aren't one hundred percent successful."

"It doesn't change my offer," I told him. "Release her into my custody and she's on the next plane out of here. Out of your way, and you don't even have to lift a finger."

Canillo smiled and looked upward. "Billy, you're like all Americans. You want everything to work out so neat and clean. The world isn't like that."

"It's an easy way out for you," I added. "No bad press."

"You would do that, wouldn't you," he said. "You don't know what a hardship it is to us down here that the United States has a free press. It makes everything so difficult."

"Do we have a deal?"

"We do, on one condition. If Señorita Malena Fonseca returns to Cuba, she dies. Is that understood?"

I nodded. "Agreed. I'll take that responsibility."

"Ah, Billy, we'll raise a toast to you tonight at the Capri," Canillo said. "Go quietly outside. I'll send her along shortly. You have my word."

Then he turned his attention back to Castro. "Another day for us, my friend. You should bless your God that Billy Bryan befriended you. He's been far luckier for you than you have been for him."

Outside, in the bright sunshine, we waited for Malena. And when the black door opened, neither of us could believe what they had done to her in a couple hours' time. Her blouse and hair were wet. In front of her, like a shield, she held a small suitcase. When she took her first step toward us, she dropped the bag and a red scarf and silver hoop earrings spilled out. Down her bare arms were a series of bruises. She was unsteady on her feet, and Castro and I, on either side, helped her down the stairs to the street. Swaying, she stared up crazily at the blue sky.

"I never thought I'd see this again," she said, and started to cry.

I stuffed the scarf and earrings back inside her suitcase.

"I was packing when they broke in," she said. "When they brought me here, they beat me first. Only then did they ask me any questions."

"Let's go," Castro said, hailing a cab. "The sooner we're away from this place the better."

"I told them nothing, Fidel," she said, her voice far away. Then again, softer, "Nothing."

Inside, I was burning with anger and hatred. I saw Canillo's face and I took home-run swings at it until it shattered into so many pieces. Castro seemed to read my mind.

"Another time, Billy," he said. "He'll be dealt with. I can assure you of that."

We got into the cab, and I told the driver simply to drive down the Malecón. Malena gazed out at the sea, watching the fortunate ones, the tourists, riding the swells in inner tubes along the breakwater. When the tears stopped, we were nearly through town, almost to Miramar, and I told the driver to take us to the beach. We sat on the edge of the sand. Castro hurried off, returning with ice cream, and we ate greedily from small cones in silence. Castro and I waited for Malena to talk.

When she did begin, the story came out in quick bursts, with long silences and frightened gasps in between. Only after they beat her had Canillo's men asked her for the pictures from the night when the bell was taken. Each time she refused to tell them, her head was pushed down into a pail of cold water that had been placed between her legs.

"When I close my eyes, I still taste that soapy water," she said. "It's in my throat and burns my nose. It was the bucket they used for cleaning the blood from their stone floors."

"Shhh," Castro said. But she didn't hear him.

"Every time they forced me down," Malena added, "I heard them laughing and I wondered if I would live through this one."

I had told the cab to wait for us, and when she was finished I helped Malena to her feet.

"You go with Billy," Castro urged. "He has a good plan. He's right, you should leave this place. You have been our eyes. Now you must show the rest of the world how evil they are here."

"Our plane leaves in an hour," I told her.

The news brought Malena around. For the first time since she had left the police station, her eyes became alert, looking at Castro and then at me.

"I'm not leaving," she said, her voice more defiant than I ever remembered hearing it. "How am I supposed to go after what they did to me?"

We got her into the cab, but her angry words continued. "I'm sick of these men. What they did today, I can never forget."

The cabbie glanced nervously at us three in the rearview mirror.

"You, Fidel," she said, going after Castro. "You said the other night that we must never surrender. And what did I do after the attack on the palace? I called you an idiot. Now I see how right you were."

"But it's too dangerous for you here at this moment," Castro said. "They won't let you be until they have those pictures."

"And they'll never get them," Malena declared.

"So you leave for a while. With me," I said, trying my hand. "You can always come back. When things have cooled off."

"Is that so?" she mocked. "Listen to my two men, treating me like a piece of china. Stop it. I hate it. Billy, if I went with you, I wouldn't come back. Not only would they guard the border against me, but I'm afraid of what would happen to me in America. You'd be too nice, too understanding. Your country would be too beautiful, too rich. I'd be lost. No, the only thing I can do is stay and fight."

"And die," I said. "If you're not on that plane, they'll pick you up again."

"I'll be safe in the countryside," she replied. "What is it you like to say, Fidel? 'The countryside surrounds the city'?"

"You'll never get to the countryside," said Castro. "Not now."

"Fidel," she teased. "How can you not see something so simple?"

None of us spoke for a few minutes. I was trying to think of ways to convince Malena to go with me. Castro was probably hatching some scheme to get the bell back. Finally Malena heaved a heavy sigh.

"I suppose that you're right, Billy. Once those pictures get printed in an American newspaper, the rest, as you say, will be history."

"So you'll go?"

"What choice do I have?"

■ ■ ■

The airport terminal was crowded. Two guards were at every door. The three of us moved into the mass of people. I took out the tickets. Beyond the final checkpoint was a small room and then the plane, beginning to board, about a hundred yards out on the tarmac.

"Let's go," I told her.

Malena shook her head. "I'm sorry, Billy. Not now. I can't."

"What are you talking about?" Castro and I stood there, letting the people swirl around us, while Malena surveyed the crowd. She had wrapped the red scarf around her neck and was wearing the earrings.

"She'll do." Malena nodded at a woman with dark hair. She was older and slightly shorter than Malena. "They'll never know," she said, breaking away from us. "Meet me by the door to the ladies' room in five minutes."

Malena began talking to the other woman. The room was filled with well-wishers saying good-bye to outbound passengers.

"Second call for the flight to Miami," the PA system blared.

"Malena, what is going on? We don't have time for this."

Malena and the other woman disappeared into the ladies' room while Castro and I stood outside. The guards watched us from all corners of the vast room as we waited.

"Something's up and you know it. Tell me. You owe me that much."

"I don't know," Castro mumbled.

"Bullshit." I looked out at the plane. "If she doesn't hurry, it won't matter," I said.

Suddenly, the woman Malena had chosen from the crowd lining up to clear customs jumped into my arms and gave me a big hug. She was wearing Malena's red scarf and earrings.

"She said to kiss me," she urged.

When I hesitated, she pulled my head down to her. Over her shoulder, I saw Malena, standing a few feet back inside the ladies' room. Her face was hideously made up, with too much eyeliner and a generous amount of lipstick.

"Good-bye," she mouthed. "I love you."

Only then did I realize what was happening.

"No, no, no," I said, my voice rising. "I'm not leaving her here."

"Quiet," said Castro, putting his arm over my shoulder and looking at the guards around us. "We have no choice. If you talk too much, everyone will know, and God knows how many of us will die."

"No, there's got to be another way," I said, looking at him. "She has to get out. She has to come with me. Think of something, Castro. So she can escape."

But he simply smiled and hugged me. "It appears she is determined to stay," he hissed. "Too bad for you, my friend. This seems to be the only course left to us now."

"I can't do this, Fidel. I can't just walk away."

"Billy, if you do not, it will be the same as sentencing her to death. This is her only hope. This is what she asks of you. The photographs, Billy. You must deliver them."

"We must go, darling," the lady beside me said, tugging on my shirtsleeve. "This must be my lucky day. A complete stranger gives me a ticket so I can go with my friends to Miami?"

"Santa Clara?" Castro said, loud enough for Malena to hear. "Tomorrow?"

From the shadows, she nodded.

"Time for you two lovebirds to go," Castro said, giving us both a big hug. Arm in arm, this imposter and I headed for customs.

"Final call for Miami," the PA system announced.

Once my new lady passed by the guards, she kept walking for the plane and didn't look back. I was completely numb, putting one foot in front of the other but not knowing how or why.

"What's in the bag?" a customs man asked me.

"Baseball bats," I said, pulling up the two handles for him to see.

He gestured for me to take them all the way out of the bag. I laid the two bats on the table. First he picked up the one I had used at the police station. Its handle was slightly cracked.

"This cannot be of much good to you," the customs man said.

"Sentimental reasons," I said.

He began to examine the other one, working his way down to the doctored barrelhead.

I desperately tried to think of ways to distract him. "You a baseball fan?"

"I go to some games," he replied.

"I'm the catcher for Habana, the Lions," I told him.

"I'm an *aficionado* of Almendares," he growled. "Your team cost us the title."

"In that case we should let bygones be bygones," I said. I picked up the cracked bat. "Borrow your pen?"

He shrugged.

"What's your name?"

"Manuel," he replied.

"To Manny," I said aloud as I wrote on the barrelhead. "Maybe next year. Signed, Billy Bryan."

With that I handed the cracked bat to him and stuffed the one with Malena's negatives back in the canvas sack.

The customs man nodded, studying my autograph.

"Yes, I know you," he said. "You'll be back next season?"

"I hope," I said.

I was the last one to board. As I was finding my seat, they closed the hatchway. I glanced out the window. There were security police cars everywhere, but no sense of alarm. I had just sat down in my seat when the lady wearing Malena's red scarf and earrings came up behind me.

"She said to give you this," she said, handing me the small photo album my daughter would find so many years later. The first picture was of the farm boy trying to control all those wild horses.

The plane began to pick up speed, heading down the runway. Holding the photo album in both hands, I closed my eyes. Outside the plane's engines roared, shaking everything slightly. I tried to block out the noise, the very world itself, so that I could somehow hang on to all that I had left behind.

Every winter since my wife died, I've driven down to Florida. I go alone, stopping to catch a few spring training games—the Dodgers at Vero Beach, the Marlins at Melbourne—before slinging out and around Miami and then down the islands strung together like a necklace until I reach Key West.

The first morning there, I am up before dawn, walking the hard white beach between Key West's main street and the cemetery. Where I stand is the closest point of land in America to Cuba.

As the sun rises I look across the water, searching for a boat, maybe a plane—anything that will remind me of the past.

I think Malena would have been proud of me. Back in 1948, days after landing in Miami, I was in New York, where I personally delivered her negatives to the papers there. Her photographs were forgotten and didn't reappear until years later, when Castro was ready to sweep down from the mountains and capture the sinful city that I loved so much.

For a long time I thought heroes could change the world. But I see now that's not how it works anymore. To be a hero in this "special period in time of peace," one must concentrate on the little things, take care of those you love, and let everything else roll by, realizing that the world has the power to hypnotize and overpower you, and when it begins to do so you must somehow fall back again on the little things, the parts of your life that maybe you can control.

The last couple years that I taught school they let me move up from gymnasium and speak to the junior-high kids about the classics. And, God, how I loved to talk with them about *The Odyssey, Beowulf, King Arthur*, and *Henry V*. Back then I believed that learning such stories could help them someday. But now, standing on this beach beside the turquoise waters, I'm not so sure. The stories we love can reassure us, maybe make us strong, but the actual deeds we must do ourselves. Perhaps the biggest injustice about life is that we're usually asked to do more when we feel too weak to consider the notion. The heroes among us somehow find a way to move ahead.

My buddy Chuck went on to play four more seasons in the majors, mostly with Pittsburgh. The year after he collected his 1,500th career hit, he retired, becoming an official greeter at the Sands in Las Vegas. He and Lola were married by then, but it didn't last. She was the one who stayed on in Vegas, becoming a dance instructor, while Chuck moved into the mountains above Lake Tahoe.

Skipper Charles had some success, even though much of it was in the minors. He was there when Castro took the mound for the last time—July 24, 1959—in an exhibition before an International League game in Havana. According to the *Rochester Democrat and Chronicle*, Castro struck out two in two innings. I saw Skipper years later at a minor-league game in Batavia and he said my oldest prospect showed good form. I'm not sure how I felt about that.

ᴛʜe others? Canillo? Oscar? The revolution swallowed them up. It was like they existed until a certain point in history, and then their ways and much of their country disappeared.

After that night in the cemetery, Eván, Cassy, and I returned to the hotel. It was clear by that point that I had not only a youngest daughter but an oldest as well. Whether it was because the day's emotions had wrung her out or she sensed that Cassy and I needed to be alone, Eván retired early. Cassy and I went out onto the balcony and sat in the darkness, not speaking, for what seemed a very long time.

I told Cassy that I was sorry she had to find out about her father's failures this way. She didn't say anything and kept her face turned away from me, but I knew that she was crying. I slid over to her, put my arm around her shoulder, and leaned my head against hers.

"I'm sorry. I'm sorry. I know what you must be thinking of me. I'm sorry that I hurt your mother," I whispered.

"That's not why I'm crying. I'm crying because I know how much this must hurt you. You lost Mom, you lost Malena. And you've spent all these years thinking that you weren't a good father because you loved someone else. Well, Dad, you're wrong. You were a terrific father and a wonderful husband."

"Cassy, I was as good a man as I was a ballplayer—never quite getting there, something always making me fall short."

"Dad, Mom loved you. She knew what Cuba meant to you. All of it. She used to tell me stories about your days down here. She sensed that you left more behind than just a game. I remember that once, when I was having problems with some guy, she told me that there are some men who have a sorrow so deep inside them that they can't even touch it. And the women who love them can't do anything about it, either."

Cassy pulled me closer to her and wrapped both arms

around me. Part of me wanted to just let go completely and join her in her crying, and part of me just wanted to scream and run away, furious at the injustice of it all.

"But you know what else she said, Dad?" Cassy continued. "She said that she had to love that part of you, too. The part that made you head off into the fields sometimes or made you sit and stare off into space. She accepted that part of you, and I know that she would accept Evangelina, Dad. I *know* that she would. And that's why I have, and why you have to."

I suppose that when you're an old man you're entitled to a few tears, and considering that, in a very real sense, I was a new father, I would have been entitled to a few more. But I didn't feel like it just then. I saved them for the trip I made to Laurie's grave the week we got back to the States. The ground near it hadn't quite completely settled, and it seemed to shift underneath my feet, but I know that as time passes, the footing will grow more solid, and it won't feel quite so much like I have to tread carefully in fear of falling down. If baseball, if Cuba, if my daughter taught me one thing, it's this: It's not the people who've never fallen or lost that are worthy of our admiration. It's what you do after you fall that's the surest test of a hero.

· · ·

Cassy and Eván always know where to find me. With all the junkets that Cassy gets through Delta, they have been all over the world. But they know when I am heading toward Florida, and they come without me having to ask. The two of them walk onto the beach without saying a word and come up on either side of me, putting their arms over my shoulders.

It took nearly every penny I had to get Eván out of Cuba. The officials that had to be bribed on both ends were as plentiful as the snowflakes on a winter night up north. It broke my heart to sell the house that my wife and I had raised our three kids in to put the deal over the top. But it was worth it to bring Eván here, to be with us.

We three look out over the water, knowing that Cuba, that strange land, lies out there, just beyond our sight. After a bit, they both kiss me and begin to walk down to the diner where we always have breakfast here in Key West. I take one last look around and then hurry to join them.

ESTADO DE LOS CLUBS

	W	L	AVG	GB
HABANA	41	32	.562	—
ALMENDARES	40	31	.548	1
CIENFUEGOS	36	36	.500	4
MARIANAO	28	44	.389	12

© Barbara Jean Germano

About the Author

Tim Wendel is an award-winning writer whose articles have appeared in *The New York Times*, *USA Today Baseball Weekly*, and *The Washington Post*. In researching his stories, he has fought forest fires in Arizona and trekked in Nepal. His book *Going for the Gold* chronicled the story of the 1980 U.S. Olympic hockey team, which won the gold medal at Lake Placid. Wendel received an M.A. from Johns Hopkins University. He lives in Vienna, Virginia.